MRS. CHRISTOPHER

Mrs. Christopher

by Elizabeth Myers

Introduction by Gerald Vann, O.P.

"Hell is not to love any more, madame. Not to
love any more!"

GEORGES BERNANOS

A THOMAS MORE BOOK TO LIVE

Sheed & Ward—New York

FIRST PUBLISHED IN
THE UNITED STATES OF AMERICA, 1959

LIBRARY OF CONGRESS CATALOG CARD NUMBER: 58-14451

MANUFACTURED IN THE UNITED STATES OF AMERICA

With love

to

WALTER DE LA MARE

The Most Exquisite Poet of the Age

and

The Kindest of Friends

INTRODUCTION
by Gerald Vann, O.P.

INTRODUCTION

It is not only when we deliberately 'practise to deceive' that we weave tangled webs of falsehood and so become destroyers, not least of ourselves. Often we mistake the nature of the ends we pursue; we are perplexed and harassed by conflicting claims or desires; we get into desperate muddles over means and motives. The Socratic theory that all sin is due to ignorance, though not wholly true, has much truth in it; as has Mrs. Christopher's remark that at the end 'It's not what we've done that will matter—but what we'd like to have done': 'O God,' says another character in this book, 'be merciful unto me—a fool!' In the end, we are told, we shall be judged on love: but we can all too easily forget this in practice, and suppose that if we learn and obey the textbook rules of right and wrong all will be well with us. It may not be so. The Gospel paints in vivid colours the contrast between the 'good, respectable' people, the rule-keepers, who did not find favour with God, and the 'sinners', the rule-breakers who did; and our Lord declares roundly that the 'publicans and harlots' shall enter the kingdom of God before the chief priests and the ancients of the people. For it is possible to act wrongly and yet be love-filled, and to act rightly but with hatred in one's heart: and in the last resort it is love that counts.

Love is the ultimate criterion. It is at least relatively easy to say what types of action in general are right and what wrong; it is often desperately difficult to decide whether or to what extent this particular thing you do here and now in these particular circumstances to, with or for this particular person, is good or bad. The christian ideal is not just to do what is right, but to do it lovingly. But this christian love is universal: the love of God and of all that is, of the whole pattern of existence. Surely it must be good to kill a blackmailer out of compassion for his victims! No, says Mrs. Christopher, 'the mistake was I didn't extend pity to *him*—the blackmailer. That's what I forgot, and it was the most important thing!' This was the lesson that Fred, the boy poet and mystic, had learnt so fully in his short life: that 'love is to love everything, it's to notice everything . . . and be pleased with things just for what they are. That's how love can come into life every minute, it's how to be compassionate and kind, how to be happy'; it is this that gives you eyes to discern beauty in a squalid huddle of mean streets, that teaches you that pain can mean an 'infinite possibility' of illumination; and that makes you cry, as Fred did, that 'nothing is unfriendly'.

It is this too that gives you the wisdom to make sense of the fact of sin, and of God's tenderness towards sinners. Péguy's words about the sinner being at the very heart of christendom are echoed by Mrs. Christopher's remark—which again, if not wholly true without qualification, has great truth in it—that 'sinners are the ones who best understand love because sin asks for love, calls it out and creates it more poignantly than anything else on earth'; she of whom it was said that many sins were forgiven her because of the greatness of her love was a prostitute; when we have 'sunk to that familiar level' at which we are 'glad to eat the husks of the swine' we can be sure that someone—our Father—will see the returning prodigal 'from afar': '*from afar*—which meant, when you came to think of it, that the someone had obviously long been looking out for the prodigal'; Mrs. Christopher, grieving over her guilt, recalls the story of how St. Ambrose, wanting to offer a gift to the Child who had appeared to him one Christmas Eve, found his writings, his prayers and devotions rejected and was told instead: 'Give me yours sins that I may forgive them'. 'Yes, the deeper you dropped into the pit the more attentive *that* Love became.'

Can we take such thoughts as these as an incitement to sin, or at least as an excuse for treating sin lightly? Of course not; the moment we become smug about our sins we cease to love God, the publican becomes himself a pharisee; indeed, any uncaring acquiescence in sinfulness must be a proof of lack of love: 'If you love me, keep my commandments'; and while the story of Mary the Sinner must console us since it means that despite all our wrong-doing we need not be finally separated from Love, it must also be a challenge to us since it means that all the right-doing in the world will avail us nothing unless we are living in that Love.

This book is a vivid statement of that challenge. It is an absorbing story, simply as a story; it has beauty in its language, its imagery, its evocations of Nature; it gives us a penetrating analysis of the psychology of temptation; but it gives us also a deep insight into the theology of good and evil. It is true of course that the author is using the language of imaginative literature, not of technical theology; and therefore there are a number of statements which, taken as they stand, the theologian would want to question or to modify but which form part of the total picture, and it is the total picture which is important, and profoundly valid. And the picture is, in a word, a picture of Love. We are concerned with goodness and sin and suffering; we are concerned with responsibility—and one thinks of Dostoievsky's 'We are each responsible for all' as one reads: 'I *am* those three who betrayed me, just as, if I hang, they will hang with me. In this world *we're all in it*'. We are concerned with death: with the idea that people 'don't think enough about death, only about dying'. We are concerned with hell and heaven, not as distant realities in another world but as states of existence in which already in some degree we find ourselves here and now. On the title-page Bernanos is quoted: 'Hell is not to love any more'; and heaven is that universal love, and that pure joy, which Fred had found: that joy which 'flourishes quite separately from circumstances, as love does, something which can come to everybody'. That universal love, which is charity, the seedling of heavenly life, is gloriously manifested in all the saints; but it is also to be found in 'sinners', which is why they must be described precisely as 'sinners' and not as sinners. True, we may well feel that Mrs. Christopher in her kindness of heart mistakenly minimizes the extent to which cold, deliberate wickedness exists (indeed in one place she seems to deny its existence altogether: 'no one does bad because they *are bad*' is, one imagines, a statement to which few, of any, theologians could fail to take exception); still the fact remains that there is a world of difference between sinners and 'sinners'; and equally the fact remains that sanctity is something far removed from the smug decorum of the 'respectable', and still farther from 'the pride and malice of the "saved" ': 'you can't really be good, with the fierce loving goodness of Christ, and be respectable also, as respectability is measured in this world!' That is why we need to pray so incessantly to the holy Spirit to kindle his fire in us.

'The twentieth century will be remembered for its attempt to destroy love and kill the heart.' It is not a pleasing thought; but it is, alas, plausible enough. And so again the challenge confronts us: for if this is indeed what our world is doing we have to ask ourselves, and to ask with brutal insistence, just what we propose to do about it. This book is therefore of very practical value to us; for it not only makes the problem vivid: it also helps us to see—to feel in our bones—just where the only answer to the problem lies.

Gerald Vann, O.P.

MRS. CHRISTOPHER

PART ONE

MRS. CHRISTOPHER

I

THEY had never seen death come so unexpectedly. Besides, the sudden mortal event was an outrage to the room which could not have looked more like an ante-chamber in a Victorian club, with its massed mahogany, plush, and bamboo, portraits in oils of obscure people like languishing fowls, a fire of tattered mimosa flames clawing up the chimney, and two gas-lights warbling above the mantelpiece. This room seemed to be making tetchy old-boy noises, as if disclaiming what had been done in it. There was something to bleat about, too. Sine, the owner of the dispiriting den, had been saying with dreamy blasphemy: "Dearly beloved, we are here gathered together to consider your transgressions in the light of hard cash!"

The next moment he sagged backwards in his chair with a chirruping kind of expostulation, the cruel smile still on his mouth and no difference in his appearance at all except that on his forehead a bead of blood like a ladybird had crept out from a bullet-hole.

The elderly woman with the curly grey hair was the one who had whipped out a miniature automatic and shot Sine dead. She rubbed the little gun slowly against her flank, as if wiping off powder or oil or the man's blood.

"Good lord!" she said with a hint of exasperation in her voice, "more than one can play at being God Almighty, dealing out orders, pains and penalties."

9

Whatever had been the woman's motive in killing Sine, she now stood to the other three living persons in the rôle of a deliverer. She had accounted for Sine, that thoughtful little man, who had been blackmailing every one of them, and on this night had invited them to his Highgate house with no other intention than to gloat over their helplessness.

There he had sat behind his desk, making his intolerable little speech in his elaborately childish voice, interrupting himself with sniggers as he savoured the revolting prestige afforded him by his nether knowledge of their lives.

"You must let me have a bit of fun sometimes," he had said in his exhortatory way, "for you're dreary scum to deal with. Yet I am a merciful man, wouldn't you say? Tee-hee! I shall name no names—or crimes. But I had the fancy to see you assembled before me, you four, my little evil ones! Do I appear to shiver with fright before such a concentration of wickedness? But I am not afraid—only a little chilly, and longing for my supper. Why need I be afraid? *You* protect me; your extraordinary wish for anonymity safeguards me from protest and . . . tee-hee . . . any misguided ideas of violence."

No one said anything. There was really nothing to say in the presence of a man who knew all the answers. He had continued to brag with paralysing complacency.

The elderly woman, standing by the fire, looked at the other three and saw them as lambs before the axe-man. The pathos, the unfittingness of the overbearing scene drove her beyond ordinary protest. She cast convulsively about for some means of bringing the disgraceful show to an end. Mindless she had become, but galvanization flew into her fingers, and, bringing out the revolver from her pocket, she shot the man who knew so many answers.

From the first the scene had been a barnstormer calling for a high-pitched conclusion. Hardly anything has the finality of murder; this, like an entity, was now in the room with flagrant dexterity, with an X-ray immobilization which hurled the people and things in its vicinity into stark relief and so searchingly isolated them that their varying constituents, cut off from the normal, appeared in total and terrifying objectivity.

In the light of this change all the security was struck from the wine-dark mahogany and the little bamboo stands with their Souvenirs of Boulogne and snowstorms waiting to be shaken up in lumps of glass. Conscious of the tensing of the minutes, Sine's victims looked round the walls and in the corners of the ceiling, as if expecting to find there the niche where the murder had been hatched.

Then the gears began to grind again. The three gazed at their deliverer with unutterable feelings. As the fact of Sine's death began to flame to their comprehension, they unknowingly drew closer together, not through fear, but motivated by a sense of gleeful battering relief as of children who, seeing the villain die at the close of a pantomime, crowd close with some vague idea of adding to their satisfaction by making it collective through impact.

Sine was dead and they were free. Bars and chains dropped from them. They felt as if they had been given a holiday for ever. They could be themselves again. Immeasurable freedom had suddenly been awarded them, freedom in which to expand— begin again. No more down-dragging reminders of guilt. No continual lowering of what standards were left to them.

The whole happening was invested for them with something heroic. They blossomed under it. Aspects of their personalities swaggered before them which made them seem strangers in their own sight. They had been submissive and maimed; now they started to effervesce. Abandonment set in. Everyone, except the elderly woman, broke out madly:

"I insist that this is the luckiest night of our lives!"

"The bastard! The bastard!"

"I knew this would come at its own hour!"

"Good night! It's wonderful!"

"Death is as good a cure for birth as anything I know."

"I'm bound to tell you that you're all hypocrites if you say you're sorry!"

The youngest of them, a doctor of twenty-eight, who had been blackmailed for the obvious reason, now took a skittish turn to the desk to make doubly sure of certainty. Under Sine's steep bony head with its needling of thin crinkled black hair a bullet was bedded in his brain. His business had been settled for him instantly. The doctor could not suppress a grunt of satis-- faction as he let the dead wrist swing free.

Power, he thought, heavenly power! Sine had it over us, then she had it over him—she had the courage to wipe him out. Beautiful power!

The other two, the good-looking woman whose christian name was Veronica, and the middle-aged man with the fixed pigeon stare and brown hair cut in a fringe on his forehead, were talking in a rose-pink haze of relief and well-being, darting grateful, deeply wondering glances at the murderer as one who had given them a world again.

She, with her charming looks and her aura of bright durable living, reminded each one of them of their mothers. This intensified their feeling of being children before her; nor could she have fulfilled the mother-figure more competently than by removing, with finality, the bogey that had haunted their lives.

"Of course," Veronica said, "there is no need for anyone to know. No question of the police—or anything. He won't be missed. Would he have had friends? Nobody could have cared for him!"

They all turned to see how the elderly woman was taking this jar—this reference to the police. She was gazing, as if she were enjoying it, at a heap of swollen wax plums and peaches under a roundel of glass on the marble mantelpiece. But she was, as a

12

matter of fact, wondering why it was, when she discharged her gun into the room, that she, too, had not dropped down dead, and wondering why the room had not fallen in on her, why she had not grown a pair of horns, why her skin had not turned spotted, why scorpions were not dropping out of her mouth— why, in short, she was still herself except for certain alien infirmities—palpitations, flutterings in her limbs, and occasional lurches of nausea.

If I'm going to be sick, she thought, where shall I *be* sick? And she looked about so as not to be taken unprepared. Conveniently close, a horrid little plant with brick-red leaves of the consistency of blotting-paper was standing in a glazed pink pot; it would do.

"What about servants?" demanded the doctor.

"He let us all in himself," said Veronica, "and I have heard nothing stir outside this room."

The doctor, Giles Bilterland, went and opened the door.

"Hello?" he called. Heavy silence fell on his shout. He came back to the others, leaving the door ajar.

"There ought to be wine, a sort of rough, sharp wine," he said, a wolfish look dawning in his blond, ugly face. "We ought to have a lot of drink to celebrate this.

"Celebrate?" broke from Edmund Macvey, the middle-aged man.

"Certainly, my good fellow," insisted Giles. "Doesn't this pretty work mean something to you? Or perhaps you deprecate murder? Perhaps you see something unsporting in killing?"

He squinted at Edmund, thinking: I wonder what *your* particular vice is, you playboy, you, with your funny little fringe! Politician with a pathic? White Slave trafficker? Unreeler of pornographic films in a nice house in Holland Park? Hoo! Something fruity, I'll be bound!

And Edmund, staring back, pondered:

Can there be worth in that insolent bag of tricks? He looks ripe

13

for hell, head and heels! Capable of anything, the cynical little...

While the two men were exchanging these common thoughts, Veronica sighed:

"Dear me, I wish I had a cigarette—such a comfort when you've had too much excitement—or not enough of it!"

Giles handed her one.

"You can't complain of the lack of excitement about this place," he said. "Whoever, nowadays, has the rich bliss of watching their oppressor turned into a corpse before their very eyes! That is an old-time fashion which has been revived for our entertainment! O, what a masterpiece of an evening!"

Edmund put in:

"I feel as if Evil personified is dead. He was that kind of man!"

At this, the elderly woman entered the conversation. So far she had been silent, staring sometimes at the pestilential figure at the desk, sometimes at the mock fruit on the mantelpiece, and every so often jerking back her head in an attempt to clear her sight which, in her overwrought state, kept blurring as though she had been drinking too much medicine with belladonna in it.

As the murder was unpremeditated, as it had happened so swiftly and with such dire finality, she could not yet take in that *she* had killed Sine, and she said to Edmund, in a reflective gentle voice, as if she had nothing else to bother her:

"What can you be thinking of, my dear? You're ever so mistaken if you suppose that Sine was Evil personified; wickedness has no *human face*, not even his. People aren't the same as their sins, they're different—they're better!"

Edmund said to her:

"Murder certainly isn't *your* face, dear friend!"

Flying from Ken Wood, a little brown owl let out its be-nighted cry which wobbled into the room with odd livingness. Veronica shivered

"Well," she said firmly, "the channels open to us for discussion are absolutely unique, but I don't know that it's the wisest thing in the world for us to remain here indulging in a running commentary on murder, either in the abstract or the concrete." She nodded at the corpse. "Personally, I should like to leave. But before I go I want to thank you"—she looked towards the elderly woman—"for the escape you've given me. Everyone has some lapses. Not many people have them perpetually thrust under their noses, as we did, and so lost our right to hope. I shall always be grateful to you for this release."

"So shall I," said Edmund. "The hope for the future is fierce! So is the responsibility. This extorting lad has . . . gone, I was going to say, but I wonder where he is now. Perhaps he's still here. It may be that we shall never be free of him till the whole thing is rounded off by an act of assassination from us all, till we have killed in ourselves whatever it was he would not allow us to forget. He can't do any more to us now—if we don't do any more to ourselves!"

"Tut! Tut! I don't doubt but you always have to say some little piece," said the young doctor, treating Edmund to a flight of wicked smiles.

Edmund bestowed on him a splendid look of menace, preparatory to some annihilating retort, but just here they were all surprised by a brindled cat which marched in through the half-open door. It made straight for Sine's hand dangling at the side of his chair. Into the dead hand it pushed its head coaxingly, but at once seemed to be aware of the metamorphosis that had taken place. The cat withdrew its head, stood for a few seconds as if annoyed, then, with a wild cry, it dashed itself against the wall. Recoiling, it pranced on its toes, and suddenly rocketed from the room, shrilling again.

The behaviour of the cat sent out something like a warning. The creeping fire, the waxy furniture, the corpse staring among its smug effects with eyes that held the blind blank glint of sequins, all turned sinister. Even the gas-lights seemed to have gone bluish. No one doubted in that moment that the dead have nothing to do with being dead. To leave without delay became the foremost consideration.

"We'll go out one by one," Giles proposed. "Obviously it would not do to be seen trooping all together from this house—as from a gala! One by one, quietly, will do the trick. I'll wait till the last. I don't mind. I'll put out the lights. I wish I'd been the one to put out *his* light! But someone must turn out the gas, and that someone may as well be me."

They all turned and gazed enquiringly at the elderly woman. She dealt with their expectations. Giving them a bright loving look, she said:

"It's amazing, really amazing the way human kind can adapt itself to any sort of circumstances. Here you all are, quite at home with a capital crime committed before your very eyes and, what's more, treating me as if everything is just as it should be."

"But, of course," replied Edmund. "And for heaven's sake don't think of . . . er . . . going and giving yourself up to the . . . to those who might, well . . . object to this night which has been without fault to us. I don't need to tell you that not one of us here would ever betray you. You are our deliverer."

"Deliverer from what?" She smiled. "My dears, none of you are under any obligation to me. I followed my own impulse, and what happens from now on is my affair. But if it should turn out, as it may in this strange world, that suspicion falls on any one of you, you are to tell at once that I killed our blackmailer. I don't know your names, I don't want to know, but it's very much in your interests that you should know mine. My name is Christopher—Mrs. Christopher—and I live in East Heath Road, Hampstead, in a place called Laburnum Cottage—just because the garden is full of lilac trees. Ah well!"

She had a pretty, happy voice, this murderer. Clearly she had come from a world far removed from wildness and crime. As she finished speaking, protesting sounds broke from Veronica and Edmund. They would never betray her! Come what may, she should never be laid hold of through them! Why, they owed her everything! How could she suppose they would ever forget that she had rid them of *him?*

They turned to give the corpse some looks of indignation and even whip up a little hatred, but the gradual settling-down of death upon their enemy seemed to be haling away the sordid guilt of his life-time, and it was difficult for them, in a presence as knock-down as death, to be sensible of the loathing they had felt for the living man.

Giles smilingly acquiesced with everything the other two were saying so vehemently. But to himself he was thinking:

The fool, the fool! She has put herself into our power. She has exchanged one master for three! Her very life now depends on our lightest word. Why . . . why, any one of us now could take over Sine's rôle and blackmail her to death's door. But that's the way to court foul play. This Mrs. Christopher appears to have rather a summary way of dealing with those who threaten her. She shows a tendency to give people rather more than they have bargained for! Just the same, she has admitted us to power over her, and any sort of power is valuable; in fact, it's the only thing in life worth anything!

Turning to Mrs. Christopher, he said:

"I am indebted to you extremely. You have given me the most entertaining night of my life, without exception. Will you leave first, and we'll follow one at a time. I'll go last and turn out the gas. It's very important that someone—now and at any time—should remain behind and douse the light!"

II

Outside a vacant moon was getting up. Its blank light poured into the long trough where London lay, dry-whitening the steeples, and changing slate roofs into mysterious grey hulks that glimmered darkly as if drenched. There was a good deal of expenditure aloft; even so, Sine's little garden was not forgotten, and his laurels were coming in for an argent filming-over, and his almond trees were full of cocoons of lavender light, as Mrs. Christopher went down the garden path.

She felt glad to see this skinless moon staggering up the sky accompanied by a little star like a bright crumb beneath it, for it was a token of hundreds of safe and merry nights that seemed now to fly, far above her head, beautifully aloof from blackmail and murder.

In Hampstead Lane she saw the lighted bus swing round by the dark tomb of Coleridge, and come dropping gaily down the hill with an air of being glad to leave *that* lone tenant behind in the open windy crypt.

Mrs. Christopher hastened to the stop and boarded the bus. The only empty seat was by the side of a drunken man.

"Why," he said, gazing at Mrs. Christopher's curly grey hair, "you haven't got hat on!"

"And you *have* got a hat on!" replied Mrs. Christopher.

He whipped it off apologetically.

"I'm that sorry," he stated. "I'm not drunk, you know, I'm hearty! There's a big difference. Y'see, I'm a self-made man and I'm all right, but I don't always think."

"Neither do I," said Mrs. Christopher encouragingly. "And we're all self-made, by the way; that's what education is for."

The drunken man gave a roar of laughter.

"I'm not educated, do you know," he brought out. "I'm a coalman!"

Mrs. Christopher then almost said in a purely automatic way: "And I am a murderer!"

But she realized, in time, how deeply improper such a glaring admission would sound. She grimaced. What a rum situation was this in which she found herself, being arch with a drunken stranger, and it was only an hour ago that she had accounted for a man's life by the unarguable method of shooting him!

The man beside her was continuing:

"Course, I'm something special in coalmen—nothing small, you know. I own five coal mines. I'm a man of power!"

"Disgusting!" observed Mrs. Christopher.

"Whadder you mean?" protested the drunk man. He shied away from her. "Isn't it something to own five coal mines?"

"Well, is it?" asked Mrs. Christopher.

The drunk man fell into a frenzy of trying to impress her.

"I can see as you don't understand," he said earnestly. "Now take me and my mines: the miners and them what uses coal is dependent on me. I can turn the men on and I can turn 'em off. I can turn the coal out or I can turn it in. Ha-ha-ha! Isn't that power?"

"No," replied Mrs. Christopher.

"What is it, then?"

"O, merely a little jungle pressure—nothing to do with real power."

Mrs. Christopher had so much crushing guilt on her own mind that she gave forth this gnat-sting of reproach quite sportively. It represented a pinch of relief.

The man breathed at her noisily. Demoralized by her lack of appreciation, his only refuge was to put her down as dotty.

"Aren't you funny?" he asked her.

"I believe I am rather," replied Mrs. Christopher.

The bus now pulled up at the Spaniards Inn, and the toper invited her to dismount and have a drink with him. Mrs. Christopher graciously declined.

"Well, good night, then," bawled the drunkard, lurching down the bus. "You have another think about me and my coal mines!"

But, very pardonably, Mrs. Christopher felt that she had something more urgent to occupy her thoughts. At Jack Straw's Castle she alighted and walked round to the White Stone Pond where she paused and looked about her. On one side hung vapory star-lit space to the heights of Hertfordshire, on the other the moon lit a vista that tilted south to the Surrey hills.

From the grassy earth to the star-spattered zenith a faint high musical hum eddied through the night—an air-borne rocking of divers sounds that took in the faint slithering of hedgehogs through the grass of Hampstead Heath no less than the blaring of taxi-horns crossing the top of London on the Spaniards Road. This mild occult sound, the trees winding down to the Vale of Health in the lichen-pale moon-shine, the dusty carmine beam upflung by the distant lights of the town, and the glittering heavens combined to give a fleeting impression of earth-caught infinity. Mrs. Christopher, who was always conscious of such things, came to the conclusion that it would not be unprofitable to linger here in the midst of so much that was greater than herself, and try and make something of those terrible thoughts which were blowing through her mind like flames.

She sat down on a corporation seat with her back to the moon and the far-flung lights of the town. Now she was staring out to Hertfordshire and the dark country humping up to the sky.

For a long time she sat there in the full access of guilt. The wonderful barbed feature about committing a murder was that, in spite of it, you continued to be aware of your own identity. Didn't it ram home that no matter what you did you always remained *yourself to yourself*, and at no time were you allowed the respite of being deprived of the responsibility of your own personality, the run of your own nature.

So now she was a murderer. Now she was a "wanted" person, someone to be watched and hunted. Henceforward everything she did would have a terrible significance—to the police.

When you read about a murder in the newspapers it was a crime which seemed immensely far away, viewed from the safety of innocence. But murder was only too dizzyingly easy to carry out; and once you had done it you had never done with it. On top of all that beggared the understanding then, was added the mystery of murder. Murder was death to the victim, but it was new dreadful life to the murderer. It could never be forgotten because no one had ever given instructions how to act and live and leave ourselves somewhere else.

Quite right, too, Mrs. Christopher decided. Why should the murderer be allowed to forget? For no amount of highmindedness or pity, even that withering pang I felt for those three people, can possibly excuse a murder. So my course is only too plain: I've lost my right to go on living. You do what you like and then you must pay. Mrs. Christopher, my dear, this is where you begin to pay—whatever price they're going to ask.

Even so, she could not help thinking that the heart, after all, was wondrous small to have so much of remorse and apprehension packed into it. Now the last horizon of life swung sharply near, that once had been so far away, and the carbonized outline against the sky was not, as before, a tree or a singing bird, but the gallows. Death. A going, where? A mystery. She shivered.

At this point in her headlong speculations Mrs. Christopher became intensely afraid. Sheer horror and anxiety disabled her. What a way to have to die! What a thing to have to anticipate— the exact known minute of an ignoble death! The prospect of having to leave the dear and the familiar half-paralysed her with terror. She seemed to be caught in the midst of a gigantic implacable malice. Death was something long thought of, but now it was coming home awfully, running wild in a new and more insistent way. For some minutes Mrs. Christopher was unable to control her panic. She wiped the sweat from her face with a trembling hand.

Good God, she thought, I've never been in such a funk in my life!

A car swished up the hill from Heath Street and gave a rush in the direction of Golders Green. Rays from its headlamps flew ahead into the darkness revealing the unsuspected—the night pouring with thousands of dusty motes, and a few moths flying like snowflakes in the long arms of powerful light. After its passage the dark surged back with quite a clap, except for a little stream of light which went swilling on over the road from the car's tail-lamp. Then it was that Mrs. Christopher became angry—angry with her own blazing fear.

Well done, you, she applauded herself ironically. Couldn't you possibly grovel a little more? Bah! Is this what all the training was for? All the education? All the religion? All the Latin tags about the good life, and the lines of noble poetry? Mrs. Christopher, my poor object, your cowardly sweat disgraces the Old School Tie, the British Tradition, the Stately Homes of England!

Stately Homes of Islington! My father kept a music shop with an eighteenth-century façade by the Angel at Islington. Among his cracked-up violins, the old Irish harp, and the trumpets, I learnt the beginning of fortitude, how to walk the whole world with myself and not be afraid.

And in that Islington backyard, smirked upon by those brave and gentle shades, one-time Islington neighbours—Oliver Goldsmith and Charles Lamb—I learnt something else, as well—to enjoy and love people, those you meet and those you never meet yet know through your imagination and the intuitive wisdom of the heart.

There it all began—in that yard which was all my world, one day when I was young, sitting on a three-legged wooden stool, with a handful of dandelions in a jam-jar before me, and thought myself in a splendid limitless garden. In the sunshine of that morning and the rich light coiling up from those golden wild-flowers, some sparks of answering warmth were struck in me. Two things irrevocably caught at my fancy then—the wonder the world was, and the thrilling possibilities of other people. That hour of loving faith and joy gave me my first readiness to give and to receive. Ay, it's the things you have that teach you, not the things you dream about. In what seems nothing there is always something.

That was the training that led to to-night's murder! How wrong something has gone! Who could understand it? Did I really kill him? There's no doubt about that death, though; there's no doubt about mine either, now. Well, let be. Let it come. When you've failed as much as I have, death can be something of a recreation!

But, for heaven's sake, Mrs. Christopher adjured herself, let's have no self-pity, let's have no conceit about it. She gave a loud laugh which caused a passer-by to retreat to the edge of the pavement and walk away from her very guardedly.

The bells of Christ Church chimed the half hour after nine o'clock with sweet and tranquillizing deliberation.

Yes, but I can't sit here all night, observed Mrs. Christopher. I must get on, and get on with things—make a decision—and I've always loathed having to make up my mind about anything, even about what I was going to wear each morning! O deary me!

She rose and turned into East Heath Road where a little wind, full of odour, courteously tugged at her hair with seeming intent to remind her that it had no objection to touching anyone, even a murderer. She trudged down the hill, sniffing the small fresh smell of the grass of the heath, till she came to where her cottage faced the open moon-bright land.

Mrs. Christopher let herself into the house. The fire was dying down in the sitting-room, and the grandfather clock, which was slow, rumbled abysmally, then brought out the half hour in a comic falsetto.

"You'd better get a move on," Mrs. Christopher reproached it, "otherwise you'll be chiming night-time in Hampstead when it's eternity everywhere else!"

She hit the sullen coals with the poker and some little low flames came out like azure moss. She sat down and looked round the room, at the rows of beloved books, the Georgian writing-desk, the elegantly fading green carpet, the Cotman water-colour, the one dark little Limoges enamel, the silver ornaments on the chimney-board, the two old-fashioned wing chairs, the little pot with the stars and griffins in bright colours painted on it. When she remembered how much of her life had entered into these things as she had existed in their midst, they seemed to be part of her heart, and she could hardly bear the thought of leaving them.

"Well, my dears," she addressed them, "what am I to do? Where shall I go with this nice bedtime story of mine? I've never done anything like this before. Can you give me a little free advice?"

Her eyes came to rest on her books; her face softened. Books don't make a person invulnerable to the big blows, she thought, but perhaps, yes—yes, indeed, they do help you to remain unconquered.

She ran her fingers through her bright grey hair, cut short, and curling round her head. Yesterday had been her sixty-fifth birthday, but she looked much younger than that. Her face with its clear pale skin, her deep ardently-seeking eyes, straight well-balanced nose, and her tranquil mouth all informed Mrs. Christopher with a look of lasting youthfulness.

It came over her that she was sixty-five and, confronted by her mortality, her mind went back to the horror she had suffered by the White Stone Pond.

That fear of death, now, what's it all about? Better see what life means, first! When you've had sixty-five years and enjoyed 'em all, it's churlish to be cranky about giving up the few remaining years during which I might easily get cancer or the "willies" or go sour somehow. Besides, death has to come; it's the only thing any of us can be sure of—the one horse that's certain to be first up the home straight some day, and we can only get on with the business of living because that's the only event in the sporting calendar which remains undated.

Where I must be careful is not to think of hanging as being the *same as death*. One is a material arrangement, the other is the beginning of that life for which we were born. What is important is not the way of my end, but the end for which I began. I must not confuse myself. People, and I'm no exception, don't think enough about death, only about dying. My fear is of the sordid and sinister trappings of execution: I am not frightened of death, and why should I be since it is love's answer to the strange yearnings of the finite human heart. It's a beautiful and natural thing, is death, and though it calls us into the unknown— usually a trembling proposition for our hidebound natures—it may not be too much to suppose that conditions *there* will be largely what we have been making them *here*. The closer you get to life here the nearer you are to eternity, as far as I can make out.

Death, eternity, the other world—we talk as if these things were distant in time and remote in space; but, in many ways, we are *already there*. Our lives even now are opening and, when we are not too vile, flowering already along those roads that run with all the roads here, the dust of one mingling with the sublime dew of the other. Fantasy? No, the ultimate reality, and the longer you live the more you become aware that you're equipped for more than can be used here, and the more clearly to the inner ear come the ineffable messages from those *other places*.

I believe death will come to me as the ocean used to come when I was a child. There was the ordinary-seeming street with the wooden setts giving the roadway a high-class look, there were the windows with lace curtains and plants in pots, there were the toy-shops with the buckets, spades, little bright flags and celluloid windmills whirring in the breeze, and then—you turned a bend in the street and beyond the cemented, sandy promenade a splendour of upflung light from the open sea was like a way up from known things into a thrilling Beyond.

But all this was not settling the assertive question of whether Mrs. Christopher should go and announce herself as a murderer at the police station by Downshire Hill, or whether—and here her mouth quirked with the stunning irony of the situation—to go and talk things over quietly with her son, Hugh, who was Assistant Commissioner of Police at Scotland Yard.

There are advantages and shocking disadvantages in keeping it in the family, as it were, thought Mrs. Christopher with what she considered shameless levity, but she could not help it.

Yes, she decided, I'll go to Hugh. But first I'll have a cup of tea. A person needs something.

In the kitchen she put the kettle on the stove, without turning on the light. Moonbeams were crossing the yard and lent the kitchen a soft suety light in which all the colour was concentrated with aniline effect in the blue gas-flames rowdily fanning out round the kettle. Some brown stew-pots on a shelf glinted at Mrs. Christopher with what seemed like pained surprise, where prisms from the gas-flames caught them full tilt. They looked at her like old comrades who cannot believe something they have heard of a trusted friend.

While she was waiting for the kettle to boil, she wondered to herself about the three she had left in Sine's house. She felt a gush of tender concern for them and ventured the hope that they would benefit and even change for the better by their release from the blackmailer; then immediately she regretted this urge.

Who am I to expect anything of the kind? It's bad enough that I killed a man, without taking to myself these fawning notions, this pride of saying to myself that I killed to give them a chance to live unaffrighted lives, or even better lives. To free them *was* my motive in getting rid of him, but it is not for me to have any *expectations* of them.

Pride! It thumbs a nose at you everywhere. Even now, as I stand here, a criminal, pride would come to trick out the very act of murder into a toadied piece of altruism. Lord! O, lord! I'm sixty-five and I've never learnt a thing. It's only too plain— you go out as you came in with the ignorance of turnips!

At that the kettle gave a furious throttling noise and began to pour over in hissing boiling abandonment. Mrs. Christopher leapt for the teapot, and soon was carrying a little tray into the sitting-room. Enjoying her tea, she thought wryly:

Heavens! You can be glad of the delicious taste of tea even after you have killed someone. In fact, it never tasted better! It's as though one self of ourselves remains unaffected by anything, but goes on quietly doing the best it can till the very end.

As she sipped and smoked a cigarette, she felt glad that she had no animals to part from. Some little nudging head just then— No. She was glad there were no animals. There were the books, of course. Cost a person something to leave books behind. But Hugh would look after them—love them in that special way that books expected and needed to be loved.

"But I must get on," said Mrs. Christopher aloud. "I've something more pressing on hand now than to sit here enjoying remorse and decorating the drama of the entire situation!"

She washed the crockery she had used. Then into a leather shopping-bag she bundled a clean nightdress, her tooth-brush, washing things, a comb, and a bundle of personal documents. She looked next for a book, and slipped in "Tristram Shandy."

"I might as well have some humour at hand," said Mrs. Christopher. "I'm going to give myself up for murder, but if I can steal a laugh or two when I am by myself—nothing unseemly—it will do me good and help me to hold on. Something tells me that I am going to need all the aids for holding on!"

When she went into the hall to put on her tweed coat, her thoughtful gaze encountered a grey bowler hat which hung there for a talisman. It had once adorned a head that now had nothing more to do but moulder quietly away in Hampstead churchyard. The head had been her husband's. This hat, a homely token of a marriage that had been an exceptionally happy one, seemed suddenly to release starts and filaments of light that flushed into the hall from everywhere. The little house was giving up its memories, the unforgettable times, stripping the years of their evergreens as an offering that could not fail to console Mrs. Christopher in whatever lay before her.

She returned to the sitting-room for the shopping bag. Her books were regimented in one mute question.

"You need not stare!" she said. "I may even come back for a few days; it all depends on what Hugh . . . arranges for me."

She turned off the light and went purposefully down the garden path where a delicious smell of damp lilac came very agreeably to her nostrils.

On the bright sky a few little tresses of silver cloud had appeared under the moon. Observing this, Mrs. Christopher felt that life in a prison cell before her trial would be endurable if only she was able to see the sky and its constant changes.

She made for Well Walk, enjoying the ashen appearance of the trees in the blue gloom, and the grass on the verge minced up between brittle streaks of moonlight and sharp shadows. The little fountain, enshrining the site of the old Hampstead chalybeate well, was like an altar made of onyx set up to a god.

Mrs. Christopher could almost hear a sacrificial chanting but, perhaps, after all, the sounds came on a wind trapped in time and were the lifted voices of revellers of the days of Queen Anne when, in this very road, the Assembly Rooms, Gambling, Card and Pump Rooms were grouped round those chalybeate waters that had made Hampstead a spa.

Further down Well Walk, the row of old Georgian houses by Christchurch Hill stood up blandly in the moonlight, their shutters tottering back from windows sparkling like liquid jet. A rich aroma of mouldering drifted off their old gardens and their attic windows in the roof seemed to lean forward to savour it.

"Hope they don't begin knocking these fine old houses down in the name of Progress or something!" sniffed Mrs. Christopher as she passed by.

Presently she came to where Fitzjohn's Avenue plunged down in two long rippling lines of street-lamp glow to Swiss Cottage. Mrs. Christopher took the long descent at a spanking pace, till it occurred to her that she need not be in quite such a hurry to go and make the arrangements for her own cancelling out. She ought to be walking soberly, dwelling upon her extraordinary undertaking of going to give herself up for murder to her own son.

Outside Swiss Cottage Underground Station a very skinny old man was knocking two ham bones together, working away with the homeless distractedness of his kind, making a sort of clacking music of the proceeding—mean melancholy work; but, thought Mrs. Christopher, it's more than I could do, or you and you—she nodded at a flurry of passengers coming out of the station—and it's a job, it's quite hard work, calling for dexterity. He is doing the best he can with the limited means at his disposal. And she gave the staggered old performer a ten-shilling note which he nearly threw away, automatically thinking that he was being fooled with a piece of paper.

From Swiss Cottage Mrs. Christopher was soon in the quiet streets of St. John's Wood where the slender lamp-posts leaned giddily and lonelily towards garden walls, pushing their luminous polls full of golden electric light into pallid falls of laburnum and lilac blossom, or glistened, bright and wild, among moist new leaves perched on the boughs like companies of butterflies.

This splendour of fizzing light and twinkling leaves made the night seem as if it were pounding out to glory on the tide of a festival; and it touched off memories of other glad nights, far off in time but brought near and decked anew by evocation.

"It's all very well for me," sighed Mrs. Christopher, hot and anguished again by her own irreparable action, "but what about *him?* What's happening to him now, sent out in a second to his judgment without twopenn'orth of preparation!"

And she walked on, her nerves tingling at the thought of the collapsed bag of bones that once had been a man, shut up among its Victorian paraphernalia in the dark den on Highgate Hill.

III

Hugh Christopher had a small house in Hamilton Place. In this treed thoroughfare he lived with a butler who had once been a burglar but whose policy had changed to a heavy-going honesty, only occasionally broken down by transports of temptation put in his way by Hugh's Amontillado. This model of reform having gone to bed early with a weeping ear, Hugh himself admitted his mother when she pulled the bell-knob.

"Why, Mamma, how nice to see you! Are you pretty well? You're rather late, darling. Poor Willie has gone to bed in the hope of comforting a very angry ear. Have you had your supper?"

"I've had everything I want, thanks, Hugh," replied Mrs. Christopher proceeding towards the open drawing-room door.

"As you've always had!" smiled Hugh.

"As I've always had," agreed his mother, "though a person can't go on like that for ever."

She settled herself in one of his Chippendale armchairs.

"Surely you haven't come to tell me that someone has put an end to your enjoyment of life?" asked Hugh.

"On the contrary—I've just done that for somebody else."

"I don't know what you mean, but have a drink. Brandy—whisky—a cocktail?"

"No, thanks. Can't you sit down, Hugh. You look so large standing about!"

He was big, nearly forty years old, and beginning to find himself cushioned here and there with areas of abundantly prospering flesh that were an affront to him. Cones of bright grey hair had come out at his temples and were starting to nip their way further back into the thick black curls which covered the rest of his massive head. His face was guarded and alert, with a big dark nose and down-drooping mouth. He was wearing a tie which informed those in the know that in his time he had been among the leading cricketers at his Varsity.

Mrs. Christopher accepted a cigarette and a light for it. She looked at her son coolly, lovingly, as he moved about. He was, she felt, an unsatisfied, ruthless and efficient man, easy to make a fool of because he knew so much. She had never made such a late call on him before. But she had never been operating in such circumstances before. O, how strange everything kept suddenly seeming, how threatening and end-of-the-world!

"How's the murder business?" she asked, throwing a glance on her fingernails.

"O, quiet, you know, Mamma—not that we have a close season in crime! I am thinking of taking an early holiday this year."

"My hopeful boy, are you really? And here I have come to make you so busy. But, perhaps, a subordinate. . . . After all, I suppose my case wouldn't engage the top men. I flattered myself!"

His smile went out.

"Mamma, what are you talking about? Your case? What on earth do you mean?"

"It happens that I've knocked a poor fellow off to-night, Hugh—killed him. I came to see you about handing myself in."

"Nonsense! *What?*"

"Killed a man, I said; this evening, in Highgate."

"Preposterous!" cried Hugh. "Mamma, you're fascinating! You'll be the death of me, d'you hear?"

"Well, I've certainly been the death of one man this evening," said Mrs. Christopher seriously.

"Mamma, I . . . *You* killed a man!"

"Yes. It couldn't be anything, of course, but a sudden revelation to dumbfounder you. I'm sorry, Hugh."

He felt all his being rush to the rims of his eyes and concentrate there in an overbalance of staring.

"Can you be joking?" he asked her sharply.

"I could be, but I'm not. This man, the dead man, was blackmailing me—and others—and, somehow, things came to a head this evening. I shot him."

Hugh said nothing but continued to glare at his mother. The lower half of his body seemed to have swum away. Stranded, he hung on to the back of a chair for support.

"There's the gun," said Mrs. Christopher, and she leaned and put it down carefully on the table beside an old glass paperweight and that day's edition of *The Times*.

"Sounds like raving! I simply can't believe this," sighed Hugh at last.

"No, I was afraid of that," replied his mother briskly. "Nevertheless, it is true. Any policeman could go to that house

now and bring you back the . . . corpse. It's a very tidy corpse—
the neatest death I ever saw. You know, for a long time I thought
he was shamming—playing a trick on us—allowing us to feel
relieved that he had gone and then saying: 'Peek-a-boo! I'm
still here.' It took me a long time to realize that he was dead.
He never changed—looked just the same—hair faultlessly parted
and everything! No one is in for messiness who goes to bring
out that corpse."

"That corpse!" repeated Hugh with wonderment. "All this is
more like Grand Guignol than anything I know! Excuse me, I
think I'll have a drink."

"Yes, do, dear; I fancy you'll need one," said Mrs. Christopher
solicitously.

Hugh took himself carefully across the room. He thought it
extremely likely that at any moment he would fall down flat on
his face. He found himself deploring his education that had never
given him the least hint of what one's conduct should be when
one's mother arrives to confess to a murder.

He poured himself as generous a glass of whisky as ever he had
swallowed.

My charming smart little Mamma—a murderer! He took a
swig of spirits at it. He wanted to get the proper envelopment
of the thing. Toasting it made it seem a little more real though
no easier to accept.

The strong reek of the drink rolled through the room and
seemed to Mrs. Christopher to take the shape of puffs of golden
vapour through which wavered tipsily the black, green, and
rose-red birds and trees on Hugh's Queen Anne lacquer cabinet.

Hugh turned to his mother.

"You say this man was blackmailing you?"

"He was."

"Why was I never told that?"

"It wasn't altogether my affair, Hugh. You see, he wasn't
actually blackmailing me, but Elizabeth."

"My cousin Elizabeth?"

"Yes, yes, my lad, who else? Before she married Charles it seems that she got herself mixed up with some high-stepping Chelsea idiots and she began to take drugs."

"Elizabeth? Drugging?" he exclaimed, aghast.

Hugh's compact world of duty and orderliness had not quite finished banging about his ears. His mother, who could almost hear the crashes, murmured sympathetically:

"Poor boy! You've never had to hear such a lot of disgraceful family news all at once. Elizabeth began to take drugs. Fortunately, before the matter became too serious, she met Charles and fell in love with him. And it is only within this last year when Charles is doing so well for his constituents that this fellow, Sine, wrote to Elizabeth and threatened to expose her unfortunate lapse—how he ferreted it out I don't know—unless she paid him to remain quiet. He asked her if she had ever considered how much harm her past would do to her high-principled M.P. of a husband were it to be published abroad. Of course, she began to pay him."

Mrs. Christopher rummaged for her handkerchief, and continued:

"When he had nearly ruined her both as to money and nerves, she came to me. With her I agreed that nothing must be done to jeopardize Charles's career. I went to see this blackmailer. I told him I would become . . . er . . . his victim by proxy. He agreed, after doubling his price. That's how I came to be mixed up with him at all."

"O, Mamma, if you had only come to me, to *me*! Don't you think I could have handled things without Charles suffering, or you, or Elizabeth?"

"No, I don't. That's why I paid the man. I was too afraid of names leaking out through some over-zealous pressman at the blackmailer's trial."

"Good God Almighty! Don't you think I could have

34

taken care of that? What am I supposed to be at Scotland Yard *for?*"

"I've never rightly known. It's always been your affair, dear boy. I could not be sure that you had power enough to keep the case out of the newspapers once we had set the Law in motion. So I dealt with Sine. Really, Hugh, it was a case of saving Elizabeth's reason."

Hugh went to get himself another glass of whisky.

"Elizabeth's reason had to be saved, tra-la!" he burst out; "and now, my poor Mamma, it looks as if your life is going to be lost. I suppose you did kill that wretch? He's not . . . well, you didn't just wing him, did you?"

He came towards her with painful intensity. She had a sudden memory of him as a little boy, leaning towards her on a Christmas Eve with a similar concentration, wearing what they used to call his fretty face, and enquiring if she thought that Santa Claus would remember to bring him a very thick story book and a humming-top.

"No," answered Mrs. Christopher thoughtfully, "I didn't wing him. I fired at point-blank range and killed him."

Hugh snorted with fear for his mother.

"Tell me," he said, "how it was . . . how it happened that . . . all at once you . . . shot him."

"Ah, yes. That must seem strange after I had gone on paying him unprotestingly for so long. Well, here's a short-winded version of the affair: I usually saw him, to pay him, in the Ritz Buttery. He liked to be about his scandalous business under the very eyes of smug middle-class crowds. But something must have scared him because, lately, he took to asking me up to his house at Highgate when he . . . when his instalments fell due."

Mrs. Christopher lit another cigarette. She continued obediently:

"When the visits to the house began, I used to take that little

35

revolver your father bought me when we lived in Italy. I did this, I own, because it made me nervous to go to that house. I thought the revolver would be uncommonly useful if ever he suddenly went off his head in front of me. I never thought he was quite right, and I used to dread . . . well, it was simply fear. But up to the minute of shooting him to-night, I can truly say I never had the least intention of killing him."

"And did he go off his head to-night?" demanded Hugh.

"No; I did—for a minute or two, anyway. Until to-night I knew nothing of his other victims. He never spoke of them. Why should he? We were all paying him to keep his mouth shut. But to-night it seemed that the poor fellow wished for a little entertainment, and what does my rogue do? He invited four of us to come to his house without, of course, any advance notice that others would be present. And as soon as the wretched little group was assembled round him, he let out his intention. He did not intend to blab, he said, he merely wanted to inspect his thralls, give them a little drilling. I asked him if he had not thought of a torture-chamber, too, with a nice fire, and a few branding-irons. He said No, that had not occurred to him, but it *was* an idea! He would keep it in mind."

Hugh made as if he would pour out a third glass of spirits.

"I shouldn't," said his mother. "You'll be too tipsy to be any use at all in a minute! And so, dear boy, there we were, in the insufferable position of listening to this maniac chiding us in a paternal way for not conforming to the virtuous standard of the average citizen. For my part, he could have droned on all night. After all, no personal guilt weighed me down or, at least, nothing *he* knew about. But those other three—O lord! The woman was so pretty, too, and the elder of the men, who was probably your age, had such a humorous hair-cut—fringe over his eyes like a child, and standing there listening miserably to that petty tyrant. It was unspeakable! I knew it would be fatal for me to look at their faces while he was haranguing them and extracting from them a horrible kind of agreement with all he said. And then . . . I did look. I saw their poor rueful faces, their anxiety as to his intentions—wondering if he would go too far, forget himself, and blurt out something. I saw their look of being trapped, and I . . . well, my mind gave a kind of roar. The next moment I'd snatched the gun from my skirt pocket and . . . sent him to his reward!"

The fire on the hearth fell apart with a heavy sigh. Hugh flopped into a chair.

"Mamma! Dear Mamma! You shot him. O lord! O hell!" groaned Hugh. Sunken-headed he stared ferociously at his glistening shoes, giving way to the utter despair of his mind.

"We'll go away!" He looked up with sudden determination. "I'll resign. I meant to soon, anyway. Never intended to remain in that nerve-exhausting job all my life. I'll resign. We'll go abroad. I shan't be able to get away for a few weeks, but the important thing is to get you away—to-night, if possible. Could you catch the midnight train to Harwich and cross to the Hook? From there you could make your way to Paris and wait for me in some quiet little hotel."

"Do you always make proposals like this to murderers when they come to confess?" asked Hugh's mother with tender amazement.

"No, of course not. Don't be silly, Mamma. But it's permissible to look on the situation with different eyes, I think, when one's own mother acknowledges to . . ."

"The crime of murder—go on! Let's not hedge. How is it different?" asked Mrs. Christopher.

"Listen, Mamma," replied Hugh, his eyes hardening with fear and determination, "there is no guarantee that you won't hang."

"I know that as well as you."

"Then, let's have no objection to your taking the midnight

train to Harwich. You know nothing about hanging. I do. I've seen more than one person hanged. If you think that I'll let you . . . hell, no! The thing's impossible. You must get away to-night."

"Trumpery!" said Mrs. Christopher rising and looking for her bag. "My poor Hugh, things are in a much worse way for you even than for me. When the only solution seems to you to run away, it is time for me to leave and go to one of those little police-stations with a blue light—which is what I ought to have done all along."

"Mamma! Sit still!"

"Then," countered Mrs. Christopher, "understand once and for all that I came here to discuss giving myself up for the crime of murder. Having killed a man I have my own ideas about my future. There are times when a person would sooner have death than life. Don't think," she said agitatedly, "I am unaware of what all this means to you. Do you suppose I'm not suffering with you and for you, my dear child? My whole object in coming to you first was to enquire if there isn't some way whereby your name can be kept out of the whole sorry business. I didn't come here to listen to plans for my escape—as if rushing to Paris were an escape! My God! Do you think there'd be anything for me in living with all the flunkeyisms which would come from running away? Hugh, I fully realize the bitter irony of our situation. It's the sort of thing one reads about and thinks—it could never happen to us. But it has happened, and the consequences have to be faced. I want your help—not to run away—but to decide how *you* shall not be involved in the business."

"I don't give a damn about that side of it," shouted Hugh in chronic exasperation. "I'm thinking about the Old Bailey and hanging!"

"I hadn't forgotten them, either," said Mrs. Christopher quietly.

Contritely he whirled round upon her.

"Mamma, I'm sorry. It has all been a terrible shock to me. I really am most devilish bothered. I hardly know what I am saying, and anxiety makes me cruel. Perhaps it is a mistake to be dunning you with mere common sense!"

A look of having been suddenly, fleetingly pacified came into his troubled face.

"Very well," he said, "you are determined to face it. We'll get the best defence in the kingdom. I know the very man. Now, what can you tell me of the others after you had shot the man?"

"Why, then, of course, they were great company! The murder put them in spirits!"

"I'll bet it did," interrupted Hugh grimly. "We don't all have the privilege of front stalls when it comes to having our tyrants removed from annoying us for ever!"

"Yes, well, they were full of their advantages. They . . . I'm afraid they thanked me. Finally I gave them my name and address in case suspicion fell on any of them—it could happen."

"Aha!" exclaimed Hugh. "Then, at that time, you had not decided to give yourself up?"

"I had decided nothing," said Mrs. Christopher calmly. "You don't kill a man on an impulse and five minutes afterwards be in full possession of what you are going to do next. At least, it didn't happen that way with me."

"So those three people know your name and address? Not that it matters now, since you are bent on destroying yourself. But had that fellow any servants? Did they hear anything?"

"No servants were in the house. We made sure of that."

"What sort of a place has he got there?"

"O, as smug as you please—he lived in a clutter of Victorian properness. He passed for a man of exceeding respectability, as many criminals do. You can't be really good, with the fierce

39

loving goodness of Christ, and be respectable also, as respect-ability is measured in this world!"

"No, you're the proof of that. O, why on earth . . . but never mind." He sighed deeply. "How could anyone as mild as you draw a gun? It's a great mystery to me!"

"How could I? I don't know, now! I'm not the same person now that I was then. People are changing every minute, and I am no exception. But when I look back I see that what moved me to kill him wasn't anger or rebellion but—compassion. It was too much to see those people standing round his desk, like lambs or something, so helpless and doomed-looking. I always knew that one day I should do something wild through com-passion. I've seen it coming—the times when I saw a child ill-used, a horse beaten on the streets, and calves kicked off the trucks outside slaughter-houses. These things have brought me to murder's edge before now. Why, it's one of the most violent goads in the world, is compassion."

"All I can say," replied Hugh, vexed, "is that to feel so keenly for unknown people seems pathological to me! Good heavens! You've brought those three people off from something! Given them security—peace of mind, a fresh start." He smiled sourly. "Yes, I can imagine their gratitude. And it's a safe bet that if you *had* decided to run for it and suspicion had fallen on them, they would have given you away without a second's hesitation."

"Why, that was the whole point in giving them my name and address," protested Mrs. Christopher.

"True for you. Even so, no one with loyalty would use the information against you."

"I think they'd remain silent, yes, I really believe they would," replied Mrs. Christopher. "They were ordinary kind and decent people who had never been allowed to forget some little moral lapse."

"Umph! You know nothing whatever about them. You don't

know what he was making them pay up *for*. We are all kind and lovable as long as we are getting our own way; but just let someone disparage our class or worth, let us be the least bit frightened or thwarted in our darling little schemes, and at once we revert to the zoological type. From sordid experience I know human nature better than you do."

"Hugh, I don't care twopence about what you know. Anyone can know. You have to be more than knowledgeable. The thing is to love."

"So it's love, is it?"

"That's it. Too many people make the mistake of supposing that brains are called for when, all the time, what is needed is love. There are teachers of this and that, teachers of mathematics and rhetoric and economics and the arts, yet these things don't take people very far, they don't make humanity humane since there are no teachers of love. We all need educating in *that*."

Because, mused Mrs. Christopher, it *was* hard to love everyone, so hard, indeed, that the sheer difficulty of the thing made it enthralling. It's probably an excellent thing that neighbourly love does not come easily. Nearly all the lessons this side the grave can be learnt in the efforts required for understanding, toleration, and sympathy. Anything that is effortless leaves the height unscaled. In the anguish of that struggle endlessly to forgive, believe in the lost, remember the common attributes of our humanity, and love the undeserving, the desiring heart arrives nearer to that luminary of freedom in which selfishness is totally broken, yet, oddly enough, the highest form of self is reached.

Just the same, it is difficult to spend one's self, to spend all one's affections on other people because of the hostility inevitably flung up by ignorance and stupidity—given and received. Yet there is nothing else. And half the battle is to *want* to do the thing. You can't, you simply can't love God and hate His people, you can't hate those whom God loves. To despise humanity is so easy that *that* alone should make it suspect. We identify ourselves with what we condemn in others. Condemn! Umph! Who dares? We scorn *that* vice and, all the time we are up to our eyes in *this* vice. So it's far better to let people see that you believe in their intrinsic worth. Of itself this makes 'em wish to do better. It makes all the difference in the world if you say, in effect:

'Dear ones, what way are you now? Why will you not remember the goodness and light within you? We're all very much better than we ever realize. We've all got Christ in us. So let's look under our muck and ignorance and what do we find but that the kingdom of heaven is not something to die for but it's within us—something to live with. We are not *going* to the kingdom of heaven, we are *taking it with us!*'

Hugh was saying with melancholy earnestness:

"I've always viewed with extreme scepticism that love-your-neighbour mania. I can't bear it. It's not only absurd, it's dangerous. Look what it has brought you to!"

"O, no," said Mrs. Christopher softly, "it was because I forgot that love-your-neighbour mania that I fell into the error of supposing that violence was the solution, and I'm now obliged to stand a trial for my life. Murder doesn't wipe out blackmail. Things can only be improved by better things, not voided by force."

"Why, it was *compassion* for those three that made you commit murder."

"Yes, but the mistake was I didn't extend pity to *him*—the blackmailer. That's what I forgot, and it was the most important thing!"

"I give it up," declared Hugh.

Above the lighted match he was touching to the end of his cigarette, he looked at her with exasperated curiosity, as if understanding of her were to be found, somehow, in her hollow temples, in her bright and lively eyes. She looked an unremarkable little woman, pleasant and mild. Yet how unconquerable she was behind that exterior of violets and lilies.

He sat, silent, considering to himself the expenditure of his mother's boundless charity that he found so hard to understand—her faith in people even where, seemingly, there was no cause for belief, and her insistence on a universal brotherhood, under the wing of God, which could be achieved through the mystery of those strange, hardly-realized affinities which exist between all who live, affinities which steal into force in the light of compassionate understanding. All that loving kindness of hers which no one wanted! What could it be called? It was much more than a mere romantic enthusiasm. It wasn't something new, either, it was her habit. All her life these ideas had *been* her life.

The way is so clear for her, he thought, because she has never allowed her brains to destroy her heart. What a victory that is, after all!

Aloud he said:

"Well, deck it out how you like, Mamma, I maintain that those three people were not worth the harrowing risk you have taken for their sakes. Not one of them would have done the same for you, and I'll wager that all of them would have betrayed you had they been given the chance."

"No, I don't believe that," retorted Mrs. Christopher. "The young man might have done so—he looked as if he didn't care much one way or the other—a wild card altogether! But I don't know. We've no right to suspect them of anything. I believe they would all have been loyal."

"Bah!" exclaimed Hugh.

Silence fell. Mrs. Christopher knelt and dropped more coals on the fire. Suddenly smiling, Hugh said to her:

"Look here, Mamma, we can put your claims to the test."

She looked at him over her shoulder.

43

"What do you mean, Hugh?"

"On this night of daring I will make a completely unorthodox proposal to you," he said. "I might as well take a hand in all these fateful goings-on."

"Are you going to ask me to commit another murder?" demanded Mrs. Christopher, throwing herself back into the chair.

"I am not so unloving! But I'd like to see you proved wrong about those people," replied Hugh, his eyes on the ornate pocket of flushed light fixed in the opposite wall. "Furthermore, my proposition will give us both a little light relief from the major eventualities ahead. I suggest that you return home as a sort of prisoner confined to the house, since you have no notion of evading justice, only of holding it back a little. You will remain quietly at home in Hampstead for a month and, meantime, I, acting as though I have no knowledge of this man's murderer, will cause it sufficiently to be advertised that . . . let me see . . . that five hundred pounds will be offered as a reward for information leading to the arrest of the murderer. Five hundred pounds! It is not a lot of money, but it's tempting enough. I'll finance the venture. I don't feel as if money or much else matters after this night! I'll pay all three at the rate of five hundred pounds per person—because if one comes and sells his information, the reward is still to stand till the month is up to give the others a chance of earning the second and third five hundred. What do you think of the idea?"

Again Mrs. Christopher saw the three faces hovering about her, ardent with gratitude, as the blackmailer lolled with death upon him, faintly smiling.

"I don't much like putting temptation in people's way," said Mrs. Christopher. "Life's difficult enough without the addition of temptations. If you offer people payment for a betrayal you don't know what needs will force them to accept your bribe. Just the same, I have such faith in those people that I'll agree to

44

your scheme. But *I'll* finance it, d'you see. I'm down, more or less, to my last fifteen hundred after the blackmailer's demands. But that would be enough. It would be akin to leaving those three five hundred pounds apiece in my will in return, of course, for their buying me the little death by hanging which awards them their money. But they won't come for it, you know. I shall hold my fifteen hundred intact to hand over to you for some police charity."

Hugh drummed with his fingers on a small table beside his chair.

"From now on," he vowed, "you can say anything you like to me, and I shall not be amazed. I declare to high heaven that I am past all forms of known and accepted behaviour. It is not too much to say that my whole life has changed in this last hour. Yes, you can finance my idea if you wish. You can pay these people for betraying you because, of course, they'll all come for five hundred pounds, Mamma dear. I am just working out how I can contrive it. It will be my last throw before I resign. Damned interesting, too; an experiment with human beings instead of with words or chemicals!"

"I don't really care for such experiments," said Mrs. Christopher.

"Well, tolerate it for my sake. My whole future's bound up in it! To believe in the human race or not to believe! If only one of those three holds aloof from that blood money, I'll have faith. Come! Give me a chance to prove something, and them a chance to prove their worth—if any. I'll arrange everything. Sir Lintot goes to Jamaica the day after to-morrow. I shall be in complete charge of all our side of things. I'll issue the notice of the reward. And I myself will interview the three of them as they come sneaking in for their cash. O, it's an outrageous, fine idea! Outrageous! And, as I tell you, it will take our attention, a little, from the forthcoming ordeal of your trial. I can be quietly arranging about your defence, as well. We'll want a first-rate counsel. What about a lawyer?"

"Use mine, Johnny Auton. He's a good man and knows my ways."

"I'll have a talk to him. He can then advise you what you are to say to counsel. You must plead temporary insanity, of course."

"I'm not a lunatic, and I won't use that sort of trick," replied Mrs. Christopher. "Apart from anything else, it's degrading to be thought insane. I'm a murderer but I'm quite right in the head. I daresay I wasn't very controlled at the time of the shooting, but I was sane; and I will not put myself to the ignominy of pleading any debasing excuse in lunacy."

"No? Well, perhaps you'll make out a list of everything else you can think of that will ensure you the death sentence!"

"I know I'm trying, Hugh," said Mrs. Christopher, "but then, so are you. You're top full of schemes for escaping this and evading that. Can't you see that all of one's being is inside one? What's the use of running to Timbucktoo to try and escape from what you have carried there inside you?"

"I should have thought that anything was better than hanging," muttered Hugh.

"It's not the worst thing by any means," replied his mother. "It seems far better to hang than to lose one's notion of honour, commonplace though it may be. Of course, I know I'm old-fashioned. Very few people bother about honour nowadays. The craze is for sincerity. People seem to think that sincerity excuses everything—even evil. Let's be sincerely sinful! Don't you read your Gide?"

"Well," said Hugh, "it's something to stick to your principles. It's something to *have* principles! Yours may make an end of you, but it seems that you know how to die—not that it should come to that. I have every confidence in the man I'm thinking of as your counsel."

"Thank you, dear. What unruly parents some children do find themselves burdened with!" lamented Hugh's mother.

46

"Yes, indeed," said Hugh. "Never mind. I would not change you for anyone. Now, darling, I know nothing. I am going to issue notice of a reward for information because I know nothing. You never came here at all to-night!"

"And are you going to . . . leave *him* there . . . to be 'discovered'?"

"Certainly," replied Hugh. "He will be found to-morrow, sure enough. Even if he had no resident servants, some poor woman must have cooked and cleaned for him; she will squawk out an alarm in the morning, or the milkman will, or some other shocked and screaming party. You go home, Mamma, and I will work for your defence, to say nothing of my little scheme to prove the worth of the human race."

"And at the end of a month you will see that I am taken into custody? Well, I shall see to that myself."

"Yes, yes, Mamma, you shall be arrested, never fear. I wish all accused persons were so willing to be locked up! Good God! How macabre all this is! I'm glad to have my little plan to think about, otherwise I might turn unreal with the force of reality. Would you like some supper—a drink—before you leave? Are you sure? Well, I'll slip out and get you a taxi."

While she waited, Mrs. Christopher caught the scent of a rose that Hugh's Willie had placed in a glass on the mantelpiece. She turned towards it as if some gay and delicate tune had occurred to her and on its faint sparkling notes all the best things of her life were coming back to her. Odd, she thought, the scent of any rose makes you feel as if life has been one long summer!

"Taxi's here," Hugh called.

He watched his mother coming down the hall; she seemed charged with a kind of poignant acuteness. He drew her to him and kissed her with lively affection.

"Nothing is going to be as dreadful as we think," he said warmly.

47

"I'm sure of that," she replied steadily. But as the taxi churned away with her, she felt grieved and terrified again.

"God help us! God help us!" she said in the stuffy jolting dark.

It was then a few minutes after midnight, a breathing space loved by Mrs. Christopher, when sweet and unfamiliar airs drifted through the streets, exciting the late wanderer with intimations of far-off contacts, when the metropolis was hushed in a trance, suspended like a giant bubble between the waste places of the sky and the muted pavements a-wash with the fine ivory sheen of arc-lights.

And as the taxi drew her up the long hill to Hampstead, it seemed as if they were crawling up an incline outside cosmic relativity. Mrs. Christopher imagined she was moving through a non-earth bound realm and, from her airy unfettered station, she gave a thought to the world of humanity a-bed, the riff-raff of anonymous ones—the snorers, the starers at the ceiling, the lovers, the dreamers, the midnight weepers.

All her faculty of love rushed out like a warm cloak round her as she thought of those common hordes who have to hurry to queue for the cheapest seats at the cinema, who wear ugly clothes, work long hours at ignoble tasks and live in the back streets, who can't wash enough or eat enough, inarticulate and rough, yet who are the salt of the earth, who never write or read poetry but who are poetical themselves, having known that suffering without which great poetry cannot be written.

These, she thought, are Christ's people, those whom He is happy to call His own and, some time or another, happy to work through. Even I, a murderer, know that all of my life has not been God-wanting. That's not vanity: what sort of people would we be if we were conscious only of our own evil? We have a right, without being righteous, sometimes to remember that we have been decent as well as other things. In this world where we are only too ready to talk about ourselves from morning till night, the very odd thing is that no one ever speaks of those times when he knew God was most busy articulating through him. Perhaps that's because we never really know our own best moments. But God's presence is not banished because it is unnoticed or denied. No one knows in what secret hour the worst of us have been struck with a shaft of recognition of truth and light which, perhaps, the very saints have not known. There's more goodness, tenderness, courage, and endurance going on in this world than anyone ever dreams of.

Still, she sorrowed, it wasn't very comradely of me to go and do that poor fellow in just because he saw the world in a cross-eyed way. Not even the thought of what is coming to me—and when you kill a man there is plenty to pay—convinces me that it is reparation enough. And here I sit thinking loving thoughts about the world at large, having committed a murder! How strange that is! But—is it? I've not changed from what I was fundamentally. It's been my habit to think fondly of people. Because I've killed one man it does not mean that I have to *think* murderously of everyone!

And then as Mrs. Christoper continued to grieve over her guilt she all at once remembered about St. Ambrose to whom the Christ Child appeared on a Christmas Eve. She remembered that St. Ambrose asked what he should give his God standing there with a flame of wonderful light at the back of His head. What about giving his fine holy writings, or his prodigious prayers and devotions? But the Child hung His head in rejection of all those gifts. Anxiously the poor old saint asked what, then, could he offer? And the child replied:

"Give me your sins that I may forgive them."

Yes, the deeper you dropped into the pit the more attentive *that* Love became. And Mrs. Christopher felt bold and glad as well as humble and shamed.

The taxi sagged to a stop at the garden gate. Above, the stars were shining with a glassy reddish tinge as if a lot of pomegranate seeds had been flung across the sky. In the garden leaves wagged amiably in the light bantering wind. Between stars and leaves a current of unearthly benignity seemed to be rolling; it caught and enveloped Mrs. Christopher as she went to open the door.

She stood with the key in her hand, and the first easing tears began to drop out of her eyes.

PART TWO

FROM SOHO

I

AFTER Mrs. Christopher left the house in Highgate the other three stood in silence. There began to prosper in the room an intensely threatening atmosphere as though violence had attracted to the place a host of elementals from the void, and now they were gathering in the upper stories and on the dark staircase, waiting to enter this room when the light had been turned out.

"Now," said Giles too briskly, "who's next? Who's leaving next? One by one does it, and I'll go last."

Edmund looked enquiringly at Veronica.

"Will you go now?" he asked politely.

"Do you know," she replied, "I'm superstitious, and I'd rather not be the second one to leave. I don't like even numbers. I fancy that to be third will be lucky!"

"Haven't you had enough luck for one night?" Giles asked her. He turned officiously to Edmund.

"You'd better make a start, then," he said. "We must get out of here. Someone may call, or the 'phone ring, or . . . What?"

"So long!" said Edmund, at the door. "I don't suppose we shall ever meet again, but we've shared a rum evening. Few people can ever have had an experience so instantly rewarding! Good luck."

"Talks too much, that one! A perfect fiend for proselytizing,

51

I'd say," observed Giles to Veronica as Edmund shut the front door quietly behind him.

He could have caught the bus, but so as to savour his new delicious freedom Edmund preferred to walk the long distance to Hampstead Underground Station where he could get a through train for his home.

The calm immaculate moonlight gave him pleasure. He looked up and saluted the moon which like a piece of bone-white china, was shining in the dark cupboard of the night.

"This mystic radiance!" he exclaimed softly to himself, his thoughts reaching out to where the moon rays would be shimmering with an effect of spun sugar on distant wet beaches. Shells would be lying about like silver leaves on the sand, and little pools gleaming like the fallen shields of heroes; while in the mouths of caves the wind would sing the long night through until the dawn when all the sound and action would rush to the brightening sky.

Edmund's mind took on the tranquil colours of a nocturne, spreading out limitlessly, peace-gathering; but all at once he came to himself and the ruder aspects of the hour.

"I feel as if I'm going home from a play!" he muttered. "Even now the thing seems unreal; the non-criminal aspect of the murderer varnishes it over like a dream. Yet she positively murdered him. Who'd have thought it of her? So gentle seeming, and modest, and all! He must have been squeezing her badly for her to rush to that extreme. But what the hell could a woman like that have been blackmailed *for?* I dunno! The longer you live the stranger life becomes. It's only when you're a child that you accept everything without surprise! Still, whatever she was or whatever she's done, this Mrs. Christopher saved us. God love her, say I, and keep her from the hangman!"

He began to review his own position. He would have more money now, no longer being drained by Sine. He could begin to make a few plans, but—for what?

I wonder, he thought, humour coming into his face, if there's any future at all for a poetic old devil like me!

He was not, as a matter of fact, old at all. He would be forty-four on his next birthday, but he was emphatically lacking in those prospects which constitute a person's "future."

He had trained for the teaching profession and, as a consequence, saw that wisdom can only be learnt, never taught. His various headmasters found him too radical in his talk and ways to be what they considered a good influence among boys, and he left one school after another, either sacked by an infuriated headmaster or departing at his own inclination.

As a schoolmaster he had brought anarchy into the classroom and dismay into the drawing-room; he had constantly outraged housemasters' wives by introducing at their parties such unseemly topics as the poor, prostitutes, and people in jails.

What had happened at Marrow, the last school that had unhappily contained him? Of an April evening the headmaster had invited him to dine. Important other guests had been present including one of the school governors. As a special treat dessert consisted of strawberries forced in the headmaster's greenhouse, and champagne had been served with them. And while the other guests murmured their admiration of this out-of-season feast, what had Edmund done? Yes, indeed! With a wicked smile on his long face, and his round fixed eyes ardently opened to their widest extent, he had got to his feet, seized his champagne glass and held it aloft.

"To the Unemployed!" he toasted stridently, and flung the wine down his throat.

Clearly he was an impossible man for any school that wished to keep up tradition; it was recognized that he did not possess the Proper Spirit. While for his part he saw that the dreadful shortcoming of many schoolmasters was that the minute they began teaching boys, they stopped teaching themselves.

So at every headmaster's request with whom he came into

contact, and not least to follow his own wishes, Edmund gave up teaching.

Since then he had passed from job to job. His inconvenient and frequent expressions of humanity for the downtrodden and their difficult sordid lot, and his open, scathing criticism of commercial immorality had lost him five or six secretarial posts. His hatred of oppression of the poor had led him to thrash several other bosses of sweated labour, and now he had a clerkship at three pounds a week, less insurance contributions, in the office of a fairly honest timber merchant.

It had been a struggle to pay the blackmailer and, at the same time, exist on this salary. Edmund could not remember when he had last been able to buy a new suit of clothes or even a book, but now things had taken a brighter turn. Jubilantly he grasped his blackthorn walking-stick, and when he came to Jack Straw's Castle he went into the tavern and ordered a double whisky to celebrate.

He stood at the counter, drinking his drink, a tall spare man with a pair of unwinking eyes. The hair-cut he affected—a fringe on his forehead which seemed to accentuate the lugubrious length of his mild face—caused most people to look at him twice in an effort to decide whether his appearance was ultra-sophisticated or just plainly hinted at the madhouse.

As he swallowed, Edmund thought to himself, in a retrospect of his days:

A life like mine seems so aimless. To come to middle life with no accomplished dream is to feel almost indecently futile. You're born, you're educated for a certain profession, then you find you've no heart for that profession, so you're on the world—with nothing up your sleeve! You marry, you beget a son. Wife and son are taken from you in one sweep—killed in a road accident. That's what you do—you hire a car for a day's jaunt in the country, but it turns out that you hired the car expressly to see your wife and child bloodily wiped out of existence in a collision near a cottage which has chalked up on a board: "Cut flowers and plums for sale." That's what you remember most vividly about it all—"Cut flowers and plums. . . ."

Why did you escape while they were killed? No one knows! O, thou blessed that tells us nothing! Who are we to have our questions answered? It's as though everything has never been. Everything seems to have become nothing. You never seem able to begin again on any safe or settled basis, you seem unable to know again what to welcome and what to reject. Occasionally you recognize a set of higher things, but what is the use of that if you do not allow them to become part of your life?

Ay, for some people the dawn only comes once! And you can only carry on because you remember, sometimes, that these things are allowed to happen to you for a reason that is good. Yes, I believe that, I accept it, but I can't always live up to it. I run wild, and that's how Sine caught me.

That little affair with Mrs. Q.! And Sine threatening to tell her husband. And—O well, she never loved me. It was always her husband with her. I didn't want to see that fairly peaceful home broken up. Mrs. Q. was only amusing herself with me. Perhaps I was only amusing myself with Mrs. Q. Anyway, a poor devil has to pay for his amusements. So I paid Sine!

But now I am given another chance. Now, that woman, Mrs. Christopher, has made things new. I ought to justify that, somehow, not go wallowing on in my present ways. I wonder if we ought to be given fresh starts and new opportunities? We don't deserve 'em and we certainly don't know how to make the best of 'em.

A woman began ogling Edmund from a corner of the bar parlour. He liked women in casual encounter and lost no time in going across to her. He bought her a whisky and, after a few skirmishes, she told him that she would not object to spending a full night in his company.

Edmund replied that the only reason why he could not show

how honoured he felt was that he had a wife and four little children waiting for him at home.

"What! At this time of night? The children ought to be in bed!"

"Not mine. They won't go to bed without kissing their poor old father good night!"

He remembered his dead little boy who never would go to bed unless offered that last indispensable embrace, and this felicity, long-lost, cherished, made him smile wryly.

"O, I mustn't break up a happy home, must I?" the woman said archly.

"No," he said, squinting under his fatuous little fringe. "No, don't do that. You'd destroy more than you know. There's no need for a girl of your attractions to be upsetting quiet homes in order to get your good night kisses!"

"No?" she jeered. "But the best men are all married!"

"Not the best man for you," he said.

He bought her another drink, and made off. Going down the hill towards the Underground station, Edmund wondered how best to celebrate the rest of his evening. He booked to Leicester Square, the nearest Underground station to his home in Soho, and went down to the trains in the lift, gaping at the framed theatre announcements on the lift walls, his mind agreeably taken up with plans for entertaining himself.

He finally decided to call on Alma Wosp and spend an hour or two in her impious room—as all along had been his intention. Sooner or later, these days, all the point of action centred on Alma Wosp. It really was atrociously unfair that at his time of life a person like Alma should be such an obsessive proposition. To-night the murder and his consequent freedom had pushed her down to second place, but the bold woman in Jack Straw's Castle had set Alma's disorderly life tune thudding through his heart once more.

Of course, the woman in Jack Straw's Castle was not actually

on the streets, as Alma was. The bold woman whom he had
treated with whisky was able to pick and choose, and need not
bargain in arcades and porches after dark; she had spoken with
an accent acquired in a fashionable finishing-school, and a-bed
she would doubtless have unfolded an ancestry going back prior
to the Conqueror. She would not have wanted payment for
services rendered—she would probably have offered to pay *him*.

But, O, the lack of real feelings in promiscuous women with
social pretensions! And, O, the horror of nice respectable women,
strung-out, desiccated, stupidly bright, and lost to every vestige
of innocence by constant greedy scheming and compromise to
be superior, rich, and well known! To say nothing of the
mechanized units of the well-educated, and the pride and malice
of the 'saved.' The mediocrity of the generality of women was
so appalling to him that this in itself had been the most violent
forcing of his interest in Alma whose life was so intensely
differentiated, and, by its hazards and humiliations, its helpless
daring and immediate responses, was so much more mysteriously
vital than that of many who lived securely and lawfully.

So there was little contact anywhere, and you ended up by
becoming so interested in a street-walker that it looked . . . it
looked almost like . . . As Edmund jogged in the brilliant,
racketing train he fixed his eyes on an advertisement for toothpaste and allowed his mind to accept that his feelings for Alma
Wosp were such that he seemed almost to be in love with her.
Yes, and wash your teeth with it three times a day!

He stretched his legs across the carriageway and put on a look
of being resigned to his own folly. At my age, too, he deprecated
again. Seen from childhood, the forties are years that glisten like
old black rocks washed by dark unimaginable seas. But when
you did grow up, when you reached the forties, what was your
dismay to find that advancing age never ruled out the possibility
of being silly, endlessly silly. Age never was any guarantee of
immunity, of safety. There was always some utterly futile road

beckoning to a person, leading as far away from reality, from the divine life, as possible. And the perennial joke was—you always thoroughly deceived yourself into thinking that the cul-de-sac actually was taking you Godward. Ay: tiddly hi! You lived your life out with appearances when, all the time, you longed for perfections, and perhaps there was more sorrow in that, to a sensitive man, than in anything else on earth.

And now he, who had always made such a parade in his inmost self of unflawed chastity and its being the pass to the Right Paradisical One, he, whose illuminated text had been "Keep clean, be as fruit, earn life," he now had gone beyond himself in a hurly-burly of warring emotions for a prostitute, a poor little bundle of vain and unclean flesh. Few men would, literally, have the *nerve* to endure such a situation. But he had the nerve all right: the thing mostly was nerves. He was a perfect exhibition, free of charge, of an acute case of "tenderness" of nerve! It was a good joke, and to hell with it.

If he wanted to settle down again he could have made a decent match with anyone: he knew women liked him; he seemed both protective and naive—a combination which women usually found engrossing. Moreover, he knew that he seemed far more educated than he actually was, because the mere academical cramming that had to be done to qualify as a teacher resulted in a superficial knowledge that enabled the possessor to discourse without end, and produce answers with the instant glib readiness of a slot machine; but not the whole of it made for a farthing's worth of real culture, or true wisdom. Still, armed with these fal-dals he could have snared a kind and suitable companion.

But no, he had to be hopelessly enticed by a little whore, and because it had cost him more to succumb to this undesirable girl, so, when he was eventually won over, the thralldom was all the more enduring and deep. So much more had had to be accepted, so much more patience, imagination, and sheer magic of tenderness had had to be expended, that the end of it all was a remarkable infatuation from which he seemed unable to cut free.

There it was. He had now travelled so far away from what he had once been in the depths of a meditative and fairly contained self, that he was afraid of ever being put to the extreme inconvenience of having to face what had happened to his ideals in the way of battery and ruin.

The train rushed into Leicester Square Station and Edmund emerged into his favourite stretch of Charing Cross Road. He walked slowly in order to relish his speculations of what was going on in all the shut book-shops now that the people had gone home. All the inner necessities that had made those thousands of volumes would be seething as entities in the silence and darkness, with sometimes one stark beam from a street lamp looking in to heighten the trance. Why, in a few square yards of space in every Charing Cross Road book-shop there was now a concentration of thought so formidable that its energy could have shifted all London had anyone known the way to trap and use it.

He looked up to catch the moon peering stockstill over the tall roofs in such a transport of curiosity that he felt like making a nose at it and shouting up:

"Mind your own business, you!"

II

At Cambridge Circus Edmund crossed into the hot violent lights of Soho. Now he went from shop to shop buying a supper to take with him to Alma's—a cold roast chicken, several kinds of salad, rolls and butter, some cheese, a basket of grapes, a box of chocolates, and two bottles of wine—Alma loved wine. He also bought a bunch of violets for her.

Burdened like this he set off for Alma's address. She had a top room at Mother Cremorne's who let off accommodation to fallen girls in an eerie little cemented court which always seemed to be full of mist. There were only four tall ancient houses lolling in the court, the rest of the space being occupied by a French laundry, a warren of down-falling little offices, and a long low warehouse for artificial arms and legs. The far end of the court was filled with a prospect of the towering trees in Soho Square, which could lift the heart by their magic rumour of the country.

In the dim light from the lamp clamped to the wall on an iron bracket, he saw that the front door of Mother Cremorne's was ajar, and Edmund, with his parcels, clumped up the long flights of dark broken stairs to the top of the house.

Under every landing window lay a feathery dandelion-clock of moonlight, and from beneath the doors of some of the lodgers' rooms there escaped long streamers of golden light. Behind one door singing was going on—the singing of a bawdy song, solemnly and with feeling, as if it were a sweet hymn. And as he drew level with yet another door, Edmund heard Dublin voices in a medley of statements and threats:

"It was the angel Victor that got so thick with St. Patrick!"

"Ah, what do *you* know about them ones, you long-snouted devil, you!"

"And what are you but a dirty political!"

"Would you like me to give you one in the kisser?"

"The priest will put a big penance on you for that!"

Edmund toiled on.

"God's truth!" he puffed; "it didn't show much sense pitching a shack of joy at the top of so many stairs! By the time Alma's gentlemen arrive at her room half their longings must have departed in cold sweat!"

Receiving no answer to his thump on Alma's door, he lifted the latch and went in. He would spread the meal and have her supper ready for her when she returned. He hoped she would not walk in with a client; if she did, he would make the fellow go and give Alma a present from the treasury notes in his pocket which had been meant for Sine. How seldom he had money to give to anyone as a little present!

He switched on the light, sighing as he looked round the room. Tidiness and cleanliness had little part in Alma's ramshackle schemes. On the table stood an enamel bowl full of dirty soapy water in which wallowed several pairs of stockings, some handkerchiefs, and two plates. Beside the bowl, on a sheet of newspaper, were the remains of a meal of egg and bacon. The broken-down dressing-table was strewn with open pots of rouge and cream, little hillocks of spilled powder, half-smoked cigarettes, a dirty comb, a bottle of scent, and a paper-backed edition of "Venus and Adonis" by Leopold von Sacher Masoch.

A dusty hat, decorated with crumpled black and white roses, was hanging on the back of a chair. Edmund nodded at it sadly. As one tree on a near ridge that, by its closeness, could emphasise the infinity of the distance beyond, so this broken hat seemed to speak of all that had gone dull and tired in life, of all that once was fresh and gay but had been changed by usage into something dingy and pillaged.

God! What a life hers is, he thought. O, the cankered muddled life! O, the sad dirty life!

He took the kettle and filled it at the tap on the landing. He settled it on the gas-ring in Alma's room, and hung her scattered clothes behind the curtain that was strung on a piece of twine in a corner of the room.

When the kettle boiled he washed the crockery, and spread out the food he had bought. Then he sat down, listening idly to London night sounds spiralling up to the Soho roofs—the blaring of taxi horns, whoops from urchins, the muted rush of traffic, sudden sallies of yelling from late hawker-men, far-sounding bells, little dry fumings of the wind on the roof, and catches of music from wireless sets.

All the time he stared round Alma's attic in the aqueous light from an electric bulb swaddled in a pallid green shade. Under the window stood an amazing pair of long champagne-coloured boots with high heels, and beside them were some tattered little slippers of blue brocade. On the mantelpiece was a framed commercial photograph of Alice Delysia, and another of Queen Victoria, yellow and dark.

The wallpaper carried an insipid design of forget-me-nots and roses, grown so pale with age that their common colour was now a dry grey. But just by the door there was a very gay panel, indeed, where the decorator had run out of the original design and, no doubt assuming that anything would do for Mother Cremorne's garret, he had slapped on a length of nursery wallpaper. Thus the visitors to the harlot's room might trace and trap some of the reflexes of their childhood in the piece of odd wallpaper on which Little Boy Blue, the Cat and the Fiddle, Simple Simon, Mother Goose, the Man in the Moon, Bo Peep, and Tom the Piper's Son went about their traditional occasions in a systematic design.

There were also two wickerwork chairs which gave off gentle reports even when no one was sitting in them, and a foot-stool which Alma, no doubt, found indispensable after a night's weary promenading through the streets.

She had attempted some heavy-hearted gaiety by ranging a row of fair-ground dolls in tinselled clothes on the milky-pink coverlet of the divan bed. And on the wall above the smirking dolls hung a jog to the intelligence done in poker-work: "This is a home, not an ash-tray."

Edmund scratched his head and yawned loudly. He wondered how many men would remember this text as an emblem of the purchase of half an hour or so of Alma's time and attentions.

In the middle of his absorption with what he represented to

himself as the poetry of the undertide, it occurred to him to wonder what Mrs. Christopher would think of him sitting there waiting, trancelike, for a whore to come in from her business on the streets and eat supper with him.

That's what loneliness and a searching for the ever sweet and ever new had brought him to—dependence on a little tart's company to colour his days! He drooped. He was too lonely, that was the trouble.

But how do you know, he goaded himself, how do you know that your loneliness isn't a gift, deliberately ordered to give you that necessary freedom from distractions which enables a person to contemplate, to the purpose that some marvellous spiritual ascent or work of lasting value might come of those hours and years spent alone to one's self? But what could God be at to offer such opportunities to me? I am not fitted for such difficult honours. Let those who can bear loneliness profit from it!

And wait a minute: while he was mourning over his night-bound sensibilities he might ask what was wrong with his feelings towards Alma? He had never once offered to use her in the way she laid herself out to be treated. Had he thought of doing so? He did not know. At that point his mind always became confused and seemed to gallop away so that he could not tell what it was he wanted of her.

He knew he wished her to give up her life as a prostitute and get a decent job. He would have liked to remove her bodily from Soho, see her elegantly and securely placed; but however much he superficially protested to himself that he was out to save her soul, beneath the vociferous high motive he knew that really he was out to make demands. He was not content merely with giving, and accepting her for what she was—he wanted to take and make changes; he wanted to get Alma away and permanently placed so that he would be free of the torment of not knowing what she was saying and doing at all hours with other men and girls as loose as herself in this top room at Mother

Cremorne's where the dolls sat in a row, and dirt reigned, and there lived a kind of ghost of his own thoroughly lost and seeking heart.

Just then Alma walked in, and broke up his thoughts in a flurry of confusion and gladness.

"O, it's you, is it?" she said in a flat voice.

At first she intended to become distinctly unpleasant. Things had not gone well to-night. She had been trying to catch a fish from the provinces, a quiet elderly man who had oozed money and secret whims. He had bought her plenty of drinks, but when it came to the final decision his courage had failed him, and he had made off with a splutter of evasion and a very red face.

With this disappointment she had arrived home to find Edmund—Edmund of all people—lounging in her room, all set to talk to her about God or something equally tiresome.

She felt she had had more than enough of Edmund. She first knew him when she was in jail serving a short sentence for being herself. He had given three lectures to the prisoners on the delights of reading, and after his talks she was the one who had bombarded him with more questions than any other little jail-bird. Afterwards she had encountered him by accident in the streets of Soho and learned, with mixed feelings, that they were neighbours.

By now she had come to the conclusion that he was queer, and a pest, and that she did not like him very much. And she was on the point of telling him to get to hell out of her room when she saw the good things on the table; these instantly rejoiced her. She laughed out loud and clasped her hands on her flat little chest.

"Hoo!" she exclaimed, throwing off the anxious and dismal feelings that had been following her home, "ain't we got up all of a glitter! You fallen into money or something?"

"Only an odd pound or two," said Edmund. "You need not make a wonder of it, you know!"

But she walked round the table poking her finger into everything and shrieking:

"Chicken, look! And grapes and chocolates! And lots of perishing booze!"

She buried her nose in the violets which Edmund had arranged for her in a glass of water.

"Ain't they nice," said Alma reverently, "reely nice! They smell just like lovely expensive hair-oil!"

She put the glass down and knocked out a few steps of a little reel of pleasure, holding out her skimpy dress with one hand, and flinging up the other with the triumphant carelessness of a ballerina.

She was always ready for immediate enthusiasm and this seemed to inform all her figure. She threw off the idea that she could move as quickly as an eel through any kind of a situation. She was very slight and thin like a little girl; to heighten this effect she wore a short dress with a white collar, and where other street girls teetered about on extravagantly high heels, Alma wore flat-heeled shoes with a button strap. It was, of course, an entirely vicious get-up. Just the same, after this initial impression of the schoolroom it always came as a shock to Edmund when she turned her face fully towards him and he saw how accommodating men she did not respect or like had hardened her little mug into a perpetual mistrustful quiz. It was a face which provoked interest because of its sharp contrasts; the top half was broad with a smooth low forehead and widely placed, upward-slanting eyes of a cold shining sapphire. But the broad upper face abruptly narrowed below the eyes; tip-tilted nose and mouth were very small, fore-shortened into the pointed chin, giving this part of Alma's face a feral look in violent contradiction to her candid eyes. And the whole was covered with a thin papery skin which seemed as if it would tear with alarming ease. She was about twenty-five years old.

She drew the joyously creaking wickerwork chairs to the

table, showing, in delighted grins, her bad teeth which were small and brown like seeds. As usual, she had applied her rouge without skill; this gave her a theatrical look and contributed to the raffish stoniness of her face; but her straight shoulder-length hair, light and thin, was combed simply as a child's, and held from falling into her eyes by a small celluloid clip.

"Go on," she ordered Edmund in her common fussy way, "git it cut up—that bird. I ain't half hungry. I've eat nothing since my lunch. Cushy, this is! And you've washed up for me! You are a funny one, reely you are. You know what—I can't make you out."

"What do you mean?" asked Edmund, doing his best to carve with a small knife and fork.

"I'd give something to know your caper, that's all."

"Odd, the way women most suspect fooling when a man is most in earnest," said Edmund, heaping her plate. "But, perhaps, earnestness is what you mean by a caper?"

At once she fired up.

"Don't you try tripping me, slappy! You're too clever altogether. I seen your sort before and you're the worst at capers. You can look! All men got games. Rogering and dodgering! That's their life—fun and games."

"It takes *me* all my time to make enough to live on," Edmund stated through a mouthful of chicken. "But permit me to say that if men play games, women wear masks, so it all seems to be pretty much of a carnival, doesn't it? Get on with your supper."

"Well, don't keep on with your clever talk, then. I ain't no use for talk. I've heard it all my life and none of it means a thing, see, not a single damn' thing. Anyone can talk. It's what you *do* what counts."

"O, I've never done anything much," said Edmund. "I've had a lot of escapades which my vanity likes to call experiences . . . but never mind that. My dear friend, I should like to take you into the country for the day on Sunday."

"Not likely," Alma replied hastily. She gobbled and continued: "Lor, no, thank you, reely. I don't care for the country. It's too . . . open, too wide and draughty. Gits on your nerves."

She went wide-eyed with resentment.

"Take trees: I don't see the use of trees—stuck about all over the place. They don't smell nice or look nice, and you trip over their damnation roots, or bump into 'em, or git your hat knocked off with the branches. You can keep trees—and the country!"

"Dear lord! You need not consume yourself against the country," said Edmund easily.

He looked at her friendlily. Her notions, he knew, had nothing to do with reason, and had therefore to be respected even more than arguments based on logic, since no matter how limited or comic the world may be to the apple-headed its unreasoned realities are more compelling than those of the more enlightened.

"I'd like to take you out on Sunday, though," Edmund went on. "What would you like to do?"

"I can't say. I don't know."

She threw down her knife and fork. She did not want to go out with him at all, and it looked as if her better feelings might force her to do so in return for the good supper. Alma detested conflicts. And she tended to flame into hysterics rather sooner than is usually expected of her sex and calling. Noting the danger signs, Edmund said soothingly:

"Right. It's all right if you are engaged."

"Well, I am," Alma lied decisively.

"Get on with your supper then."

He filled up her glass with claret. She picked up her knife and fork, and struggled for a minute with one of the chicken's legs.

"Here!" she cried, seriously at a loss, "can I pick this up in my hand and eat it?"

"You can do what you like with it," said Edmund.

"O, I will!" She giggled. "You're a real decent slob! If you had sixpence you'd give the other fellow fourpence of it! I'm sorry about Sunday, I am. But a gentleman might be taking me somewhere for the day. I got to hold myself ready, see? Don't do to upset a client in my line of business. *You* know that," she jollied him, wanting the baffled painful look to leave his intent eyes.

Most of the time Alma kept up a cheerful front and was kind in a spirit of casual, automatic public service. She was naturally gentle, and so there was something dreadfully contrary about her turns of rapaciousness, her times of being inconstant and vitriolic. It made Edmund cringe. It was to that gentle side of her nature that he pinned his faith, just as it was the pathetically childish line of her little body that called out a passion of protection and pity in him, which she could kill in a second when a certain whine came into her voice, a certain calculating look into her sad and vicious face.

"Yes, I understand your difficulties," he replied. "There has to be some diplomacy, I suppose, even in your cut-throat game! You know, I should like to see you differently placed. You weren't meant for this kind of life."

"Wasn't I? Fancy!" said Alma with melancholy boredom. She stuffed her mouth with grapes and began blowing out a little shower of pips. "What was I meant for, mister clever?"

Hearing the childish munching noises she made as she ate, Edmund felt as if his fondness for her was getting too much for him.

"What were you meant for?" he said. "Why, a home, and children, and a decent man to protect you."

Alma guffawed.

"Git off of it! You'll have me bust out crying before we know the next thing," she told him cheerfully. She gulped her wine and held out the glass for more. She had had too much to drink when she came in; now she was quite tipsy. She said sincerely:

"I wisht I knew what you was playing at."

"I haven't time for play, dear friend." He looked at her levelly.

"Aw, you!"

Frowning, she stared him in the face. "You give me the creeps, sometimes," she went on, unamiably, "sitting there staring and staring like I don't know what. You might be up to anything. You may be off your head. Ain't you got a funny hair-cut! Why d'you have a fringe like a little girl's? You look like an old-time newspaper photograph of a murderer of young women. You look like . . . for all I know, you might be another Jack the Ripper."

Her voice rose. She had thoroughly frightened herself.

He listened to all this half stupefied. Where was the point of direct contact with this wronged and slippery little outcast? Negotiating was her trade, but in her inmost self she was completely unnegotiable; she could not deal with values beyond flesh and money.

"That's it—another Jack the Ripper!" she repeated, coming close to panic.

"Don't be a bloody ass!" he said.

Alma recovered on hearing this homely injunction. It was the sort of thing she understood.

"I hope I haven't hurt your feelings," she brought out at him glibly. "I never meant to, I'm sure. I just gits the whimsies sometimes, that's all! And Jack the Ripper must have been a gent like you—with a long nose like a cathedral spire—quiet and staring as he went scrimmaging about. I daresay he threw in a bit about Jesus, as well—same as you're always doing—as he knifed 'em. S'funny how tarts make men want to talk holy! Jesus and their sweet selves! S'funny how good us girls seem to make men feel. It's the contrast, I suppose. They've just had one little fall with us, while we're fallen all the time! Yet we wouldn't be—what we are, if it wasn't for men. That's where the joke comes in, see? Though I don't know who does the laughing!"

"O, nobody much. Trouble is pretty evenly handed out one way or another in this world, and there isn't much time to grin. And, look here, Jack the Ripper attacked women much older than you. They were all in their forties. So you've nothing to worry about from his successor—if any. I say?"

"Now what?"

"Why don't you let me try and get you a decent job away from all this, eh?"

"What kind of a job?" she asked warily, eyeing him with disgusted anticipation.

"O, I don't know—job as a waitress, maybe, or perhaps behind the counter in a nice shop."

Alma listened to these proposals with extreme repugnance. What all these reform gents never seemed to realize was how dull, terribly, horribly dull, their idea of a "decent" job sounded.

All the anonymous encounters of the life she led were not without their sense of adventure, they kept the pace hot. Her chancy life possibly resembled an old drab dress, as one of her clients had once told her, but those perilous eye, word, and body communions with total strangers were spangles that made the old frock gleam and obliterated the melancholy fact that the whole fabric was falling to pieces.

"I wouldn't thank you for any of those jobs," Alma replied with fervent opposition. She lit a cigarette. "If you want me to go straight set me up straight so's I don't have to work at all but can sit at home the whole day long, nice 'n' cosy, thinking up little schemes to save my blasted soul!"

"Well, don't be petulant with me. You can't be pleased with your sort of life. Come! I should have thought that any job was preferable to waiting about on the streets in all weathers for all sorts of birds."

"Well, it ain't," she said querulously. She contracted her eyes against the cigarette smoke.

"Hell!" she broke out into the vivacity of rage, "what's it got to do with you, anyway? You go and mind your own yard! I must have my drinks and little things; them jobs you mention don't pay enough for a girl to buy what she fancies. There ain't no percentage in 'em. I know Me foot to the lot of them! You suppose I ain't never had a scheme to try and cut clear of this dog's life? You suppose I *like* it? God's trousers! Why, the only place where I can call my soul my own is in the water-closet. *There* I'm Someone: I even feel as if I got civic rights—the right, anyway, to use the public drain! I've done plenty of wondering about cutting clear, don't you worry. But there ain't no prospects, see! The wages they pays shop girls in some o' them stores is so poor the girls is obliged to do a bit of solicitin' on the side so's to be able to make enough to eat proper. Don't talk to me about decent jobs till they's paying decent wages. I may be low, but I ain't daft—not altogether."

"Drink up," he said, "and shut up. You work out a good answer, but you're cooking your figures! You don't want work at all, that's the size of things. So don't yammer on the key of self-pity. You and your water-closet! It's the only place where *most of us* are kings of the castle! Think that one out!"

"I never think," retorted Alma. "Where d'you think I'd be if I thought?"

"Not on the streets, anyhow," he said angrily.

"I see you're in a paddy," observed Alma owlishly.

"Well, you can overlook it," replied Edmund. "It won't cost you much. Anyway, I'm off." He jumped up, and found his walking-stick. "It's late, and I must get some sleep."

He put two pounds on the table.

"Might help."

He heard her calling him back but he went on down the stairs taking, as he sardonically recalled Keats' line "the journey homeward to habitual self," while midnight struck from St. Anne's Church.

71

He had a small flat in a Queen Anne house in Feng Street, Soho. There he lived among ochreous little shops for contraceptives, Egyptian sweetmeats, wine, horsemeat for human consumption, little books setting out propositions of barren sexual play, groceries, and foreign newspapers; there were also Chinese eating-houses, Kosher butchers, European café bars, club rooms, creameries, and private houses where tailoring or cabinet-making went on in the front parlour with the windows thrown widely up. Edmund's street smelled with a rousing continental stench in which the predominant stinks were Algerian tobacco, dirty drains, cooking, and rotten fruit. The district was full of colour and rude zestful life. At nights there bloomed a sort of wild hanging-garden of many-coloured Neon lights.

Making his way towards his flat under the street lamps which appeared to him as flaring green plums in hollows of glass, Edmund remembered that through these very streets Thomas de Quincey had once hunted for Ann, and William Hazlitt had roamed scorched by love for that prim slut of a lodging-house keeper's daughter, Sarah Walker. But Hazlitt had known what he wanted; he had wanted the girl for wife or mistress—for love. De Quincey had known what he wanted; he had wanted a comforter. But he, Edmund Macvey, did not know, really did not know what he wanted of Alma or how she could appease the fever and the fret which worked in him so diligently, producing so many devilish, odd, and beautiful moods.

I'm like William James, he thought, I've had to give up logic!

When he got in he found he had not put his gramophone away from the previous evening's use, so he played the record on it which happened to be the waltz from the film "Un Carnet de Bal." He could not have explained why, but the sombre little whirl spoke to his longings and he played it through three times, listening attentively, with his hands in his pockets, before he went to brush his teeth. He studied his face in the wall mirror, looking at it with severity and a kind of horror.

"If it goes on, I shall become depraved or something," he said softly, broodingly. "Is it 'being in love'? I take leave to doubt that remembering what I felt for Clara, my sweet wife. But it's being in *something*. What? Am I practising a sort of masochism upon myself? What am I doing? Which way does the wind blow? I long for a state of affairs in which I control every minute of her days and nights—marriage, I suppose; but that's fantastic, not because she's a prostitute—prostitutes have made excellent wives before now—but because, constitutionally, she could never endure a bond. And then, we have nothing in common, nothing at all. It's simply those eyes of hers—that's what it must be. When I look into her face, where her eyes are, I find myself so unaccountably, irrationally, and scandalously fascinated, that what has been my life's reality till now goes up in smoke. 'O eyes, O mortal stars, the authors of my harms!' I swear I'm mad. There are certain obsessions which we have no right to indulge. We all know when we have gone beyond the boundary of what is lawful for us. I've gone beyond it. What an idiot I am! To be lacerated and baffled without end is the quickest way I know of getting hard. Let's harden then—you break the sooner—and then it's all over and done with. O God, O God, be merciful unto me—a fool!"

III

On the night of the Sunday which Alma had refused to spend in the country with Edmund, he was sitting in a tavern in Charlotte Street with a tankard of beer in front of him, and some dolorous cheese sandwiches on a thick white plate. In a corner of the bar an automatic piano was grousing through

"I Kiss Your Little Hand, Madame," accompanying itself with convulsive starts and rumbles from the depths of its ancient bowels.

It was early in the evening and the bar was not yet crowded when Alma came into the tavern from the streets, with her little girl's style of hairdressing, and her little girl's slippers on her feet. Not perceiving Edmund, who was sitting in a far shadowy corner, Alma went to the counter and obtained a cheap drink which she carried off to a distant table.

Unrestfully he watched her. So much for her being engaged and unable to go out with him!

"You bitch!" he mourned.

When she had been sitting there a few minutes, a poorly-clad youth went and sat down beside her and began to treat for a session of her private company. From where he was Edmund saw the entire little drama in mime, being too far away to hear what was said.

The young man was persistent, Alma was adamant. It was easy to guess the trouble—the stranger clearly had not enough money to pay for his pleasures. He flung off at last in a bad temper, and Alma got up to provide herself with another drink. At the counter her vulpine little face attracted the attention of a hulking gentleman in big brown boots, with a face like a piece of glazed grey pottery; he evidently could rise to Alma's tariff. After a brief haggle and a few drinks they went out purposefully together.

All the time Edmund had gone on eating and drinking. It was astounding, he thought, the way you could go on doing everyday things such as solidly munching hunks of bread and cheese when you were in such a ferment you felt you were going to burst at any minute.

He had sudden notions of cutting free—of going to live abroad—of giving himself a lethal dose of something—of letting fly and going through Soho at dead of night, disembowelling

street women, as a protest, in imitation of Alma's horror, Jack
the Ripper

He could not carry on. He had become outlawed from
known experiences and was shining to himself like a bit of
rotten fish in a dark cellar. What sort of a man was he, after all,
to allow himself to become so wretchedly involved? The manure
heap, he knew, had never been far from his door, but now he
had gone out to live upon it altogether.

Let him tell himself, in a confidential tone, that the object of
his tenderness and yearning was a little night-walker, a haunter
of loose men, with a sly little face under a child's hair-cut, lips
blackened with the lees of cheap wine, and a body under that
short dress on which anybody, anybody at all who could pay,
had left their mark. That was the proposition. Yes, and wash
your teeth with it three times a day! There had occurred to him
the advertisement for toothpaste in the Underground train at
which he had looked, with his head full of Alma, on the
night Mrs. Christopher murdered Sine, and so gave him,
Edmund, another chance to rise in the world. Rise! He'd never
rise.

The horror of an intense obsession, and the unfairness, even
in an affair of this decrepit order, was the curious extension of
one's dote into every branch of life. Here she was now even
associated with advertisements for toothpaste! After a time it
would become impossible to live because there would be no
escape; high or low, there would be no escape.

The white shining of the rain on roofs became identified for
ever with the short dark dress and its little white collar; a hole
in the heel of any stocking had a murderous pathos that could
upset the most carefree hour; the pitch of her blasted voice was
in every town sound, in brooms knocking, in sparrows dis-
coursing, in traffic plaints, in barrel-organ music, in footsteps on
paving stones, in all the promiscuous noises of the great metropolis. Her silly name hung like a sign before every door; there

was no entering any place without the golden expectation of finding her there; there was nothing seen or heard or touched or tasted but it became invested with some extension of his infatuation. There was no rest or peace from dawn to the heel of the day, in dreams or out of them, with or without the dominating girl, and existence became one vast fret in which the least little sign might mean all the world—a state of affairs which, if it went on long enough, could be the ruin of a person, bringing about either the mind's collapse or a dereliction of the body in some fevered and wasting disease.

And the real horror lay in this: the person most affected in the obsession was not to blame and could not help at all, because the image so feverishly carried about was not even true of actuality; it was a subjective image, the creation of the pursuing ego, and never really existed at all outside the enslaved and demented mind of the follower.

So it was rather wonderful that one could sit mopping up damp bread and cheese, and swilling down beer, without perishing of self-hatred and misery. And just as Edmund was thinking that his mad singleness had changed the honest light of life to the vague dark glow of dreams, everything stopped racing beyond his control, and he found himself remembering, of all that there was to remember, Alma's eyes—her one wonderful feature, still largely saved from the arrant bankruptcy of the rest of her being. Flowering thus before him, reflecting a mild melancholy concentration, seeming to implore some further abysmal understanding from him, he said to himself that Alma was something more than the little drab of Soho doorways.

Using that soiled body as its meagre tenement dwelt a God-made immortal soul, capable to-morrow or next year or some time of purity and unselfishness, and of rising, formidably un-beaten, above the shameless struggling days, as an articulation of the love and power of the holy Trinity. No one at all was just a lump of sin and no one was just a fragrant hive of goodness. Good and evil dwelt together in humanity, and in the morning a bun eaten in the brotherly warmth of eleven o'clock could release the one, while the same evening a woman's leg, and not necessarily a pretty leg, could shoot out the other.

Edmund now began to put all his money on goodness, and the virtues shone like stars in the reeking pub as he sat at the sloppy table—the virtues which were not mere dull expedients to vex the population, but golden keys that threw open entrances to splendid surprising vistas, such as could be seen sometimes from a humble cottage door set open to show a passage-way straight through to an exquisite and unsuspected garden blooming at the back. Life, so far from being cramped by a pursuit of goodness, became infinitely rich and expanded, the unhampered spirit travelling into regions of beauty and stimulation.

Edmund saw Alma, and the fancy idea he had always envisaged as himself, caught away into the good life. Alma was all right. People like Alma did not go to hell, for all the moralists' blather on the subject. Sometimes, in expansive moments, Alma had chatted to him about the desires and demands of her clients, and he had known terribly conflicting emotions thinking of the lunatic naiveties, the inflamed oddishness of lust that she was called upon to satisfy. Just the same, thought Edmund, pushing up his fringe with his fist, there need not be any difficulty in forgiving all the bits of girls like Alma who, up and down the world, got their living by such ways: because this kind of catering was so atrociously silly that the girls who provided it were, in the final analysis, only like ignorant and uselessly meddling children. Their Father would forgive them because they did not know what they were doing.

Why, you had only to look at Alma sometimes when she had forgotten for the moment that she was a rather successful little tart, when her vicious sophistication had left her face, and you could see what a child she was, after all. Once he had caught her gawping with the heartiest satisfaction at a Punch and Judy show in Soho Square. That was the sort of thing which gave Alma such unexpected twists of personality, which seemed to avow her untapped sources of tenderness and receptivity, and which, together with her vitality and mysterious urgent nether life, could make so deep an impression on a man like Edmund who took scorching pleasure in the poetry of the commonplace, the whimsical, the dangerous—of life seen as a whole.

He went and brought another tankard of beer back to his table, thinking that Alma not only looked like a child, she *was* like a child, and such innocence, dwelling in the midst of depravity, had a kind of wild density through which real premeditated evil could not pass. Ah, it did not need Erasmus to point out Christ's word that the harlots and publicans would go into Paradise before the Pharisees.

Edmund suddenly wondered where these thoughts were leading him. By their token, could he not see, once and for all, that there was nothing wrongful in his interest in Alma? These thoughts proved that he was out for good. He was right to cherish this girl, and he would go on doing so.

His mind, which for so long had been roaring with fury and rottenness, became hushed and peaceful, and his heart, which had been frozen to a chip, warmed and gushed with sweetness and love.

With a frightful organic spasm the automatic piano near him belched into a wrathful rendering of "Broken Doll," in response to a sailor's penny. But Edmund did not mind the racket. He was in bliss. No one was hurting him. He was at peace. He sat on and on, just enjoying being alive.

During the next few days he saw in the newspaper the announcement of the reward of five hundred pounds for information leading to the arrest of the Highgate murderer.

At first, it never occurred to him that he might gain from the situation. He thought only of Mrs. Christopher, and felt glad that, so far, she had successfully evaded the police.

78

But half-way through the morning, as he was checking a column of figures on his counting-house stool, it came over him that *he* could go and claim that five hundred pounds, and . . . and . . .

His guts suddenly seemed as if they were on fire. He could have groaned aloud with the shock and potent of the whole thing.

"You all right, Macvey?" demanded the chief clerk, breaking in on the welter of Edmund's thoughts.

"Yes," he replied. "Why do you ask?"

"You look so damn' queer—such a rum colour all at once. Thought you were ill."

Edmund attempted to return to his columns of figures. They would be dismissing him if he slacked like this. And what would that matter? He need never slap empty pockets again when he could go and pick up five hundred pounds in five minutes! He shuddered. Whatever was decent in him stood apart, as it were, at this point, and waited to see how far he would go.

He went so far as to consider himself in the part of an informer—knocking at an official door, going in:

"Hello, there! I've come to sell a woman named Christopher. Christopher, yes, that's right. That's the name, old boy. Christ! Christopher! Come to sell Christ for thirty pieces . . . no, have another go! Come to sell Christopher for five hundred pounds!"

The wind began to stamp on the office roof like an army.

Gale warning, thought Edmund. Lots of bloody gale warnings!

He listened to the din going on all round him, the boiling wind, the crash of timber in the yard, the tearing shriek of the great toothed knives in the sawmill, and he felt as if he were rocking in a bottle in the depths of a disorderly sea.

Times without number he found himself staring at his work, the figures meaningless, the pen in his hand without sense.

"They'll certainly kick me to hell out of here," he said, "and who'd blame 'em."

At lunch-time he went off to the cheap steamy little café where he ate, and while the waitress was bringing his order, he opened the newspaper and slowly read the police notice again. He stuffed the paper into his pocket. Let the police take and ram their five hundred pounds. . . . He was above such things. Smiling with pride at his invulnerability, he received his portion of steak-and-kidney pie and chips.

"Have a nice half-day, yesterday?" he asked the waitress.

"Not bad. Went in the country with a chap. Picking prim-roses!"

That was just what Edmund had planned for Alma and himself! Picking primroses! He began to eat.

But, of course, it was easy to understand Alma's point of view. What was there in the country for a little tart who never had had time, so far, to understand any realities save the facts attending her livelihood got in the alleys and avenues of the town. If he were to do anything for Alma it would need to be more than trips to the country. It would have to be something more than an invitation to go and pick primroses. The country might come on afterwards, but first she would have to be lifted in some permanent way from one part of town to another. He must give her a fresh start, a new life. The five hundred pounds would just cover the expenses! And he was pushed back to where he had started. Leave off! Shut up! Stop! Caution! Go. . . .

He tried to remember if he had ever met anyone more odious than himself. He slashed at his food so savagely that he soon found himself with a lap full of chips and pastry. The waitress hurried to help him.

"You in love or somethin'?" she scolded. "You'll have to send this suit to the cleaners. You ain't half in a mess!"

"I know," he answered. "And I don't think the cleaners can do much to help!"

"Try 'em and see. Will you have another order of steak and kidney?"

"No, thanks. Bring the sweet, whatever it is. And I'll have a cup of coffee."

That evening when he reached his flat he found a note from Alma in the letter-box. She had never written to him before. She never wrote to anyone if she could help it. She thought letter-writing a silly, dangerous game, and in her set, so it was What the devil, then, had happened to cause her to write now?

Alma had not wasted words:

Something serious. Can you come. ALMA WOSP.

Alma Wosp! Bloody silly name! Her father was said to have been a Dutchman. Some Dutchman! The Flying Dutchman! Flew off and left Alma and her mother, whoever *she* was.

Edmund still had five pounds left from the ten he had been taking to Sine the night the blackmailer was killed, and he put this money in his pocket. Whatever was wrong, cash would be needed, for a certainty.

Without delay he went round to Mother Cremorne's. Although the little court where Alma lived was wreathed in its usual gloom, her high apartment, when he reached it, was in a flood of evening sunlight, thin, and still, and warm. He found Alma stretched on the divan, carefully nursing a bandaged leg; a bottle of cheap cooking sherry was standing on the floor beside her.

"Hello," she yawned. "Decent of you to come. I'm in a hell of a jam!"

"What on earth has happened?" he asked, nodding at her bare, bound leg.

"You might well ask," she said sullenly, speaking out of a world that was even more troublous than usual. "I'm damn' near dead! Sit down, can't you. You're like a squirt in a bottle! This 'ere happened last night. There's always something! I was out with a client, late on; he'd had a drop too much, blast him, and got the staggers. Next thing was he fell. That wouldn't have mattered, but as I was hanging on his arm, I come down as well. That's not all. I fell on a rusty tin what was cocked up, and it went in my leg. I've got blood poisoning, and what's to become of me? I can't go out to get any men and they won't come to me here. I ain't never done any advertising of my premises—it ain't allowed. And I ain't got no regulars. I never was one for askin' 'em in for a whole night's easy, once a week. Gits on your nerves, regulars does. So here I'm stuck. I've only got eight shillin' and I've got to go to the hospital every day in a taxi 'cos I can't walk more than a few steps on this leg. For Chris' sake, what am I going to do?"

"Poor old thing!" he said. "I am sorry. But don't worry. We'll soon have you well again."

"Who's 'we'? You and God Almighty, I suppose! And what's going to become of me while you're getting me well?"

"I'll see that you're all right, of course," he said.

Confusion and pleasure thrilled through him that in her distress Alma had turned to him. This accident would put her into his keeping for the time being, and he would use the opportunity, somehow, to change her life, to direct this wayward unredeemed little wretch to dependence upon him.

He looked round the room. The usual mess reigned jocundly in the canary-yellow light. He would clear up, for a start. He must lay himself out to please. He must try not to get on her nerves. He must remember that her world was as choice and as specialized as a duke's, a sporting man's, an artist's, or a dustman's, with intricate rules of behaviour, positive taboos, and forms of bad manners which might trip up at once the superior and differently enlightened. He would have to go warily. He threw off his top-coat.

"Have they told you that you can drink?" he asked, indicating the bottle.

"Who? The hospital? They never said nothing about it."

"Don't think you should drink with blood-poisoning, especially that muck."

"O, I must have my little drinks. I can't do without my little wets!"

"I'll go and get you a bottle of burgundy, then. Don't drink any more of that filth."

"I'd rather have a bottle of gin," Alma suggested helpfully.

"She'd rather have a bottle of gin!"

Edmund loudly addressed the ceiling. "What is it that makes her think spirits and blood-poisoning go together? Does she want to die?"

"No, I don't, silly," she said. "You're right. I remember it was gin what finished off my old Gran. Cancer of the face she had, poor old duck! She wasn't supposed to drink with it, either. But she got the craving, see. And one morning at opening time she sent a kid round to the pub for two shillin'sworth of gin. When it come she swigged it down without waiting to kiss her hand to anyone, and it sent her mad with pain. She run into the street, and what with the gin and the cold—it was November, see—her face seemed to fall wide open and began pouring blood. She run and run through the streets, roaring and screeching, till she dropped down dead. I bet that annoyed her—if she knew she was kicking the bucket, I mean. She'd always meant to pass out in style in the workhouse hospital."

Alma sighed noisily.

"No, I don't think I'll have no gin."

"I shouldn't, dear girl," said Edmund, washing up with a brisk clatter. "There's too much of the Lyceum flavour about gin."

Alma studied him.

"You're a good sort," she brought out. "You got the human touch! I don't know anyone else who'd have come here and helped me like you."

"Think nothing of it. Anybody would have done the same."

"Like hell they would! I ain't got a friend in the world, see.

That stinking old Mother Cremorne seen me this morning when I come in from the hospital. I was crawling up the stair and she shouts: 'Nice bloody pickle you're in, ain't you! But you hadn't better get behind with your rent!' Fancy harping on the rent when you see a poor soul with a busted blood-poison leg! It don't give you no heart, do it? It ain't human. Gawd'strewth! The lousy people there is up and down the place!"

"You can't measure everyone by her."

"You have to in my little old world."

"What would you like for your supper?"

"Now you're talking! Let's see: how about a nice big paper full of hot fish an' chips?"

"O, we can go one better than that. Wouldn't you like a steak or chicken or something? I'll order a proper meal to be sent in from a restaurant."

"My, my! Ain't we slap up! But, here," she said, contritely, "I don't want you to go and get your pockets dusted down over a few victuals. You got to live, same's me. I know! See can you get some fish and chips. They're awful tasty. I like 'em ever so, reely. Take that there basin off of the shelf and put the chips in it."

"Why!" he exclaimed, his eye falling on the china basin with its sprinkling of black clover leaves, "my mother used to have a little basin exactly similar!"

"Your mother!" she scoffed, as if it were an affront to her to hear such a word mentioned in her room. "I stole *my* basin, if you want to know something," she went on violently. "It was in another girl's room, and it took my eye! That's my sort! D'you still want to go out and buy me a supper?"

"Yes, of course," he said. "I'm going out now to order something nice to be sent in. You must have a decent supper. Will you be all right by yourself for a few minutes? Can I pass you a book or something to read?"

"No, ta. You know I ain't no reader." Alma yawned. "Waste of time, reading. When you've read all that blather they put in

84

books where do it get you? Now that chap I was out with last night, him what fell and brought me down, he was a reader. Before we went out we was sitting in a pub and he was shouting about books—something about 'magic doors'! Him and his magic doors! He had the face to tell me I'd never have sold out so cheap if I'd read books. I told him quick there was many a married woman—respectable so called—what could afford to buy every book the minute it come out, and did buy 'em, and did read 'em, and was no better than they should be! It ain't books what keeps you straight, I told him. It's something that's done to your bloody heart early on in life, when you ain't no more than a child!"

She gazed with troubled severity at the rich evening sky.

"Well done you!" said Edmund, who was hanging up her clothes in the curtained alcove. She brought her attention back to him.

"That's what this sniggering maniac said. Just the same, he would keep on about some book or other that I had to read. Said it was one of the greatest books in the world; said it was whole education in itself."

"What was it called? Who wrote it?" asked Edmund, a book-lover.

"Ah, now you're asking. Them as knows can tell!" she parried. "Let's see. Harrum! I forget the name of the old buffalo who wrote it, but the book was called 'Dan Quick Soap.'"

"Really?"

"Ay, something like that. It's in that top drawer. He gave it me. He told me to go in his overcoat pocket and git it. How many times do a man ever give a girl *permission* to go through his pockets, eh? Ask yourself that! So I goes and gits this here book. Pass it me. I've changed my mind. I will have a read of it while you're out."

Edmund handed her a pocket edition of "Don Quixote," fished from the litter in the top drawer of the dressing-table.

Her little face turned glum as she ruffled the pages.

"Looks horrible daft!" she said.

"It is daft," said Edmund, "that's why it's so good."

Some bell-ringers were dealing forth a peal of chimes from a distant steeple. Alma threw down the book to listen. She lifted to Edmund eyes that were shining with nothing but innocent pleasure.

"O!" she exclaimed, "the sound of bells gives me such funny feelings, I don't know why."

"Blessed are they who can *hear* bells," he said.

"Aw you!" she retorted. "You've always got the honey! What you always so considerate for?"

"I'm your guest, you know."

"Guest? I don't have *guests*. I only have *men!*" protested Alma with furious scorn.

He had got his outdoor things on again, ready to go and buy their supper. With his hands in his pockets he stood looking down at the little street girl with amusement and pity.

Whatever happened, the last word was with her—and for her. The sordid and abortive experiences of her life, and the intimations, every time one looked at her, of dreadful consequences only biding their time to blight her, gave her a strange ineffable charter of suffering which softened judgment and invested her— the victim—with more than a hint of positive and lasting triumph.

IV

Edmund took advantage of the chief clerk's error in supposing him ill and absented himself from the office in order to look after Alma. The next morning he went round to take the girl to the hospital.

As he went in, Mother Cremorne appeared at the top of the

stairs which wound down to the deep dismal basement where she lived. Mother Cremorne was tall and carried about herself, as a sort of perpetual luggage, many heavy packages lumps and p rcels of gross flesh. From between her painted lips two foolish b ue teeth threw off some indication of the rodent properties of her mind. Her much-dyed hair had arrived at a permanent tint of tomato red; this was worn short and frizzed out like a Zulu's. She gave off something fusty, something unpleasant and elderly. There was a piece of fried fish in her hand at which she sucked vigorously.

"You goin' to pay her rent?" she jerked her head in an upward direction.

"Whose rent?"

"*Her* rent."

"Sorry," said Edmund. "They use names where I come trom."

"You're that smart," said Mother Cremorne, unruffled. "You and your names! What name do you give that funny little fringe of yours? Never mind. I know. What I don't know is who's going to pay the rent of Miss Halma Wosp what's a lodger of mine?"

"Miss Wosp will be paying her rent."

"That takes a load off my mind! When will she be paying?"

"When it falls due."

"So long as we know——"

"Now you do know. And I'll tell you something else."

"Go on! Let's have it."

"Hoppit, and don't mind other peoples' business till it becomes your business!"

Edmund climbed to Alma's room.

Nearly all the morning was taken up with the visit to the hospital. The queue, flaunting injured anatomical sections, picketed in the out-patients department was very long, just as if there had been a deliberate conspiracy among the public to get itself unusually and copiously burnt, bitten, cut, scalded, bruised, crushed, and poisoned, simply to waste more of Alma Wosp's time and fray her nerves. She did not take kindly to the clinical surroundings. She was badly scared, and she was glad of Edmund's support. Combustible through fright, she took it into her head violently to resent what seemed to her the ruthlessly inconsiderate way in which the nurses and sister in charge treated the patients.

"Give theirselves airs, don't they!" she observed loudly and offensively to Edmund. "And why? 'Cos the patients around here is too no-account and sick to answer back. But see the difference in these starched stuck-up scutts when they're out of their uniforms, when there ain't no doctors around to make sweet eyes at. Poor little objects they are with no one to boss and a tuppeny cup of coffee as much as they're worth. I seen 'em in the cafés around here when they've time off! I know 'em!"

Just here the sister hustled out a trembling and recalcitrant old man.

Alma gave a loud and indignant cry.

"Here, you!" she called to the sister with rich hate, "leave that poor old sod alone. Stop shoving him about or I'll lift the skin off you!"

"Shall I tell you something?" said Edmund tranquilly, while the sister, unheeding, continued to hale the protesting old man down the passage, " 'Before fording the river, don't curse the alligator's mother.' It's an excellent proverb, dear girl."

"What you talkin' about—alligator's mother!" asked Alma peevishly.

"Don't you see, donkey," he said, "that woman will be dressing your leg when your turn comes, and here you are antagonizing her like anything."

"I'll agonize her!" declared Alma. "I'll pulverize her! She hadn't better start dressing or undressing no legs of mine. Cor damn it, I hate it here, what with these nurses and . . ."

"Don't let little things worry you," he said. "The idea is to get well again. If these girls annoy you, be above it. They don't mean to offend, you know, and often that sharp manner is cloaking about as much real goodness as you will ever find in this world."

"Cloaking it! Smothering it, you mean!" protested Alma. She found herself pained. "Why, you twicer! What you sticking up for them for, eh? You're a nice bloody friend! Are you on my side or ain't you?" She turned a blazing face upon him.

"Of course I'm your friend, Alma, but be fair. True sympathy is not shown by soft talk, any more than mere church-going is real religion."

"O, you've got on to religion now, have you," said Alma; "any excuse for a ha'porth of holiness—that's you! Well, I don't care what you say. I hate this place. It's the smell. The smell don't half upset me. Next door to death, that's what it is!"

"It isn't exactly roses," said Edmund, "but at least it's clean."

"Clean! Who wants to be clean?" asked Alma, resentfully. "Let's be comfortable is my motter."

"How amusing that is," said Edmund. "You remind me of the beetle in Hans Andersen's story who said that cleanliness greatly exhausted him."

"And so it does me," snapped Alma. "O, Gawd! If that baby don't stop crying in there, I'll throw myself out of the window!"

"Hello, it's your turn to go in," said Edmund. "Come along. Take that look off your face. They're not going to kill you, you know."

"I *don't* know," retorted Alma, limping off into the presence of the surgeon. Her wound was probed, Alma shrieked, the surgeon lost his temper, and high words floated out to the delighted queue beyond the door, Alma insisting in a piercing voice:

"I ain't come here to be butchered! You go and try your tricks on in a slaughterhouse!"

At last Edmund was able to lead her away to an appeasing lunch in a restaurant in Tottenham Court Road.

"How would you like to spend an hour or two in one of the parks?" he asked her over their coffee; "that is, if you are not too tired."

"Me? I ain't tired, not in myself, but tired a bit in my head," she answered. "I can say this to you, seeing as you've never took advantage, but helped me on account of you're being egg-senterick; but, d'you know, gitting hurt and going to that damnation hospital has made me think. When you're laid up you ain't got nothing special to put your mind to, and then you begins to think. When you thinks you sees and when you sees you thinks. Not my idea of a picnic!"

"No, nor mine. I prefer just to—live."

"Lucky you can live, scabby! Me—I ain't never even done that. I've just dragged through—hoping."

"Poor old thing!" said Edmund. "Cheer up. There comes a time when hope turns into what we wanted. The only snag is we usually have to wait so long that we have changed completely by the time our ship comes in, and what was our heart's desire once upon a time is then the last thing we want on earth."

"Mebbe you got hold of something there. You're always sounding off about this and that, but sometimes you do hit the nail on the head. I suppose *you* thinks often—about dying and such like?"

"Yes," he replied softly, remembering his wife and child. "I often think about death; can't help it, it's part of life."

"What you talkin' about? How can death be part of life? If it was, I wouldn't be afraid." She seemed suddenly to be the youngest thing in the world and dashed-looking.

"What are you afraid of?" he asked her, quickened to sympathy.

"O, I dunno. Just the thought of it makes me go all goosey.

Death's a very goosey thing. A person knows nothing about it and I . . . well, I like to know where I stand."

"So do we all," observed Edmund, blowing out an accumulated billow of cigarette smoke. "Point is, my dear, we're not very often meant to know how we stand."

"Aw, it's easy for you to talk," protested Alma. "You been educated, and though you don't strike me as a saint, you ain't never been low. Now—I'm low, and for people of my sort death is fearful, and religion and such like is too far away and high up."

"My God!" he said, "what's education got to do with it? It isn't educated people who matter, it's people with *feeling*. There's almost no real feeling in the world to-day, that's what's the matter with it. That's why religion means so little. Religion is nothing without love."

"Love!" Alma laughed without being either cheerful or amused. "Love ain't for the likes of me. You can cut that lark right out!"

"But have you forgotten Mary Magdalene?"

"Forgotten her? Never heard of her! Who's she?"

"She was a little bawd who lived about two thousand years ago."

"O, ay. What about her? What happened to *her?*"

"A man loved her."

"And then she woke up!" exclaimed Alma derisively.

"Well, she did rather. The man happened to be the son of God."

"You mean Jesus Christ?"

"Certainly."

"*He* loved a prostitute? *He* did?"

"Yes. Didn't you ever hear about it- -anywhere?"

"No, course not. I never been anywhere to hear anything. I was delikit as a child, see. I never went to no schools."

"Who taught you to read and write, then?" he asked.

"O, a lady. I was put to her as a skivvy when I was fourteen. I was there three years. She learnt me. She learnt me to read and write at nights when me work was done. But she never said nothing about this here Mary Muddling."

"Magdalene."

"Have it your own road. Course, when you come to think of it, there was no need for her, in them days, to bring it home to *me* that Jesus Christ loved a prostitute."

"Didn't she ever tell you about Him—Christ, I mean?"

"I never heard her mention His name, 'cep' when she tripped over something or anything startled her. I never reely heard much about Him till they put me in prison that time for solicitin'. I went to prison to hear about God! Funny—that! If they'd told me a bit more about Him outside mebbe I'd never have landed inside!"

"Doubtless. Why didn't you remain with this woman?"

"No, I couldn't." Alma chewed at her thumb, reminiscently.

"Why?"

"She went and gassed herself. She committed suicide."

"Perhaps that was the result of never talking about Jesus Christ."

"O, no, it wasn't. She done it 'cos some feller she was sweet on went off with somebody else," Alma told him instructively.

"Umph! Well, what about going to the park?"

"I don't mind. Here! Would you take me to St. James's Park?"

"Willingly."

What in the world could be jollier, he thought cynically, than an hour in the park with a tart! Who could withstand it! I'm coming on! Every day I get more like one of those pathological cases who can't seem to find their manhood except in the company of freaks and monsters. I'm well on the down-grade: in fact, the road's blooming well greased!

"I like it there," pursued Alma. "It's near Buckingham Palis and we might see the King 'n' Queen. Ain't you fond of 'em? I am. There's something about 'em—well, they make me feel *safe*."

They drove in a taxi to St. James's Park. During the ride Alma regarded her companion with melancholy wonder.

"This is the first time I ever ride in a taxi," she said, "without someone trying to take advantage of me on the way. That's the big tell of a decent cove—how he behaves hisself in a taxi!"

"Thanks very much, but I'm no trapper of virtue," he replied, bored.

"O, damn' funny! He said 'virtue', you notice," Alma observed to an invisible onlooker. "Don't act as if you didn't know . . . what I was," she said testily to Edmund. "I got my good points but virtue ain't one of 'em, see!"

"It all depends," said Edmund, "what you mean by virtue. If you mean always to be chronically la-di-da and correct— pouf!" Edmund forked his fingers at such a notion of virtue.

In the park he found two deck chairs and placed them in such a position that Alma had a good view of the Palace and the lake.

"This ain't half the life of the idle rich!" commented Alma with much satisfaction. "Sitting in the sun in St. James's Park, waiting for the King 'n' Queen, and watching the chickens on the pond."

"Chickens!" He looked with awe at the industrious scattering of moorhens, black-headed gulls, cormorants and pelicans.

"Ain't they chickens, all of them birds?" said Alma, indicating in her collective noun the different kinds of wild fowl congregated and busy on the water. "Course they are! Give us a gasper."

They smoked in silence for a little time listening to the syrupy notes of a robin; them Alma said:

"Ain't it nice to be out with a man and not on business! O, it do feel funny—indecent, almost."

They both began to laugh, then stopped abruptly as if hit.

After a while Alma exploded:

"Here! Something I like to ask you—what did that Mary Muddling *do* when she found out that Christ loved her? Did she get advantage from it?"

"Mary Magdalene? O, it came as a bit of a shock to her to think that anyone like Christ should be interested in her sort, and *more*, that He loved her."

"I bet it was a shock—shock and a half!" said Alma. "A little story like this is just what the doctor ordered! It'll make me laugh, see, then I'll feel better! So Mary Muddling comes over in a daze, does she, to think of being picked out like that?"

"Yes, and mark you, it was love without any illusions. He knew what she'd been and what she'd done, and those Eastern prostitutes are much more low than those over here, my angel. And, of course, it was a great comfort to her to know that this love came straight down to hell to her, and was not given on any false basis—no loving her because He thought she'd been forced against her will to being low, but understanding that she had thoroughly enjoyed it. Love, in fact, because she was a howling sinner and not a whacking great saint."

"So what did she *do?*"

"What would you have done?"

"Don't ask me! I dunno!"

"That was just how she felt, too. But she had a quiet think about it all, and it seemed to Mary Magdalene so amazing and wonderful that anyone like Christ should be waiting to give her something instead of waiting for *her* to give something, that she threw up the life she had been leading and followed Him. And now she's one of the most golden saints in the calendar!"

"Ho, is she!" Alma gave some reflection to this priceless career. Finally, she said resentfully:

"Ay, it was all right for *her!* She copped it nice. It ain't at all the same for me. Jesus don't go about loving prostitutes now. All that happened two thousand years ago."

"What's two thousand years . . ." began Edmund.

"It's a hell of a long time," Alma broke in.

"Be still. There are some things time cannot topple. All that was done Then for us Now. See yourself in it. But you've got to do more than want that love—you've got to look for it. God is about, but quietly, you know—no trumpets. I daresay you'd often run into Him, Alma, in the streets at night, if you kept your heart open."

"Who? Me? Run into *Him* on my beat? What you talking about?"

"God."

"I see a lot on my rounds," said Alma slowly. "On wet windy nights after twelve o'clock I see enough in half an hour to last me a whole life-time. But I never see Him. No, nor never will."

"You won't unless you look."

"That all I got to do? Well, let me tell you something: it must be a very interesting stunt going looking for God in dark doorways, but my business is to go looking for my supper. I'm starving, see, while I'm hunting around for the Almighty! Besides, if they caught *me* looking for God they'd clap me straight in jail. To them it would seem worse than looking for clients—the likes o' me on the prowl for Jesus God Almighty and love. Anyway, there ain't no God on the 'broad road that leads to damnation,' as they say. There's only people like me."

He laughed. "It isn't the broad road which leads to damnation, lamb: the broad road leads to the kingdom of heaven. It's only the way to hell that's narrow and shut in between high prickly hedges—exciting, damn' stupid!"

"Wherever it is, the kingdom of heaven ain't for me, that I do know," replied Alma.

"O my! Did you suppose that the kingdom of heaven was only for church-goers? There are more rum people in the kingdom of heaven than anyone ever dreams of. God would not have been fit to be God if His love had been only a special reward for the virtuous."

"God's good—according to you!"

"He's more than that, He's loving. It says somewhere in that perpetual 'best-seller' the Bible that God's delight is to be with us, for if we need Him *He* longs for us."

"Go on! You trying to say that God *longs* for the likes of me?"

"You're just as important and desirable to Him as anyone else," he answered, amused at the rôle that had overtaken him. "I don't suppose it's ever occurred to you to remember what a privilege it is to be a woman."

"Privilege!" echoed poor Alma faintly.

"Yes, privilege. No one's ever tried to make you see how fine you are. Silly though some of your notions are of what woman-kind should be, the very fact that you're of the sex which was chosen to fulfil a divine promise is enough to make God love you with special attentiveness. Whatever did you suppose God was for if not for love?"

"To deal out penalties, of course."

"It's something, at any rate, that it occurs to you there is a God at all, even if His only function is to deal out penalties; poor dear girl, this must seem so to you, but it wasn't God who contrived such little joy for you, it's the various inhuman human factors that have touched your life at every level since before you were born. God, my dear, is Love, to the extent that some mystic or another has been bold enough to crow: 'I know that without me God cannot live an instant.' "

"Ain't it nice to know that! I don't believe it," she protested. "Why, if it was really like that nobody would ever do anything wrong any more."

"Yes, but it really *is* like that, only people find that they can't believe it. You may praise a man to the skies and he loves it. But tell him how important he is to God and the idea of so much floors him. He can't rise to it, so he tells you he doesn't believe."

"Do you believe it?" she asked.

"Yes," he said.

"Pshaw! Anyone ever tell you that you was good at fairy tales?" Alma enquired.

"I am, rather," replied Edmund, nursing his knee. "You have to be, you know, because the odd thing is that life is the biggest fairy tale that ever was told."

"Life ain't been no fairy tale for me, it's been a dog's dinner!"

"Certainly it's been a fairy tale. You've had the worst part first, which is precisely what happens in most fairy stories, and is for the making of character, you understand, nothing merely malicious being intended. There's only one reason ever for being put out into the dark, and that is to find the light. The brighter time is to come, perhaps sooner than you think."

"I know," said Alma with rapt mockery, "the shining lights, the fairy godmother, three wishes, and Prince Charming! You can go and tell it to them chickens on that pond!"

"I'm telling you."

Alma looked round the sparkling parkland, at the green living flesh of the grass, and the pond across which the wind was blowing an idle and complicated pattern; enlivened by the arcadian prospect and the poetic life of Mary Magdalene she said carefully, ponderingly: "Course, I think I could give up the streets if I had enough to live on and a nice little flat to myself in this classy neighbourhood near the Palis, and the King 'n' Queen."

"Why the King and Queen?" he asked.

"I told you—they make me feel *safe*. It's something to feel safe—it's everything."

"Is it?" said Edmund. "And, of course, no one at all is ever safe."

He spoke agitatedly. Something had whipped into his mind. Five hundred pounds would secure that flat for Alma near "the King 'n' Queen" where she would feel safe. Five hundred pounds would make her infamously his. All he had to do . . .

Ticklish profundity of a temptation! What colour is temptation? It is red—red as blood. It gets in the blood, too, swirling round and round, going the full circuit in all the waking hours. Food nourishes it, as well as thought. It is a monster.

Alma, bent forward, was looking at him with wonder.

"What's up with you?" she said slowly.

"Nothing. What are you staring at? Do you see a portent in my face?"

He leaned away from her, putting on an expression that he hoped was collected.

"You look dicky all of a sudden. You look . . . you look *hollow!*" persisted Alma, frowning at him.

"I'm perfectly all right," said Edmund. "Should you be annoyed if I asked you are you serious when you say you'd leave the streets if you had a flat in this district, with enough to live on?"

She turned to him, caught between tittering and sobbing.

"I don't know about serious, but I'll tell you something: that doctor what was butchering me this morning, him what looks a bit of a sis and ain't no more than two piss-pots high—well, he told me yesterday that if my leg don't get better in a few days, I've got to have all my teeth out, else the blood-poisoning'll go all over me and I'll be done for. All my teeth out—for God's sake! What am I going to do, I ask you? Think of me without my teeth! It's a nightmare! I'll never get no clients—I'll be done for, anyway."

"But, forgive me, the clients aren't interested in your teeth."

"I know that as well as you," she said, nettled. "But, well, hell—they got to be led up to the main interest, such people. They want to see a nice front and then it makes it like poetry for 'em to come and pay for the dirt underneath!"

"You've got no illusions, I must say."

"If you mean that I never kid myself, you're perishing well right. Nobody could kid theirselves over a future like mine.

I don't know what to do, or what's going to happen. I feel
like a rat in a trap!"

"So do I," said Edmund softly, one base thought after another
flopping into his mind.

"You look it," Alma remarked. "You look half mad over
something. What's eating *you*, I'd like to know?"

"Your troubles are a great grief to me," he explained.

"I'm sorry about that, I'm sure," she said irritably. "What's
the use of worrying? You can't do nothing."

"I may be able to do—something," he said sharply.

"What? Go on, tell us."

"Not for anything! We'll say no more now. Shall we go to
the cinema, or are you too tired?"

She gave him a long, calculating look. Then she said:

"I'm tired to death, but let's go to the Pictures. P'r'aps we'll
see a story about someone who's worse off than us. They say
there's always something worse could happen than what does.
So let's go and git a basin full of it. I could do with something to
cheer me up!"

V

The windows of Edmund's sitting-room looked to the flaring
life of Feng Street. Below, the children shrilled, vans hooted,
foreign voices soared in despairing rage, cash registers pinged,
brawlers roared from the taverns and dram-shops, housewives
gossiped, and shady transactions hummed to conclusions among
close-gathered groups on the street corners. But his bedroom
window overlooked a well of silence; immediately outside, the
walls of a great block of offices rose many feet into the air, built
on this nether side of white glossy tiles so as to make the most
of the light in the narrow area.

Edmund wished that these tiles had been of some other colour. White called to his mind daisies and sea-foam, polar-bears and similar jolly things of which he did not wish to be reminded as he looked out, galvanized by the temptation to go and betray Mrs. Christopher for five hundred pounds. What affinity had daisies with blood money? No. The tiles ought to have been black and mired, or harsh and burnt-red, not this gentle wooing white which seemed to complain of him to himself.

"You know," he said aloud to the battery of white tiles shining to him so persuasively, "she gave us permission to go and tell of her. She herself gave us her name and address for that very purpose."

"Quite right," replied the white tiles. "You were to go and tell of her *if* suspicion fell on *you*. Are you in danger of being arrested for the Highgate murder?"

"No," said Edmund.

"Well, then?"

"But I might be," he protested lamely. "It might come at any time."

"So might the end of the world," said the white tiles.

"But, look here . . ." began Edmund.

"No, you look here," replied the tiles. "You leave aside why Mrs. Christopher gave you her name and address. Forget everything except your words to her. You told her that whatever happened *you* would never betray her. You never would assist in hounding her, you said."

"You go on as if I were not within my rights to go and give the police information about her. After all, it is murder. It is my duty as a citizen to . . ."

"Your duty? You righteous prig! Have you *ever* known what was your duty?"

"Perhaps not. I'm nothing much, and you are very discouraging. But I want that money so as to help Alma—to lift her. Mrs. Christopher would be the first to applaud me—I know."

"All this is not a matter for Mrs. Christopher though it is very much a matter of Mrs. Christopher. Her crime is her affair. This charge is upon you. *Your* word will be broken if you betray her. It will be a ruinous thing to do."

"Shut up," said Edmund. "Go to hell!"

Three days went by, three days of occasions lit up by rapids of the most keen and disturbing awarenesses and sensations in the park, the harlot's den, and the hospital.

Alma thrived on this time of inconsequent hours and outings, of leisure, and good regular meals provided by Edmund. She was not using the harsh slashes of rouge while she had no need to go out and catch someone, and the absence of this alone gave back something of lost integrity to her face. Her eyes seemed to prosper with a new remote beauty giving the contiguous skin a kind of opalesque mirroring of their fine light. Peace and the cessation of commercial amours contributed a general expression of tranquillity. It was only when she took it into her head to be gushing that it struck out like a blow what she was; then two little fans of tiny lines ran out at her eyes, she held her face forward, and it broke in a smile of gay and superb falsehood.

On the fourth morning Alma was dismissed from the hospital, her leg being considered out of danger. She was instructed in the future dressing of her wound, and the house surgeon sent her about her business with:

"And get those teeth drawn—every one of 'em—the sooner the better—if you want to make old bones."

"Him and his 'old bones'!" sneered Alma in a fright.

"Yes, but it's really serious," said Edmund. "Bad teeth are the very devil; they can be the death of a person."

"Don't you start," said Alma. "I ain't never heard such a fuss about teeth in all my life."

"Pity! Early fuss would have prevented early extractions."

"Early to bed—early to rise! What you loses on the swings you gains on the roundabouts! A rolling stone gathers no moss! I know a lot more, as well," she flashed out savagely.

"Don't be childish."

"And don't you preach."

"Sorry. Let's go and have lunch."

That evening in her room, Alma announced:

"Well, now that me leg's so much better, I must git a move on: business as usual tomorrer—for me!"

Edmund heard this with a terrible pang, although he had known it must come. He had been looking out of the window at the fancy evening sky where streamers of bright rose were passing slowly over a background of smooth water-green acres. He knew that the time of decision had come. Now he began to trick out the naked guilt of intended betrayal by representing it to himself as a course to be taken in which the elderly Mrs. Christopher was sent to her death so that a different kind of life could be given to this young woman. There was nothing wrong with it. If you came to that, it amounted to spiritual daring to face up so bravely to an evaluation of souls, and make the difficult choice!

He swung round and said to Alma:

"Suppose I could give you a little money—enough to live on in a flat until we could find a really enjoyable career for you— would you give up this way of living?"

"Pardon," she apologized. "I was listening to the music. What did you say?"

Mournful little thumps of an old popular song were jolting from a barrel-organ in a nearby street—"Melancholy Baby." Alma was listening with earnest attention.

"Pretty, ain't it?" she said. "I always had an ear for good music! What was you saying, ducks?"

"If I were to give you enough to live on for a year or so,

would you go and get a flat in Victoria—near the King and Queen—and live free of these clients?"

"Course I would. I'm sick of obliging. You never know *what* you're bringing home—lunatic, p'r'aps; you never can't tell, reely, whether they's wrong in the head or not till you gits men private; then the blinds go up, the lid comes orf of it! Gits frit I do, sometimes. And now there's me teeth hanging over me head . . ."

"I'd want you to have your teeth seen to, Alma, if I go and . . . if I give you this cash."

"Would you? Ain't that nice! I'll git everything seen to when I'm living near the King 'n' Queen! O, ay! You can git anything seen to when you got enough of the ready! But you ain't got enough to keep me. Don't make me laugh! Look at you! Frayed collar, and your shoes want mending."

"You forget yourself! Those items are my choice not my necessity."

"Looks like necessity to me," she said pertly.

"Too many things have seemed like necessity to you," came his brutal rejoinder. "Let's make an end of some of 'em. Don't go back to the streets, for a start."

"I don't want to," said Alma, "especially after this nice rest you've give me. I've been living like a human being, I have, and it makes a nice change! But don't keep on with your soft talk. You bore me. People don't go giving away large sums of money. For one thing, they ain't got it, and for another, if they've got it they wants something for it. You talk . . . well, sometimes I think that the only person in all the world who ain't loopy is me—poor Alma, the tart, but sane! And you know why? It's 'cos I never think, see, 'cep' when I got a busted blood-poison leg; also, I got a short memory. With them two advantages you can do anything, and, p'r'aps, git somewhere!"

"Interesting. I'm sure you're right to say you're the only sane person alive. I know I'm crazy. I'll see you to-morrow—let's say to-morrow night. Don't go out till I come. Don't go looking for clients. Promise?"

"And what do I live on till to-morrer night? Promises?"

"This will keep you going till I come." He gave her a ten-shilling note—the last of his spare cash.

She laughed and put the money in her purse.

"I never see your equal!" she said.

"No, nor I!" he retorted. He went home. When he got in he went round the flat drawing curtains, and making a bob at the evening star which hung in the heavens like a glittering spider.

He went to stand at the mantelpiece. Wound up to his purpose, he went over his defences again. "Mrs. Christopher didn't do it for me!" he declared aloud, glad that his curtains and the dark were shutting out the insistent white tiles which, in these last days, seemed to have become a tenement for his conscience, for it had grown too tempestuous for him comfortably to contain it. "Mrs. Christopher didn't kill Sine to oblige *me*. She was taking care of number one. She was thinking of herself. *She* wanted him out of the way—silenced. I . . . I was paying up, and so were the others. Mrs. Christopher got tired of paying—she killed him. It was a benefit to all of us, a great benefit. But that's by the way. Only the peculiar circumstances made it a boon for other parties. She still remains a murderer. Let's be fair. The woman's a criminal. Probably going about settling other differences with her little gun! That mild sort are always ulterior. Too good to be true—a face like hers! She *ought* to be under lock and key. The stunt is five hundred pounds for some information about her. It isn't as though I should be dragging her to them by the hair. No, no. They probably won't catch her, anyway. She's had plenty of time to hop it. She'll be in America or on the Continent by now, I'll wager. Too astute to get caught! And that money means Alma's salvation. I can't allow her to go back to the streets. I don't want anything for myself. It's for Alma. There isn't a thing wrong with doing one's

duty by the law and using the . . . er . . . proceeds for services
rendered to help a wronged soul to its salvation. I am right to
do it. I will do it."

It sounded all right, but it did not make him feel all right.
Somewhere there was a grievous flaw. Edmund wished the flaw
would occur to him. Then he could demolish it, and all would
be well.

He had been staring at the large framed print he had of Pieter
Brueghel's "A Wedding." It was not only a satisfying and
delicious sight to the eyes with its vigorous sixteenth-century
merry-makers, its harmony of line, its side vista of a long treed
avenue which reminded Edmund of Constitution Hill as it
swept round Buckingham Palace (the King 'n' Queen), and its
trees with their unique and beautiful character as if sixteenth-
century trees had a different individuality from those of the
twentieth century—not only all this, but Edmund had had the
picture for so many years, and had gazed at it so often from the
depths of moods and speculations that, as a tune trembling from
the heart of time will often evoke a whole forgotten sequence
of life, this picture had become a depository of himself, to the
end that when he looked at it in the present he could often
recapture extensions of the past, caught away in those sixteenth-
century trees and jocund clod-hopping feet. It was so now,
because some forgotten pent joy suddenly rushed at him from
the picture, and exhilaration stirred within him.

What is this, he wondered. How can such happiness arrive at
this moment when I am making up my mind to go and sell
Mrs. Christopher?

And he fell to cursing and marvelling that no one was ever
wholly this or wholly that, but every person rushed with the
smithereens of hundreds of moods and impulses, as he himself
now demonstrated, being top full of despicable intentions yet
capable of the most exquisite joy remembering, through what
was stored in his picture, a winding canal where meadow-sweet

foamed on the banks, and tall crags rose up on one side with a waterfall dropping down the rocks at immense speed, its waters joining the canal under a damp lichen-spotted bridge. He had leaned and caught handfuls of the icy water, drinking breathlessly, the draught going down like a striking sword, wounding, cleansing.

He trimmed up this little gleam till he had extracted from it something of consolation and glamorous meaning for himself. He had been allowed this happy memory as a reward for not shirking the hard struggle with his conscience! That's what it was. He had not flinched. He had made the fullest use of that great gift which had come to everyone with the Incarnation—the gift of containing within one's self the ultimate recognition of what was wrong and right, and deducing from that, untrammelled, the course of action to adopt. True, it was a grave responsibility, but courageous men did not shrink. Brave men fought out every problem even though that "Know Thyself" business was a full-time job, a whole life time's occupation, and even in the last hour it could be seen that after learning so much you still knew nothing. Well, he felt he could now claim to know a little. He became quite exalted as he thought of what he had set out to do—deliberately to betray in order to save a soul from a greater betrayal. Why, the thing had a daring Crusader ring about it! He felt himself to be someone quite special and set apart. Not every man had gone through the experience of working upon his own baseness till he had changed it into a matter of principle! Yes—even high principle!

It was afternoon of the next day before he arrived at Scotland Yard. During the morning he paid a call at his office to collect his sick-pay and inform the chief clerk that he would report for duty on Monday. After this, he went to buy himself a few drinks as fortification. The drinks lasted him till lunch-time. As he could not visit Scotland Yard during the lunch-hour, he endeavoured to eat a meal in a public-house which provided noonday snacks. Then he drove in a taxi to his destination, locomotion which he could not afford, but it gave him greater confidence.

"When you're out to collect blood-money," he told himself, "you might as well do it in style!"

At Scotland Yard he was shown, with expediency, into a room where Hugh Christopher was waiting for him. Hugh sat with his elbows on the desk, smoking a cigarette, his handsome face set in a show of nonchalance.

Edmund advanced to the desk. Hugh did not invite him to sit down.

"I am here in connection with the Highgate murder," Edmund announced.

Through the windows he could see the Thames glittering in the sunlight; clouds like small white whales were puffing across the sky. As he spoke, an old slow barge named *Frantic*, which was waddling past, gave a horrid groan of derision.

Hugh Christopher took one elbow from the desk, and said, with a sudden leer:

"So you have come to lay some information, have you? What do you know?"

"I know," said Edmund, "that I'm saying nothing until I'm assured that my part in the matter will be kept secret."

"I daresay I can conceal your furtive virtue," replied Hugh scornfully. "What's your story?"

Edmund stood and brought out his account of the murder under the hooded gaze of Mrs. Christopher's son.

"Incredible!" exclaimed Hugh, as Edmund concluded.

"You mean you don't believe me?"

"Lord, yes, I believe you," answered Hugh. "I'm going to pay you in a minute; your information tallies with certain knowledge already in our possession."

"What's so incredible, then?" asked Edmund.

"Listen," said Hugh, narrowing his eyes, "don't use that tone to me. You're being rather well paid for a few dirty words.

Keep a civil tongue in your head and have the grace to concede that it's an extraordinary thing after the undoubted service Mrs. . . . er . . . Christopher did you *all*, apart from herself, in blotting out this gentleman, that you should come here and give me the information which will enable us to commit her for trial. People come here playing the Judas almost every day, and their motives generally run to revenge, hatred, greed—such things; but I must say, you're the only one who has ever come here to betray a benefactor." And to himself, Hugh was fuming: who'd have thought it, who'd have thought it of this mild-faced owl!

He opened a drawer in the desk and threw a roll of five hundred pounds in notes towards the informer.

"Here!" he said. "Here's something for a good boy! You have put a right criminal in our way. We simply can't have citizens going about settling their business at the point of a gun. What a lawless and dangerous old filly this Mrs. Christopher is, to be sure. Dreadful type!"

"She wasn't a bad type at all," mumbled Edmund. "I seldom saw a more decent-looking, decently-spoken woman. She might have been a little eccentric—that's the worst I could say of her."

"But not the worst you could do to her, eh?"

"It's not within your province to air your comments to me," protested Edmund.

"Isn't it?" said Hugh. "But I'm leaving at the end of this month, you see, and I need not trouble about what constitutes polite behaviour—especially to you. I don't have to be tolerant or judicious or pleasant any more. If I don't like a fellow's face, I can tell him so. If I want to express my contempt of an informer, I'll get on with it. And what are you going to do about it? Nothing. Except slink off with your money. Well, now you've got it. Get out!"

"There's no encouragement to citizens to do their duty," said Edmund, turning away.

"O, there's every encouragement!" protested Hugh in a shocked voice. "We'd never get any information unless we offered encouragement in the shape of rewards. You'd never have dreamt of coming here with your story about Mrs. Christopher unless we had given you five hundred pounds for your trouble! Without a reward, you'd have thought yourself a beast to come here and split on the old girl after she had done you such a good turn, albeit in so unorthodox a fashion. But with a reward of five hundred pounds the thing becomes a matter of duty! Doesn't it? Doesn't it?" he bellowed.

"I know what you're thinking," said Edmund, "and you are right. But I needed the money!"

"Yes," said Hugh. "Money talks. Get out."

Edmund left. He felt so put out and ashamed that he went to a shady little club, of which he was a member, and got drunk, the club serving drinks at any hour of the day or night.

Another member of this club, also endeavouring to drown a personal humiliation, became Edmund's companion in the vinous concentration to restore lost prestige.

"If it hadn't been for Alma," Edmund suddenly announced from a grave silence, "I'd never have done it—couldn't have done it!"

His companion, a short-faced man with a squint so violent that Edmund's head reeled every time he tried to meet the fellow's gaze, had no idea of what Edmund was talking about, but he thickly and solemnly concurred.

"Thass it! It's all Alma's fault!"

"No," Edmund corrected him haughtily, "not Alma's *fault*—her inspiration. If it hadn't been for her . . ."; he leaned forward with an air of black conspiracy. "I could tell you things that would make you an anarchist in half an hour!"

"What things?" demanded the boon companion.

"Things about the Police, about Scotland Yard. Understand?" said Edmund in a voice calculated to impress.

"You couldn't tell me anything about them—not me, you couldn't," vowed the companion. "I *know*."

"Whaddya know?" asked Edmund petulantly. He was disappointed at not having caused a sensation. "Whaddya know?"

"I know . . . what I know," declared the companion, pompously. "Beyond that, I am not prepared to speak."

"Neither am I," replied Edmund, offended. "All I will say is that it's . . ."

"Alma's fault," volunteered the other.

"No, not Alma's fault," said Edmund reprovingly; "but if it hadn't been for her . . ."

They both put on faces to indicate that they were contemplating something infamous. They would not speak, the subject had become too deep for mere comment. Besides they could not think of anything else to say. Their swollen lids fell down on eyes made pig-like by excessive boozing and they reeled off into noisy slumbers.

About seven o'clock Edmund awoke. He was a little time in coming to himself. The boon companion had gone, so there was no assistance from him. But gradually the day pieced itself together for Edmund, and he ordered a whisky and soda to help him to bear it.

After an attempt at supper at the club, and several more drinks to sooth his shamed and outraged ego, Edmund drove to Soho in a cab. It was then just after nine o'clock, and from the bottom of the chasm of Alma's court he could see stars like specks of lustrous egg-shell, clotting the strip of dark blue sky.

Alma was waiting for him.

"The hell with you! Thought you was never coming. I'd given you up. In fact," she said sulkily, "I was just going out."

"After your promise?" he said.

"I don't remember no promises," she answered. "I told you, I got a short memory."

He stared at her morosely. He had been through the afternoon's horribly degrading experience all for this shrewish little . . . But he must not be trivial. He drew a bottle of sherry from his pocket. "Let's have a drink," he proposed.

"Sure." She went and rummaged for the glasses. Her mood began to turn golden at the prospect of a drink. "Ah—I'm sorry I spoke rough. It's the worry of things makes me flare up." She gaped at him cheerfully. "You've been boozing!" She gave a delighted giggle. "I never see you in drink before. Ain't you an eyeful!"

"Yes, nothing short of a swine! You must excuse me," he mumbled.

"O, I likes to see a gentleman with a load on! Shows he's human. Them what never does anything wrong ain't human. That's what being human means, don't it, that you *do* do wrong sometimes."

"Your words comfort me strangely," said Edmund, leaving off drinking to reward her with a wavering smile.

"Fancy! No one's ever said that to me before—not with your meaning, anyroad." She drained her glass and offered it to him for more. "What's new?"

"Nothing much," he replied. He tilted the bottle. "I've got a present for you."

"Ain't that nice! What is it this time?"

"Five hundred pounds."

Alma sighed.

"Ah, for God's sake! You always was one for fairy tales morning, night and noon. It's a gift! Don't you ever come down to earth?"

Edmund drew the big roll of notes from his pocket, and held it out to her.

"Here you are. All I ask is that you will go away from here and set up house-keeping somewhere near the . . . er . . . 'King 'n' Queen.' There's enough to do your business for you—buy you a few sticks of furniture, and pay a year's rent at least. You will be able to live on what's left until heaven sends you some decent and pleasant kind of livelihood. You can also have your teeth seen to; that really is rather important for the sake of your health. Go on, take it, it's yours."

Alma had backed away from the extended hand with its considerable largesse.

"I couldn't," she spluttered. "I never see . . . Hey, I feel funny! You can't mean it?"

"Yes, I do," said Edmund patiently. "Come. Take the money. It's yours."

"Why are you giving it me?" she asked, not looking at him.

"I've told you, poor dear. So that you can go away and be free of . . . your clients."

She sat down on her divan bed among the fair-ground dolls.

"But you're not doing this for *nothing*. You must want something."

Now she looked him full in the face and, noticing the sad mistrustfulness in the little harlot's eyes, Edmund felt glad, for the first time, that he had got the money for her.

"Dear," he said, "I don't want anything. You must not suppose that everyone who makes you a present requires some offering in return."

"I just can't believe it," said Alma, disabled. "I never heard of such a thing. You . . . you must be *crazy!*" she burst out.

"Well, I am. But take your present." He went over to her and tipped the roll of notes into her lap.

"You want me . . . to go away . . . and live nice?" she enquired.

"That's the idea," he answered.

"I'm certainly sick of this life," she said. "But what I can't make out is—*why* you're doing all this for me. Five hundred quid at one blow! 'Strewth!"

"I'm your friend. I always said I was. Friends help friends."

"Not as much as this, they don't. It makes me afraid, somehow. You'll have me getting what they call emotional in a minute. I've never . . . why, it seems as if, all along, you meant what you was saying when you used to tell me about Jesus and love and Mary Muddling."

"You needn't bring Jesus into it," he said uncomfortably. The name of one betrayed made him think of another betrayed. Christ and Mrs. Christopher were two different theorems that worked out to the same answer. Even now, at this very moment, the police might be arresting her, taking her away in the big official car, putting her through the preliminaries for the hangman. Yes, and he had arranged it all for her. They had paid him five hundred pounds for his help. Through his sick disgust he heard Alma saying:

"But I will bring Him in! It's Christ-like to do what you're doing."

He found the irony of this insupportable.

"Well, I'm off," he said, making for the door. But she called him back.

"Don't leave me," she entreated. He came slowly and stood before her. "You don't understand," she said. "Try to see it for me. I'm not used to goodness. It makes me feel ever so frightened. It's thrown me all of a heap. You know what—I've never been so near to suicide in all me life. If there's . . . goodness like yours in the world, see, then I've been wrong, wrong as hell to live as I have been doing, and before I always thought I was right. I figured as it didn't matter what I did since everyone else, in different ways, was just as bad. But now . . . Don't go—ah, please. Don't let me be here alone just yet. Let me talk about it a bit and that will help."

He looked down into her eyes, widely-opened eyes lit with a gleam as if they had just been ambushed while gazing into far and marvellous stellar spaces. She's no right to have such eyes, Edmund objected.

"Here! Sit down," she said, and when he was seated at her side, she fluttered out an avowal:

"I never met anyone like you before—straight, I never. Course, gentlemen often got on to me to lead a better life. I've told you before I've often laughed to think how going with a prostitute makes so many of 'em feel soulful. I suppose it's the remorse that comes over 'em immediately afterwards. I suppose they feel as if they've got to restore theirselves in their own eyes after going with the likes of me. And so, while they's paying me they's saying, 'Change your life, ducky, or you'll be damned for sure'! Ay! And sometimes they forgot to pay an' all, so serious they got about me an' my little old soul." She laughed. "But you," she continued, "you're different—too lovely for words. You've never asked for anything all along—only helped me—with my busted blood-poison leg an' everything. And now, you give me all this money to go straight with. You act as if . . . as if . . . you loved me," she said, staring at him with shining wondering eyes.

"Love!" exclaimed Edmund. "I sometimes wonder if any of us have the least idea of what love means. Anything is called 'love' nowadays. But does anyone know what real love means?"

"You do, at any rate," declared Alma. She suddenly bent and kissed his hand quickly and shyly: she was not used to giving a kiss of homage.

The effect of this on the half-tipsy and distraught Edmund was electrifying. The timid decent gesture virtually sent him off his head. All that he had refused to face and inhibited of his feelings for Alma now burst through his careful defences and did for him. He seized and clasped the little figure in his arms.

"Little deary thing! Little deary thing!" he called, beside himself. And he fell to kissing her in a way that Alma had come to expect only from her clients.

After the first shock of sorrow and indignation, Alma allowed him to go on. She realized that it hardly became her to object; it was, after all, an episode terribly natural in her sort of life; *that* was what she was there for, and she had been so very well paid—

not a penny short of five hundred pounds. So she allowed him to go on, to pass into the full temper of desire, and to yield to it. Afterwards, when he wanted to apologize in an agony of shame and misery, she said:

"No, it's all right. It's quite all right. I understand. I know you never meant to. You were going and I called you back. It's quite all right. I know you've had a drop too much—I know, I know. You needn't feel bad about it."

She paused, then said as sorrowfully as ever she had said anything in all her life:

"I gave you a little kiss on your hand, and I suppose you thought . . . well! Yes, yes. Shut up! It's only very clever people who can understand that sometimes . . . sometimes a kiss given need not be returned. Yes, course I'm all right. Yes, yes, I'll go straight from now on. *You* were my last client!"

"Your last client!" he repeated.

His eye fell on the joyful panel of wallpaper with the nursery-rhyme characters, and it seemed, somehow, to put the finishing touch to his opinion that he was scarcely human.

He took a wretched leave of her, floundering down the dark stairs.

As he went something occurred to him for the first time: she had never once called him by his name. At no time had she ever addressed him as Mr. Macvey or as Edmund. And why? Why, because she was not accustomed to think of any man as a *person*, or even as a name. That was the last thing men wanted to give Alma—their names. And so she never thought of men as anything but anonymous flesh; this included him. And because it would take some time before he could face the real cause of this day's disasters he now took a precarious refuge in the foolish opinion that everything might have been different if she had thought of him as Edmund Macvey. He emerged into the quiet sinister court. Under the solitary lamp a lonesome mongrel stood afflicted by an ague. Edmund reeled out of the court followed, it seemed to him, by looks of cynical reproof even from this poor and ill-conditioned hound.

After he had gone Alma lay and stared at the ceiling. Many an expression went through her mind—a tattoo of pain, bewilderment, indignation, yearning.

The silly fool! O, the silly fool! It's what he wanted all along, only he wouldn't own up! Takes some of 'em ages to tell you what's on their mind—well, on something else! What do they call it their soul for when they mean something else? It's what they all want, every one, none of 'em is different—or better. He was just the same, reely, as anyone who'd stop me on the streets—half a crown for half an hour! But *that* wouldn't have been nice enough for *him*, O, no, not by a long chalk. He had to deck it all out like a fairy-tale. Him and his fairy-tales! So he had to lead up to it with talk of love and living respectable, and the price he paid had to be that big it went beyond *payment* and became a gift—it had to be disguised as the means of my salvation. Ugh! *Men!* He needn't have give me five hundred pound for what *he* wanted. I'd have obliged him for nothing if I'd known! Him and his looking for God in dark doorways! All of a piece, that stuff, with his educated talk and his funny little fringe an' all. *The educated ones is the worst!* From what I see of it education makes 'em able to face up to everything 'cep' facts. Well, I'm ... I'm glad he turned out like the rest. For a minute, to-night, he nearly done what he's always been yapping about—he nearly saved my blasted soul! For a bit he had me deceived into thinking there was one decent man in the world. I'm ... glad there ain't. Yes—*glad*. It 'ud have meant I'd have ... loved him, and love ... it'd have been too much, too perishing much. Ah, well! It just shows. There ain't nothing at all 'cep' what you make for yourself. Nowhere, beloved, will you ever find anyone to look up to, for there's no one, *no one* that's any better than your goddamned self.

She suddenly found herself weeping. Her life for years had

been lived with the tears just out of sight, and now, when she gave way to them, as if some secret of melting and fusing had been lost for ever, these difficult tears brought her no ease from the perplexed pain of her disappointed heart.

VI

Haunted by his own iniquity, the days dragged by for Edmund. His treacheries, first to Mrs. Christopher and then to Alma, were so painful to him that he was sure he had never heard of anyone as idiotic and depraved as himself. I must have a trivial character, he thought, to agonize so much over these matters. A really formidable and aloof nature could put them by and not exhaust itself on such drastic and unremitting atonement for wrongs done. But I can't get rid of the guilt, can't get rid of it.

There was so much to gloom over that he did not quite know which particular disaster to allow to occupy him the most, and he permitted everything to fall on top of him at once, vast and accumulative, enough to anæsthetize him, with only now and again some particular jolt of shame or quake of agony isolating itself from the anatomy of disasters. O, to have to take thought for things done! To have to push the wrung heart into the piercing fire of loss and betrayal and shame. The only consolation, it seemed to him, was that he had, at last, touched rockbottom. Now horror was so complete it was akin to an ecstasy. He couldn't fall any lower or suffer any more. The obsession, the dream, the indefinable hope were shattered. He had served neither God nor man. He had lost everything—including himself.

Yes, but he must not sit about so much, gradually coming to the end of what he had been allotted in the way of endurance.

It was unthinkable to perish there by himself of himself—of the inferno of his own thoughts.

The first thing he could do was to go and see Alma—go and face her and beg her pardon; he must help her to find a flat, get her away from Soho. The side of all the dark happenings that made for upward progress must not be allowed to lapse for a minute.

When several days had gone by he went to call upon Alma on a bright Sunday morning. For once the front door was not ajar and he had to use the rusty iron knocker. Mother Cremorne opened the door. She was eating, as usual; this time she was engaged with a cheese and garlic sandwich.

"You again?" she said, a blast of garlic accompanying her derisive grin.

"I've come to visit Miss Wosp," he said curtly.

"Have you now. Bit late, aren't you?"

"Late? What do you mean?" asked Edmund.

"It's easy to see as the lady don't keep *you* informed of her whereabouts, and you such a nice gentleman, too—the only 'regular' she ever had! Well, she's gone." The merry crone looked pleased at being able to put him out.

"Did she leave her new address?" Edmund asked.

"People what lives here," replied Mother Cremorne, "don't leave no addresses when they hoppit. That makes it easier for me to tell the blinkin' truth when the police come here looking for them!"

"You ought to do something about your own address, too," remarked Edmund walking away up the court towards the plane trees of Soho Square. Mother Cremorne shouted an obscenity after him and remained in the doorway bawling till he could hear her no longer.

He began to cross Soho Square. Down through the plane-tree leaves dropped brilliant diamond scrolls of sunlight dappling a little bashed-about horse which was pulling through the Square a small cart dazzlingly piled with flowers, plants, and bay trees in tubs, all on sale at Sunday morning prices.

At the corner, under the square tower of St. Patrick's Church, Mrs. Palmer-Pinto was standing, her face full of bitter indignation, calling in sudden loud spurts:

"Rebecca! Rebecca! Rebecca!"

Edmund did not look to see whether Rebecca was animal, vegetable, or mineral. He knew there was no Rebecca to be seen except in Mrs. Palmer-Pinto's own crazy mind. She lived alone on the ground floor of the house in which Edmund had his flat, and she had been certified insane but quite harmless.

She had a small income of her own, and she passed most of her time standing on street corners calling out christian names in the imperative mood. She was not ill-favoured. She wore her hair neatly shingled and she had a pleasant face when what was on her mind was not occupying her too strenuously. Her eyes were by no means vague but full of a fury of purpose so much so, indeed, that this concentration, as if to mash the universe, was the first clue she gave of what was amiss with her. She spoke well, and dressed like a retired schoolteacher.

Sometimes as she stood at street corners when night was falling, queer men picked her up, so as to be able to boast of the experience of having "been" with a mad woman.

Now as Edmund went by, she gave him a wrathful stare, and after his retreating figure she hurled her "Rebecca! Rebecca! Rebecca!"

He went into an Oxford Street bar, to think about Alma having gone away, helping himself out with glasses of cheap grog.

Wish she had let me know her address, he thought ruefully. Yet—why should she? I cancelled out any gratitude she might have felt for that money—gratitude which might have been an incentive to her in looking for a better life. What did she call me—her last client! God!

I shall never rightly know how it happened—that night. I was going home, actually leaving her. I'd made for the door, and she called me back—made me sit down beside her to talk about my goodness—*my* goodness. She spoke of love—she kissed me. And I was drunk. It was all too much for poor old Edmund!

Yet, it need not have been too much. The trouble is that in concentrating so much upon Alma's spiritual welfare—ha! ha!—I long ceased to care for my own soul. That is a heartrending mistake. It's the root of most trouble, if anyone asks me! Once you neglect the divine selfness of yourself you become selfish and inhuman; you lose the central point of all action. Ya, ya! Preaching Willy, don't be silly!

"Pink gin," he called to the barman who was coming round for orders, "and I'd like a newspaper." When this came he went scurrying through it, as was now his daily practice, for a report of the arrest of Mrs. Christopher. She must have got away, else they'd have arrested her by now, he thought, and tried to find some relief in this from the stupefying sorrow of his betrayal of her. Then he returned to considering Alma.

Don't suppose I shall ever hear from her again, he thought, deeply troubled. Lord! What a lot I had to learn from her, yet I was the one who tried to teach her—always talking to her about love and God. She knew nothing about Christ, and so cannot be said ever to have offended Him. But I was always saying my little piece about Him, yet I was the one who in betraying my own conscience betrayed Christ. That's the way it goes, tell your mother!

I've only known God and love *in words*, not in my behaviour. You have to do more than talk the Truth, you have to live it. I've only talked and never acted. Been righteous and never been right. Been blind and thought I could see. Been æsthetic and thought I was being religious.

But Edmund did hear from Alma. About a month later a

letter arrived for him by the Saturday afternoon post. Recognizing her dreadful writing on the envelope he left off drinking tea and eating muffins to tear it open in some excitement, thinking: she's got her flat near the King 'n' Queen! She wants me to go round! She's forgiven me! She wants me to go and help her choose some furniture—or approve what she has bought. She wants me to . . .

These thoughts were so assured and congenial that he could hardly believe the evidence of his sense of sight as he went through her letter.

Alma told him she thought he would be glad to know as how she had retired at last same as he had wanted her to, and she wanted—not half. She was sick and tired of obliging, that she was. Now she need never oblige again, thanks to him. With all that money he had given her, she had set up in a little house by the docks, and hired six young ladies to oblige seafaring men. The rent was a bit high, but the young ladies' earnings would take care of that. Alma went on to say that she gave the young ladies a good percentage on their takings, because if you wanted to get the best out of people you must give them a good percentage.

She did not know how she would get on as a "Madam," but she thought she would be all right. She had a sharp tongue, personality, and there were no flies on her. Many of her clients had told her she had personality and that there were no flies on her. And she had bought a beautiful black satin dress because it was a well-known thing that all "Madams" wore black—satin if they could get it. She had got it.

Furnishing all the rooms as bedrooms had taken up a lot of the money. But she was sure he would be pleased if he could see them. She had pink everything in all the rooms, because pink was restful, and gentlemen looked for it.

She hoped he would not mind how she had spent the money. In a way, she deserved a present from him though, perhaps, not as much as he had given her. She deserved a present for all the time she had wasted listening to his clap-trap about God. If he didn't mind her saying so, God was only a luxury for gents such as him. She didn't understand about God and didn't want to, seeing as how all those who had clicked with God made him out so dull. Sometimes she felt sorry for God on account of the funny people who seemed to be his friends.

In conclusion, she adjured Edmund to keep smiling, and she was his respectful Alma Wosp. She added a postscript to the effect that she was not going to have her teeth out, after all, because she found that it would be too expensive!

"We'll certainly keep smiling," said Edmund, dazed by her valedictory words; "we'll smile our heads off!"

He turned the envelope over; it was post-marked from a sea-port in Wales. He sat thinking to himself: a whoring establish-ment, eh, with pink everything in all the rooms because pink was restful, and gentlemen looked for it! Did they? That was something new. That just about completed his education. Gentlemen looked for it! Well, it was nice of her to let him know. It showed consideration for him—great consideration!

He began to laugh, he could not stop, because the more the situation came home to him, the more it seemed quite the best joke he had ever heard. You gits your wages according to your job—as Alma once said. O, he must go out immediately and tell someone—let someone else share in the gale of laughter at his expense.

He rushed from the room. When he got down to the hall, the mad woman, Mrs. Palmer-Pinto was standing at the door of her flat in high heels and an olive-green tailored suit. Edmund was about to pull the street door open, when she called in her wild way:

"Humphrey! Humphrey! Humphrey!"

Edmund paused, arrested. He turned to look at her where she stood, a sorrowful lurid woman, with the early evening sunlight falling beautifully through the Queen Anne fanlight on her stern demented face, the white lace at her throat, and the green gems in her ears.

"Humphrey! Humphrey! Humphrey!" she called again, now on a lower note of melancholy uncertainty.

"Here I am," said Edmund, going towards her. He took her hand and walked her into her flat.

"Here I am," he said again, peeping into her face. "Someone has answered your call at last. And you shall have the entertainment of listening to the best joke of your life! I can tell *you* the truth, the whole truth, and nothing but the truth, so help me God! Nothing so mad *you* ever knew for all that you are out of your mind. And *that* makes you the best possible listener. Only the sane scoff. Who would listen as compassionately, as tenderly as you? Come! Sit down in your embroidered chair. The informer shall confess in full to the lunatic, and together we shall laugh—until we cry."

PART THREE

FROM SOUTH KENSINGTON

I

WHEN Veronica left Sine's house on the night Mrs. Christopher accounted for him, she went up Hampstead Lane, walking up the hill with quick grace. She wore no hat, and her black bobbed hair, which was of a shining fine texture, blew about her head. A pair of good-naturedly mocking blue eyes and a tilted nose with proud little arching nostrils carried the character of her face. It might be said that she over-painted her mouth, but when it was without its carnival slash of colour its line suggested a sweet gravity which was not necessarily consistent with integrity or wisdom. She was dressed in unremarkable, modest clothes, yet a finely-wrought slenderness, eyes that in their pride saw only what they wished to see, an air of dying-off aristocracy, together with a bearing of habitual verve seemed to urge a one-time familiarity with the regal, the sparkling— even the sumptuous.

As she walked, Veronica looked about her. She began to enjoy the moonlight which was scouring the chalky tombstones in Highgate cemetery to china blue, and spreading out into a kind of luminous pearly canopy in the higher air all the way down to the town where lights were heaped like golden radishes on the vast dark platter of London.

This moonlight makes you melt away to a hair's breadth, thought Veronica, and you're caught up in it, and you become it, turning grey-blue and flattened-out; you take to yourself the life of light.

I can afford, Veronica ruminated, to think expansive thoughts this night!

Here she arrived at the top of the hill where Coleridge's tomb was, and she knew it. She crossed the road and, thruogh the railings, peered down into the dark open crypt.

He used to walk in these very streets, she observed to herself, wandering about, making up poetry, with that awful mouth of his open. O, *what* an ugly mug for so exquisite a poet. And I daresay he stank of opium and stale medicine, and looked seedy, with a big uncared-for head! I don't suppose many pause here and give a respectful bob at his tomb. I wouldn't, either, but that relief gives me the leisure for fanciful goings-on.

Some lines from "Christabel" occurred to her. Her old horror of the poem returned. "Hush, beating heart of Christabel! Jesu, Maria, shield her well!" When I first read that poem, mused Veronica, going slowly away from the railings in the direction of the Underground station, I might have qualified for the sweet innocent Christabel, but now the part of Geraldine would fit me better, with her "mark of shame."

She smiled wryly. How did I ever come to be interested in Coleridge and poetry? I certainly got no example in my own home. My father never opened a book unless it was a stud-book, and my mother counted it a social asset to say: "Of course, I never read books." I wasn't even sent away to school to learn to love books, but to pick up the accomplishment of passing my life in a splendour of nothingness (men not caring for girls who know more than they do) in order to catch a rich and suitable husband. I was being trussed and got ready for the market!

But during this sad process I went and fell in love with the English literature mistress. Loving her, I naturally loved the things in which she was most interested. Does that always follow? Did I love the things in which my husband was most interested? O, I did not once, but now I do, now that I no longer love the things my lover cares for most—parties, running round for a little drink here, a little drink there, a good time all the time, a time in which to shine and conquer everybody. But I loved these things before I loved William, long before I ever met him. Indeed, since we did meet there have been fewer parties and a lot less of a good time.

Veronica was a married woman, but the man to whom she was going home in South Kensington was not her husband. Her husband lived in a large house in Leicestershire, sustaining, as best he might, the loss of a wife whom he passionately loved, who had loved him, and who, with an unaccountable change of heart, had left him two years ago for another man. The scandal had not only alienated Veronica from her husband, but from her family.

In the circles Veronica came from, a man, such as her lover, was known as "a damned low-born cad"; perhaps, as Veronica often thought, that was why he had attracted her so much. Perhaps a woman like Veronica could have too much of the society of those who were not damned low-born cads.

The cad to whom she was now returning was a man of thirty-nine years named William Phenyl, and he sometimes earned a trifle by writing short stories or metrical abominations which certain obscure little magazines were pleased to publish under the denomination of poetry. Otherwise William lived on what Veronica earned in various capacities.

William found that he was unable to take up employment himself in an office or factory to keep him and Veronica till he could write what people would read. To have worked in an office, or worked anywhere at all would have interfered with what William called his artistic temperament. So Veronica worked, usually as a typist and sometimes as a waitress. She was not very bright at her work; her education had never been designed to equip her for earning.

The union of William and Veronica was neither easy nor happy. Sometimes the disaccord and vexations of their life together dealt Veronica such prodigies of melancholy exasperation that she gave serious consideration to the proposal—popular because painless—of gassing herself out of existence.

Poor old Veronica—she would open an examination of her wrongs—life was nothing but one torment after another; there was always nagging remorse, and the fact that she had not ceased to love her husband—it was just that she loved William more. And much credit had to be given her for the daily fret of coping with her lover's difficult, mean, and exacting ways.

Do you love your man? Do you? Then for God's sake have a little patience with his close resemblance to a jungle beast. And don't overlook the trial of having no real friends, only William's impossible consorts. Anything else? Yes, you might as well mention the ordeal of having to go out and do work, in offices, which seems totally unreal work to you, and having to mix with gross and uncongenial colleagues who hate you, suspecting you of being a rich author come among them to cadge a little real-life copy. It's your finishing-school accent that finishes you for these good people! You may conclude your list of woes by saying how dreadful you find it, so often, not having enough to eat.

At first Veronica had been blithe enough to sacrifice everything for William. Then, only her love for him had filled the world hugely. But after two years Veronica had slipped very considerably from the heights. She saw that romantic love was not enough: many kinds of love had to be put into a union to make it successful and lasting; romantic love was only the beginning. Nowadays old claims and ways and values had begun to assert themselves, strong with the persuasive force of things known from birth, causing the faithless Veronica the searching pains of the exile.

Besides all these predicaments, there had also been, till tonight, the horror of Sine's blackmail which Veronica had borne alone, not wishing to upset William with her oppression though, as a fact, had it not been for William Veronica would never have been in a position to be blackmailed at all.

A year ago things had been so hopeless financially that Veronica had stolen from the office where she was then employed, the sum of seventy pounds. Her light-fingeredness had been discovered by her employer, a singularly christian man, who forgave her and did not insist on a repayment of the money when he heard how driven she was. He himself had had to explain the matter to his auditor. The auditor was an innocent friend of Sine's, had mentioned the matter to him, and thus the blackmailer had obtained his power over Veronica.

But now Sine was dead. From to-night Veronica was free of that series of humiliations; no more pinching and desperate scheming to scrape together each month that pitiful four pounds for his silence about her theft. And now after so many friendless days perhaps everything was going to be different and better. Sine's death might be the signal that a new world was emerging from the ruins she herself had brought about. Her thoughts turned gratefully to her deliverer, Mrs. Christopher.

What on earth, wondered Veronica, what on earth could Sine have been blackmailing Mrs. Christopher *for?* That ardent simplicity of hers might, of course, be as suspect as the devil. Veronica had now lived long enough in South Kensington to know, without the physicists telling her, that appearance was not reality. Yet Mrs. Christopher looked—well, she might have been my mother, thought Veronica. But being blackmailed doesn't give a person the *look* of being blackmailed, any more than what a person is being blackmailed *for* stands out in the face. No one, to look at me, would suppose that I have been blackmailed for stealing. No. Things don't show, though they must be being registered *somewhere*, I suppose.

She frowned. Flaws were appearing in the good evening.

She gave a little shiver and hurried into the Underground station as if to escape something intolerable.

Once in the Tube train the bright lights, the bustle of passengers coming and going, the instant homage she saw in certain men's glances when they rested upon her, and the amazing unlooked-for knowledge that she was free of Sine for ever, restored her spirits. She had to change trains in Leicester Square Underground station, and when she stepped into the second train she immediately heard the type of voice that had dominated her old world:

"So I went to Benton of Wimpole Street to get it confirmed, and he gave me six months to live—such a bore!"

But Veronica's attention was not taken up with a high society woman's attempt to show how well she was Taking It; Veronica was staring at the woman's little girl who was sitting gravely beside her mother. This child was nine or ten years old. The little figure was clad in a dark green cloak the hood of which was tumbling off her long brown hair. Russet stockings had been pulled over the child's slim legs. Her beautiful vivid little face with its rosy cheeks and shining eyes was composed in some remote dream; she looked like an estrayent from the wild wood. It made Veronica's heart contract to look at this poised and entrancing little girl, who seemed as if she would be loving as well.

Ah! Dear lord! If only you were mine!

Veronica glanced down at her own flat stomach. "I ought to have a baby in there," said Veronica naively to herself.

The little girl caught her eye and smiled in instant friendliness.

Dash it, don't smile, my little one, my dear, you only make things harder. Nevertheless, Veronica grinned in return, while all that unworked aspect of creative love confronted her anew: O, to have a baby! I wouldn't mind even a sick baby with a big waggling head, a delicate baby who'd need dosing and cosseting till it got better—then I could give it things it would gobble and enjoy. You see, she voicelessly and dispiritedly addressed some hovering fancy of deity, I'm not asking for a beautiful well baby, I'd be content with an ill baby—agitatingly ill—so long as it were mine.

The train flung itself into South Kensington station and Veronica came up into the night again. The little girl had started up a most desperate yearning in Veronica's harassed heart. All her strong delicate frame of female sex tingled with longing for a child of her own. She looked up into the sky, seeing a round of stars as a daisy-chain to go over a little girl's head. But it wouldn't do to become too fanciful. She began to whistle "Irene," throwing out the notes into the impassive night as if they were her cares and so she got rid of them. She really must not grieve to-night. She must celebrate.

She made her way towards a delicatessen. When you had extra money your first thought always flew to food. Here she bought a supper in cartons—potato salad, cooked salmon, a long length of French bread, a bottle of mayonnaise, a bottle of fruit salad, and a pot of cream. It was seldom she and William had such a supper, but to-night they could afford it. In her purse, Veronica had the money she had been taking to Sine who now had passed beyond the tearing need of anyone's bitterly saved-up hush money.

She came to where she lived: this was one of those short old streets of neat cottages, such as are to be found in many a metropolitan district of London. The cottages have little weedy gardens, bright brass door-knockers, soft violet, glossy lime-green, or fiery scarlet doors with snow-white steps, and flower-boxes; there are a few trees and an air of leafy dreaminess. Somehow, these little ways, right in the heart of London, have managed to invest themselves with the tranquil character of a country village street.

Veronica's little backwater opened off a South Kensington Square, and the cottage had been lent to her for an indefinite period by a friend who had conveniently gone away to India. The garden in front of the cottage had been clamped down under the rigors of patterned concrete, and only enough dusty earth had been spared to nourish a single almond tree which every spring lent its cool glory to the relentless crazy paving and the street. Its blossoming for that year was done, but it dipped its hood of fresh green leaves in the night wind, and laid itself out to be transfigured in the bland gold rays of the street lamp.

This tree, had they let it, would have been an egress for Veronica and William out of the pell-mell of their senseless and unlovely hours. The mystery of its life in this flagged London enclosure was no less profound than theirs, and in its essence were gleams and beckonings of its image above and beyond the world, an image of which it was a moving metaphor in space and time. In pursuit of this tree's transcendency they could have lost themselves, forgotten what was and discovered the might-have-been.

But William had only taken notice of the tree on two occasions and each time he had gone and relieved himself against it, drunk, in the dark. And Veronica, when she noticed it at all, felt that it was a nuisance and called it "that thing" because it darkened the tiny drawing-room at the front of the cottage. They had no thought of it for itself alone, only of its misuse to them.

She now walked past the strangled little tree without so much as a glance in its direction, and let herself into the cottage by way of a buttercup-yellow door. In the kitchen-dining-room at the back, she soon had the supper spread, then sat down among the cheap bright arty effects of the little place to wait for William. Once her eyes had rested on the beautiful colours of a Van der Borght tapestry as she waited in a room, or on the delicate green and blue panels of a hand-painted Chinese wallpaper. But Life had shot out from the gracious to the garish. And these cheap raving modern colours were symbolic of the change—for the worse.

II

William came in half an hour later. He had a humorous jaunty
little walk, and was, as usual, wearing a very wide-brimmed
hard hat. Arrogant well-being poured from him. Habitually he
wore a slightly truculent air, but to-night something had put
him in a mad bursting good humour. He was hungry and
exploded with delight when he saw the supper.

"What's this, Veronica? Celebrating something?"

He threw off his hat and long overcoat, and stood square to
the eye in a suit of dark-grey whipcord—a rig which he thought
invested him with bohemian glamour. He began pulling satisfied
grimaces under the electric light, a bull-necked burly man, with
a plump clean-shaven face, hard and handsome, a face that gave
nothing away yet did not repel because of a certain impudence
that prevailed upon the interest. He had a thick white skin, a
lard-like skin which looked as if it would have to be cut into
deeply before blood could be discovered.

The suggestion of diminished commonness which never left
him was provided by his early environment in a South London
slum, and the abundant measure of prim cocksureness and
alacrity constituted the effect of several years in a grammar
school at which he had been admitted by a scholarship.

"What's all this?" he repeated. "What are we rejoicing
about?"

"O," said Veronica, sitting to the table, "I found I had an
unexpected shilling or two, so I thought we would have a decent
meal. It makes a pleasant change. I'm tired of bread and cheese
and watered beer."

William seated himself opposite to her.

"Well, I get tired of muck, too," he observed. "D'you know
I thought for a minute that perhaps your loving father had at

last forgiven you for taking up with someone below the salt, and had given you a cheque as a sign of his newly-acquired socialism."

Without comment Veronica began to break up her piece of flabby salmon. She was used to his treating her with the rowdy condescension of the propertyless. Most of his time William seethed with the crotchety snobbishness of those who had never possessed anything but snobbery.

"I heard a good one about your father to-day," William went on, usually unable to refrain from poking into Veronica's family affairs. "Fellow I know saw the old boy playing golf at Roehampton and said he always looks like an actor playing the part of an old gentleman!"

William waited, but Veronica imperturbably ate.

"Meaning, of course," persisted William in his harsh, bitten way, "that there's something which looks bogus about the old boy. I daresay it's one of your humble ancestors looking out through him. How long is it, Veronica, since your family was in trade?"

"They were merchant princes in the time of Henry IV," said Veronica through a crammed mouth; "prior to that, I've never bothered to enquire. It's all down in the family tree somewhere."

"Never mind," said William, "I'm not really interested. I say, doesn't it seem sad that at his age, the chief concern of your noble ancient father should be an exact and loving care in putting a ball into a hole on a golf-course. To come to the end and have no ambition but that! Awful! Why doesn't someone go up to him sometime and say, as he pats his ball into the little hole: 'You're on the verge of a hole yourself, old man!' "

"I daresay that occurs to him," replied Veronica. "He's pretty wide-awake. And with so much waiting just round the corner, it's probably relief sometimes merely to knock a little ball into a little hole."

"He'd be better off saying his prayers," retorted William.

"You're quite likely to go before he does in this uncertain world," said Veronica. "Do you say *your* prayers?"

"No, I don't," William replied. "Prayers are only for the old and the superstitious. Besides, I haven't as much to pray about as he."

"What has my father got to pray about?"

"O, having been so idle and so rich. And then, there's you—his beautiful erring daughter. You and I have lived together like anything for two long years all among the gamboge stucco and lily-livers of South Kensington! I don't suppose any member of his family has ever sunk as low as you—running away with a man like me!"

"No," said Veronica, "I don't think they have."

"Living in sin in South Ken," persisted William, speaking out of the vocabulary of snobs, "with a ghastly little tick whose parents kept a fish-and-chip shop!"

"Did they really?" asked Veronica with interest. He would have been astonished if he had known how much she understood and sympathised with his snobbishness, for she recognized that children who have nothing still have dreams, and upon those dreams, good or ill, depends all their future life. To herself Veronica was perpetually excusing William, not for what had been his life's actualities, but because of his dreams.

"Haven't I told you before?" he asked belligerently.

"No. You've only hinted at some George Gissing kind of a background. A fish-and-chip shop is really something definite. My aunt, the Lady Eugenie Pot, is in a similar line of business. She runs that little 'Dish o' Tay' place in Mayfair and is famous for her anchovy teas. Exactly the same, you see, though I daresay my aunt's charges are a little heavier. But then, so are her overheads."

William stole a wary glance at her. Her face was mirthful. He was ever apt to hope that his ill-bred way of wanting always to be right would throw Veronica into a rage, put her on the defensive, but he had no such satisfaction. He supposed she was too well bred to be touchy. Ah, well, she came of a thick-rinded class which had no spontaneous feelings. They never committed themselves, probably because there was nothing to commit. He was in the habit of awarding himself these consoling portions of thought because *he* was the one who was empty, and he knew it. He was so empty and famished he was always trying to create values with which to fill himself. In his bewildered yearning for higher and better things he read Proust, which would give him, so he argued, a value over those who, like Veronica, had had the benefit of an expensive education (denied by circumstance to him), and who yet remained dolts because, of course, all the schooling in the world did not make an educated person. Top circles were crowded with vacant little faces under hats—faces that were of the best breeding in the land!

Veronica was not bookish or clever; her head was top full of clap-trap about babies and some steamy little kind of family life they ought to be having together. She was just a clod, really, and he despised her.

But in being his mistress she gave him one of the values he craved because she was the daughter of a peer—a rather shabby and back-bencher peer, it was true, nevertheless aristocracy, an old name, not some upstart who had only just been jumped into the lords and creaked with the newness of his title, but genuine old stuff, choice and quiet. William had never loved Veronica— he was only in love with her sparkling background.

But apart from her social value to him he admired her ease and grace, the way she spoke, just as apart from the snob value of "A La Recherche du Temps Perdu" he found genuine pleasure in reading the book. He had an eye for beauty and was wistful for it. Phrases from the novel would linger in his mind and delight him. " . . . . dinner in some restaurant along the coast . . ." His satisfaction in such words as these did not lie in

the fact that the Baron de Charlus and the socially inferior
Morel were dining together, but in the romantic spaciousness
the phrase opened up, giving him, as it were, the freedom of the
whole coast of Normandy, of innumerable beaches, plages,
Majestic Hotels, with always a wind that blew in regular
sequences of little pecks as if to provide a humming travesty of
the phrase from Vinteuil's sonata, and an immense grey sea
coldly rolling in, with a lonely light frigidly winking at the end
of a shadowy pier.

"You're not eating," said Veronica. "Have some more
salmon?"

He had been sitting glowering and at a loss, turning over her
remarks about her aristocratic aunt; he felt the need to assert
himself and embarked on something clever, saying with a
merry air:

"Lord, yes, every class now is copying the pursuits of its
opposite. Just think, Veronica, only this afternoon when I was
sitting in a theatre waiting for the 'Cherry Orchard' to begin,
my neighbour turned out to be a Maida Vale postman whom I
knew by sight from the time I had a flat there. This person gave
me a wan greeting, and in the course of a little desultory conversation informed me that the analytical psychotherapeutical
treatment he was having was definitely checking his coprophobia!"

He waited. She said, unabashed:

"But what on earth *is* coprophobia?"

"It's fear of inconvenient bowel action," he said severely.
"Didn't you know?"

"No," she said, "I didn't. Only fools know everything!"

"Why," he protested, "the whole point of the story is lost,
since you didn't understand."

"What *was* the point?" she asked.

"Only that one doesn't look for the lingo of the educated
classes in a postman."

136

"No," she said; "it's a pity when a decent honest man of that type deteriorates into a mere intellectual and so lives with only half of himself."

"The intellect is everything," he said.

"Even I know that you're wrong there," she replied. "It's only a means—it doesn't show you how to live only how to think. Life is a good deal more than taking thought. The fullness of life comes from response and that doesn't come from thoughts but from feelings." And as she finished speaking she thought bitterly: yes, and somehow, it's you, William, who have killed all responses in me to everything but to yourself. You are ruining me.

William was brooding, too. This essay had not been successful in scoring one over her. He tried something else:

"Sold two short stories to-day."

"O, well done," said Veronica. "I am glad, my dear. Which magazines took them?"

She stared at the chunks of fruit in the thick juice in the china dish. She wondered if he were speaking the truth. She would not look at him till he gave her more details; he might see the unbelief prickling in her eyes. William had two dreadful failings: he was an inveterate liar and his heart was hard. These are faults you cannot know in a person all at once. They have to be learned slowly and bitterly as intimacy develops. Veronica was learning; she was going through the mauling experience of seeing a loved and rather unlovely being gradually emerging from all his disguises.

William reeled off the names of two little magazines.

"Nothing very startling," he admitted, "but it's all getting my name known!"

Self-obsessed, it was his indefatigable aim to get his name known; he was always looking for something to this purpose, and always entertaining himself with sweet imaginary conversations in clubs:

"William Phenyl! O, yes, the chap who ran away with the Hon. Veronica Soter."

"O, Phenyl—the man who had that brilliant little thing in 'The Passport' the other day . . ."

"Have you met Phenyl? You must—he's a coming man!"

He sat at the table now, in a happy dream, nursing his name.

Veronica asked:

"Are the fees good?"

"You would ask that," he replied with an air of superior weariness. "What does money matter to the artist?"

"It happens that the artist must live," she said.

"Veronica, you *are* sordid!" he informed her loftily. "Your mind is always running on the importance of cash. So it may please you to hear that I am to have five guineas each for my stories—so my agent tells me."

"That's very good," Veronica commented. "We are doing well!"

"I always told you it was only a matter of time before I began to do something big in the literary world," said William from the depths of the warm opinion he held of himself. "Look, honey," he went on, "I want to spend that money on a subscription to a good club. Must mix with literary men, you know. Must get my name around!"

"You have to live up to an exclusive club," said Veronica mildly.

Instantly he flew at her.

"You mean I'm not good enough?" he demanded. "You think I cannot mix with the members of a decent club just because I did not have beautiful friendships with them at Oxford or Cambridge?"

"Not at all. You haven't the means. You'd be mixing with men of considerable incomes, and entertaining and keeping up appearances would run away with far more money than you've got—yet. To begin with, you want a new suit, my dear, before you can belong to any club."

He darted a suspicious look at her. No. She was not trying to make him feel small. He was obliged to acknowledge that she never got up to anything mean. And he had to admit the sense of what she had said.

"Very well, then. I'll get a new suit," he declared, "then the money from my next acceptance can buy me into a good club. And I must have some cards. I find they are really indispensable." He laughed jeeringly. "My blessed mother never left cards," he confessed, "only debts!"

"She must have been a remarkable woman," observed Veronica, "to have done so well for you."

"She never did anything," he said sourly. "She always thought I was an idiot. She would have joined with you at once against my excellent idea of belonging to a good club where I could show myself off to advantage. You seem to forget I have a position to keep up."

"What position?" she asked sincerely.

"Why, I . . . my position as an author," he said firmly.

Veronica said:

"Don't be silly, William. The only people with positions to keep up are those who have nothing except money."

"And don't you despise money," he retorted. "It's everything."

"Perhaps it is when you've got nothing else."

Veronica looked at him. She assumed that the day's good fortune would have mellowed him and melted one or two of his implacable prohibitions. And so she said to him with some resolution:

"William, darling, clubs and things like that don't matter two pence. If it is in you to be a great writer, that is what you will be, and membership of all the clubs in the world won't hasten or alter the outcome. And listen, I shall have a little more money in future—a rise in salary, sort-of, and, well, now that you are having more stories accepted, don't you . . . don't you think, dear, that we could have a child?"

"God, no," replied William in instant alarm. "I don't. Isn't it just like you to be bringing *that* up the minute prospects seem to be brightening?" He chewed dismally, waiting for the next attack.

"Are you always going to refuse?" asked Veronica.

"I wonder you aren't sick of this subject by now. *I* am," retorted William. "Sitting there looking injured! I don't know! Haven't you got any progressive thoughts in your head? You're deplorable, really you are, Veronica! Good heavens above—women do make me sick! I wish we could do without 'em. Why is it that you wish to tie me down to a prospect of squalling brats and everlasting poverty?"

Throughout his scolding, he had taken on a horrid air of wishing to get away, to escape—and for ever. Daunted, but determined in her need for an enduring token of love, Veronica said briskly:

"You argue from the impurity of your heart. I know I am persistent, but what I ask for represents the whole meaning of our being together. Our love hasn't much purpose without a child—children. Surely you can see that, too?"

William threw himself back in his chair and stared at Veronica. Returning his gaze she noticed with pitiless clarity the debased vacancy in his eyes. He, meantime, was wondering what kind of a retort to deal out to her. He decided, as he regularly did, to take refuge in the underhanded.

"Look, Veronica," he said with quiet brutality, "don't you think that I, too, want a child? Do you suppose that you are the only one with feelings? But I want a decent home for my brats, and I want 'em born in wedlock. Do you see?"

Veronica saw.

William was looking at her with sharp attention. He was

always interested in the effects of his cruelties which themselves were the result of a life-long attitude of self-defence. Then again he was so constituted that even the highest form of affection of which he was capable was held together by tight thongs of cruelty which often slipped, showed up, and caused suffering. But perhaps he had gone too far this time. Veronica's face wore a revolted and weary expression; she turned from him, disgusted and speechless.

"Of course, I know it isn't your fault that we can't marry," William shrugged. "Your thick-headed husband won't divorce you. But that isn't my fault, either, and I won't have an illegitimate child. It's difficult enough to make your way in this blasted world without being loaded with a stigma like that," he muttered virtuously.

"What cant that is," said Veronica, "coming from you!"

It made him wild to hear this said. It was unthinkable to let her words pass without lash and fury.

"I daresay it sounds cant to you," William answered loudly; "you were brought up without any morals—your set are all the same. You seem to think that title buys you immunity from everything including sin and its consequences. *You'd* have a bastard, you'd have a house full, simply because that happens to be what you want. Hang everything else—hang what I want, and the children's own feelings—the handicap illegitimacy would be to them!"

He bubbled with his suddenly acquired passion for *comme il faut*.

"All your objections are grossly silly," said Veronica, going to the mantelpiece and lighting a cigarette. "Illegitimacy is no handicap. As for the children themselves—children need love, as much love as can be given to them, then all the other things will look after themselves. Love-children, anyway, ought to get the most love if their parents live up to the circumstances of their birth."

"Yes, and they don't get it," William replied, "in fact, they usually get less of it. Anyway, I'm not having any of your love-children. If you can once get that idea firmly fixed in your noddle you will save yourself a lot of useless argument."

"You certainly take the heart out of everything," Veronica cried, letting everything go in her hopelessness. "You must have been told many a time how dreary you are! You never seem to think how quickly life is going by with nothing done while you are playing at being an author and I am playing at mean stupid commercial work in offices, and together we are playing at being in love. It's the waste, the horrible godforsaken *waste* that is so shocking! Can't you see it? Good God! How I wish I could tell you how much I hate what we have come to. We're just an appetite—one for the other, without romance, or dignity, or anything fine. We've got nothing—only what each gets out of the other—and it's not enough; I tell you, it's *not enough!* I used to think only prigs called a deliberately barren sex love selfish: now I see how trivial it is. Even if you actually believed in that rubbish you talk, you would, if you were a true lover, want a baby, too, because a child would be the justification of the love we've had no business to snatch."

"I see what it is," he shouted, "you don't love me any more, that's why you're talking like this."

"On the contrary," she replied, "it's just because I *do* love you that I . . . William don't you like children?"

"No," he said violently, "no, I don't like kids, and I won't be burdened with them. I'd rather write books than have children."

"Write?" she said; "do you know, you'll never write anything till you get some manliness."

"Manliness!" he spluttered. "What do you mean? You're surely not trying to suggest——"

"O, no," she said ironically, "hardly that."

"What do you mean by manliness, then?" he demanded.

"Godliness," she replied.

He smirked.

"No, my dear girl, you've got it all wrong. A man must realize *himself*. That's the important thing to be doing. To hell with God!"

"And how are you going to realize yourself or anything else without God? How can you be a man without God?"

"That's easy," he said. "Look at me, darling! I *am* a man."

"Are you?" she said.

"Yes, and I'm getting tired of hearing about God. You'd better go and ask God for a baby. You won't get one from me!"

"Thank you for making yourself so clear at last," said Veronica. She lit a cigarette with unsteady fingers, and continued: "I have just been through a year of the most harrowing and degrading misery for your sake, yet you will do nothing for me. It's a very one-sided arrangement, ours."

"Now what are you talking about?" William demanded. "Gone through hell for me? What do you mean by that?"

Veronica told him. He heard how she had stolen to keep them solvent, how she had been blackmailed and of her painful struggle to scrape the monthly payments together to keep his and her father's name clear, and how only to-night was it all ended because one of the victims had ushered the blackmailer out of the world in no uncertain fashion.

William listened to her story with alarm and fury. At the same time there was something in such a tale for his highly nervous, tortured, and treacherous type that filled him with a sort of wild wonder.

"Well," he ranted, when she had finished, "you *have* been mixing with some nice people! And what the hell did you want to go stealing for? Really, Veronica, you'd stop at nothing! Of all the irresponsible silly bitches you do take first prize! Stealing! What a flair you've got for the unruly! You might have been sent to prison and got my name linked with yours in the Press! Have you no consideration at all for me—for my name? You know how carefully I am trying to keep it from dirt and scandal!"

"Just a trifle out of proportion, aren't you?" said Veronica. "It was consideration for you that made me steal. We weren't getting enough to eat, our clothes were rags, and you were on the point of being arrested for a twenty-pound debt. Don't let your priggishness drown rightness, will you?"

"I thought you got that money for my debt from your brother," said William, angrily dragging at his ear.

"That's what I told you at the time, but of course neither of my brothers has remembered that I am still alive since I set up housekeeping with you."

"Nice lads they are," he sneered, "with their gold-mounted monocles and their hard stony mugs!" He was waiting for her to go on and point out that if he had been man enough to work there would have been no need for her to steal. But she did not hit back with that. She sat looking scornful and helpless, as if something had tipped over inside her and she was suffering from shock.

A little good nature began to hobble back to him. He began to understand what she had been through. The poor dear must have had an awful time with that blackmailer! He, William, would have been scared to death! He would have collapsed with the sordid exasperation of it all; he was always terrified of what his nerves would do to him. He could not have borne the situation bravely and in silence, as Veronica had done. So he need not be so beastly about it. Really, she was a decent brave thing. In his sentimental fashion he began to accredit her with all the salutary virtues. He began to speak to her with what, for him, constituted kindness.

"Damn," he said, with a sort of shame-faced mirth, "I oughtn't to go off the deep end about it. That money was a godsend even if you did deceive me about where you got it. What a liar you are, sweetie! You've got degenerate ears, on my word of honour! But we'll say no more about your dreadful tendencies. I'm not a particular man! And what's a theft here or there so long as you don't get found out! Yes, it is reasonable of you to hope that I would not mind. I properly appreciate that you were trying to please me by stealing in the first place and afterwards paying that man to keep his mouth shut so that my name should not be harmed. You're a good little thing, and I feel as if you are deeply devoted to me. But don't pinch anything else, you little fool! Think of my career."

She let his insufferable words fly about her head without losing her temper, but she came near to laughing out loud at him. Used to the careers of the scholars, statesmen, soldiers, and artists of her line, quietly pursued and achieved, the spectacle of William's fatuous occupation as a contributor to tenth-rate magazines, and the earnest common din that accompanied it, savoured of lunacy to Veronica.

This is the man I love, she thought, appalled, this strange clown, calling himself an artist, yet totally lacking in that response to life and depth of emotion without which there's no art at all. He'll never write anything worth while till he finds something higher than himself. Do I really love him? No, it isn't love. It's a black attraction which has gripped me with the power and the glamour of craziness. If only I could tell him to go to the devil! But she saw how pitifully tenacious the human heart is even of those impulses which can only end in known ruin.

She went to wash the supper things. She was very careful with the two cups in which they had had their coffee and from which, in the morning, they would drink their tea; these cups and saucers were the only two of the kind they had, bought by Veronica with an office bonus from a tray of oddments in an antique china dealer's shop. Sometimes you had so little left of your one-time high heart that you had to cling to so small and pitiful a token of lost elegance and gaiety as the bright panels of

flowers spiralling across the cerise background of two Rocking-
ham cups and saucers.

William had clattered off to the little drawing-room to pay
tribute to the last inch of whisky in the house, and to Create.
He was writing a memoir for godless intellectuals, working in
all the ingredients that gave them satisfaction and pleasure—
scepticism, gloom, hopelessness, pretty melancholies, ennui,
iconoclasm, derision, some little fancies of windy despair, and
the pleasures of non-being, the whole sicklied o'er in terms
lifted from the jargon of the many sects flourishing in the name
of psycho-analysis.

Veronica having finished the washing-up, seated herself at the
kitchen table and wrote an application for a post advertised in the
evening paper and offering a higher salary than she was earning.

It was getting late when she went out to post her letter. The
pillar-box stood in the square at perpetual dumb military
attention, and Veronica was just in time for the midnight
collection.

As she turned away from the scarlet box the hour struck
swiftly from the church in the far corner of the square. The
chimes fell out into the night in a little pandemonium of indignation as if the bells were having an argument with the clock
tower and something had affronted them. The staccato notes
were abruptly throttled in the high air, and a distant train paid
the ensuing silence the incivility of a gross hoot.

Veronica stopped and looked about her. In the deserted square
the borough lamps threw off a hard crafty glitter. The trees
rocked and expostulated among themselves with acrimony. A
suddenly tigerish wind was extorting a fandango from a paper
bag. Overhead the moon flamed wildly in a hole in the vast
plain of bulging silver cloud. It was an hour of unrest and
rebellion. Veronica had never felt so lonely and wounded. She
seemed to be coming to the end of what she could endure. She
flung her protesting spirit against the hushed houses, chafing

against her own bitter mistakes, longing for something different and wonderful to happen, and so release her from William, South Kensington, and, above all, from herself. O for a little sense from somewhere!

For so long now she had felt what it was like to be homeless, really homeless, to have no place where the spirit and heart could rest. She felt most grievously abandoned. "These days," said Veronica, "I'm always wanting to cry."

An aspiring novelist, whose art still floundered among the apocalyptic brevities of graffiti, had scrupulously chalked on a house wall:

ETHEL C. LOVES CYRIL O. SHE IS A TART. BERT F. SAYS SHE IS A DAMNED FOOL.

Observing this, Veronica thought ruefully: Ethel C. might very well be me! Lord, she sighed, your life goes over your head in long washes of memory and you see that you've never done anything to be proud of, learnt nothing, and become even less. You live so close to yourself you can't learn anything from your own follies, and you never have the wit to learn anything from stories told or the mistakes of other people.

She moved on haltingly.

Sometimes you smashed your life with no more thought of what you were doing than smoking a cigarette. She sighed. She knew that William was ruining her. Their irresponsible life together was not living at all. She saw how all her nature was beginning to change by William's use of her. She was just a plaything, and this was all she would want to be the more William exhausted her and thwarted her subjective need to fulfil and complete their love in a child.

O, how cowardly it was in her to tolerate this flabbergasting state of affairs, cowardly not to cut free, and return to her husband. If only *that* union had been blessed with a child, William would not have had a chance, could never have snared her. But, perhaps, if she went back to her husband, this time a child would unite them. What had that fellow said to-night after Mrs. Christopher had killed Sine? "He can't do any more to us now—if we don't do any more to ourselves!" Well, it looked as if the blackmailer wasn't dead for her yet, because she still loved William! She could not let him go. In spite of his monstrous selfishness she still loved him too much to leave him. Perhaps such knock-down egotism was what fascinated her in him, used as she was to men of different courtly ways. Whatever it was, she was trapped—a prisoner whose will was paralysed. She was going to the devil and she longed for some intervention outside her own power—some other thing equal to to-night's murder—by which everything would be arranged for her and changed, so that if she had to suffer any more at least to her burden would not be added that turn of the screw—that she herself was to blame.

Now she had arrived at her own little street. She went up the path, dodging, as usual, recognition of the almond tree, and went into the house with a wild head from the wind. William was emerging from the drawing-room.

"Hello," he said. "Been taking the air? Been getting a bit of consolation somewhere?"

The light from the room fell across his big face with its broad brow above the intent eyes, and the soft brown hair piling back in thick disorder. The triumphant heartlessness of his character was concentrated in two brutal lines which drove into his face from the bridge of his nose to his wide mouth. And yet, thought Veronica with a pang of love-hate, faults and all, this is the face that has driven me out of my wits. My God! What a dangerous thing it is to fall in love after one has turned thirty! You bring so much to it—all the past, all the best that's been rushes forward and mingles with the present in so exciting and irresistible a way that it would be a death to give it up. And then, what few people seemed to realize, even those who indulged it most, was that physical love could become so approfundized as to be a power akin to what, on a higher spiritual plane, trapped the interest and souls of saints and philosophers.

William, too, was enjoying some stirring of amativeness. As Veronica turned to hang up her coat in the little hall, he was thinking:

I could have done worse. An "honourable" for a fancy girl, eh! Who'd have thought it? From a round of fish-and-chips and drubbings to going to bed with a peer's daughter!

And he experienced a surge of fondness for her because she represented the whole of a world which, seen from his dubious hit-and-miss existence, was the only endurable and possible life, a world of family seats, shoots, and trees, in which everything was stupefyingly correct, which began with being entered at birth for Eton, gave one the privilege of wearing coronets on stationery and chamber-pots if the fancy ran to it, and soared to its zenith in becoming domesticated with royalty—home and foreign brands.

All that was Veronica's world. She had the exclusive accent, the right little ironies, the courtesy, the correct walk; she had been born in the proper postal district, and the men of her line had done the right thing down the ages from hunting queens and princesses up palace back-stairs to tracking down the rogue elephant in Ceylon. Veronica knew the rightness of everything— wines, clothes, clubs, manners, the sporting calendar; in her elaborate and insolent civilities, so it appeared to William's romantic ideas, she seemed to possess and transmit to him, in some exhilarating way, the whole of Burke's peerage. And if, in spite of all these attainments she had not very much strength of character and knew very little of fundamental things, did that matter much? No, it did not. Character had nothing to do with getting to the top!

Money and Birth are the only things that matter, thought poor William, facing one who once had had Money but now was left only with Birth. It would do.

And Veronica, seeing about him signs of softening, cried:
"O, William, don't be cross and withdrawn. Let's be loving;
I can't bear it if we're not loving!"

He took a pace forward and crushed her to him. She forgot
the littleness of his aims and his cruelty. She could only think of
the immediacy of the moment, and that, whatever he was, she
loved him. You made people what you wanted them to be,
even where the material was most suspect and frayed. Reality
dunned them as one thing, but Love waylaid them and decked
them as something quite different. O, life would be so easy—and
so dull—if only whoever had planned it had left out love.

III

He used to be disgusted by his own meanness. All the way
down his years of cheating and compromise it had filled him
with repugnance that he never could be straight. Being intelligent, he realized fairly early on that unless life could be lived in
accord with a voice within, rather than with all the voices
abroad, the whole show turned lamentable; nevertheless he did
not change because, on the whole, he found that uprightness
meant too much trouble.

"I'm going to get better at once," he would declare, and then
diligently look round for excuses which would put off reform
indefinitely. In this state of mind he nearly always found that
the urgency of things tended to sweep him off into schematic
baseness. Here, now, was this matter of the Highgate murder.
William was the one who saw in the newspaper the announcement of the reward of five hundred pounds for information
leading to the arrest of the Highgate murderer. He did not take
it in all at once, but suddenly he remembered Veronica's story,
and whipped back to the significant paragraph. Five hundred

pounds! William lifted the newspaper close to his eyes and made grunts of approbation at it.

During the last few days suddenly whipping-up events in his life had made money even more of a raging necessity than usual, and now he sat in a café and thought productively about the offer of the reward.

When William returned home that evening he was carrying in his hand a gay little plant in a pot. This was a peace offering to Veronica. His manner towards her just lately had been abominable, but on this evening William was airing himself as the repentant lover, a rôle in which, from long practice, he excelled. He was a far better actor than ever he would be an author, but neither he nor any leading stage-producer had ever discovered this interesting fact.

At supper William gave Veronica the plant.

"Thought this little fellow would please you," he mumbled.

"It was nice of you," stated Veronica, without looking at him, "to think of me."

"Nice of me? I'm always thinking of you, Veronica." He began to put on a look of injury.

"That's the explanation of it, then!"

"Explanation of what?"

"That you've hardly spoken to me all the week. But I understand now. You were thinking of me!"

He reached and took her hand.

"Don't think ill of me," he begged. "If you knew the disappointment I've had to face these last few days . . ."

"But I don't know," protested Veronica. "You never tell me anything, yet you expect me to understand and sympathize when affairs go wrong, and pardon your uncivilized behaviour in the house."

William preferred to say nothing but sat with an effort at wretchedness in his face.

"What's wrong?" asked Veronica. "Come. I want to know."

"But I don't want to bother you with my troubles," he objected.

"Yet you don't mind upsetting me with the effect your troubles have on you," said Veronica. "What a wretch you have been all the week!"

"I know. I'm sorry. I've been so tired of everything. Do you really want to know—could you bear to listen to my . . ."

"That's what I'm here for," she said. "We're supposed to help one another."

He listened to this with the utmost satisfaction, then broke into his story:

"What happened was I met a fellow who was at school with me. He has become something influential with Mell and Mell the publishers, and, just think, he offered me a place on their board of directors for a mere token of five hundred pounds! He might as well have asked me for five millions! I've got to refuse this really glorious chance simply because I haven't got five hundred pounds—or pence, if it comes to that!"

"O, William, I *am* sorry. That is really galling for you," she said.

"Well, now you see why I've been sulking. Lord! If only I could get that money! Apart from the thing providing me with a decent regular job, you see, I could obviously get my own works published there—my major works, that is, when I write 'em. And all I lack is five hundred pounds!"

"I wish I had the money," she said, "I would give it to you as quick as quick!"

"Of course you would, you darling. You have always been splendidly generous to me."

"Isn't there any way—wouldn't your friend hold the position open until, well, we had looked round a little? Not that I've the least idea where we could pick up five hundred pounds."

"I've got to give him my decision on Monday. He's holding it open that long as a special favour because our association goes back to our schooldays. But I must let him know on Monday."

Veronica said:

"If only we could get the money by then!"

William directed upon her a gaze of calculated intentness.

"Well?" she said. "What is it? What's the matter now?"

"I hardly like to say," he answered slowly.

"O, don't let us have any more injured silences," she cried. "For God's sake, what is it?"

"Well," he said, still keeping his eyes upon her, "we could get that money. At least, you could."

"I? Whatever do you mean?"

"Veronica, haven't you read the paper to-day?"

"No, I haven't had time. What do you mean?"

"O, I dunno. Perhaps I ought not to . . . No. Forget it."

"What is all this, William?"

"Very well, then."

He got up and brought the morning paper to her.

"Have a look at page five, top of final column."

Veronica did as she was told.

"O, I couldn't! I couldn't!" she said at once. She threw the paper on to the floor. "No. That's too much."

"I was afraid so," said William, hanging on to his temper. "But you would have me tell you, wouldn't you?"

"Yes, but I had no idea . . . I thought I could help." She turned distressfully away.

"Obviously you can help. Do you think that I would hesitate if you were the one who needed that money so badly?"

She began to feel frightened. Even to think idly of such a suggestion, still less to make it the subject of a serious argument, opened up absolute worlds of looseness in which assent could be given to almost anything. She cried out:

"William, it's selling the woman's life. I don't think you realize that. It's infamous. I couldn't do such a thing."

"Good lord, that is very dense of you! Since when have you become squeamish about betraying people?"

"William!" Her voice was full of pain.

"Well, Veronica, *really*, what's the difference between betraying your trustful, doting husband and mentioning that woman's name to the police? I think the husband business is much worse! After all, this old girl *told* you her name, she gave you permission to use it to the police."

"Yes, but only if suspicion fell on us," Veronica countered. "The need doesn't arise. I could not go and betray her to them simply to make things easier for you . . . for us."

"All I can say is I wish you had mentioned her name to me when you were trotting out your silly story. I would go straight to Scotland Yard myself. In this world you have to make use of every advantage."

"William!"

"That's it—squawk William! Be all shocked and horrified! Blast it! What are you quibbling about? That woman won't be in this country now. You can't suppose that she just sat about waiting to be arrested. She'll be in America or Timbucktoo by now. You can't do her any real harm. Besides, don't forget, will you, in your awful indignation, that the woman is a murderer. Nothing excuses the crime of murder," he concluded virtuously.

"Don't let us argue about the moral of it from *her* point of view," said Veronica. "The moral here concerns us—concerns me. I cannot go and betray her. Besides, I owe her so much; she freed me from that blackmailing dog."

"Freed *you?*" he cried in a shrill voice. "My poor Veronica, when she shot him, she was attending to her own affairs. He was blackmailing her, too, don't forget. She wanted to free herself. It was mere chance that she released you and the others at the same time. Yes, and do you suppose that *they* are as scrupulous as you? While we are sitting here clutching at your doubtful virtue, I'll bet anything you like that one or both of the others are on their way to Scotland Yard, if they didn't turn up there this morning." He fell into wild impatience. "O, why don't you get up and go and get that money now? What are you sitting there for like a stuffed dummy, eh, Veronica? You'd let someone else go and grab the five hundred pounds rather than help me whom you're supposed to love! 'We're supposed to help one another' you said just now, you hypocrite! When it comes to the testing, you'd let someone else have that money instead of getting it for me. I'm so tired of you and your notions of love!"

He kicked the fender. Really, the woman's scruples were absolutely intolerable! He began to be afraid that he would not succeed in breaking down her resistance. O, she must not oust him from his plan like this. Veronica, meantime, was saying:

"Such amiable remarks, William! Especially warm and rich coming from you! There are occasions when you are a most unlovely specimen, poor dear!"

"Yes, I am unlovely," he conceded quickly, giving her a look of real enmity, "and what about it? Only the rich can afford to practise the virtues. Goodness is a luxury which I can't afford."

"The Oscar Wilde performance doesn't become you at any time," she said wearily.

"Look here, Veronica," he said with his ill-bred directness, "tell me that woman's name and I'll go to the police myself. Well? What about it?"

"I am smiling at you, of course."

He rocked with rage. His eyes fell on a modern painting hanging over the fireplace. No one knew, except the artist, what this non-representational work was supposed to mean, but it seemed like a crimson bar of metal upon a background of geometric and glittering purple devices. It was entitled "Equation." William felt glad that abstract art could mean the first nonsense that entered one's head, because now he used the apparent piece of iron or lead as a sort of lever with which to jerk out his raging and convicting thrusts.

"It's enough to drive me crazy thinking of conscience worrying *you!*" he shouted at her. "You're a thief, a runaway wife, and you submitted to a blackmailer! Your excuse for these lively demonstrations is that you love me! Laugh! So what is eating you now? This is just a little matter of handing in a name and address to the police to assist them to perform their duty— their *duty*, mark you! That woman cannot possibly mean anything to you, whereas I . . . But, of course, the meaning of this extraordinary attitude of yours is that you no longer love me. That's what it is. I see it all, now. But don't disguise your falseness under a sudden show of morals. Just when we have a unique opportunity to live in style, free from want, just when it would mean that you could give up your job, stay at home and have your precious baby—that's the time you choose to let me see that you no longer love me!"

Veronica rose abruptly and went into the kitchen. She took things off the shelves and put them back again, not knowing what she was doing.

He *would* say that about a baby, she thought bitterly. People come to dish up your dreams and you can't pay the price! O, how curtly you could be paid back if ever you'd been mean or treacherous! And she wished to know if anyone had ever been more tormented than she.

While she fretted in the kitchen, William, left alone, stood taking the Holy Name, and teasing himself with alternative schemes. After brooding over a likely set of effects for some minutes, he prepared a new form of attack, and suddenly displayed himself in the kitchen doorway.

"I'm sorry, Veronica," he said, enticingly earnest. "I didn't mean what I said just now about your not loving me; I know you do, you're splendid. But you make me say terrible things in my disappointment because you won't help me. If it were you—I would do anything for you!"

"Would you, William?"

He managed to meet her level gaze.

"Yes, I would," he broke out defiantly. "I know I've not had a chance to show you much devotion since we first met, but if only I had a little freedom from anxiety—some leisure and security in which to live like a civilized being—then you would see what tenderness means. Then you could have your baby—dozens of babies. O, can't you see why I have objected, Veronica? Do you suppose I have liked refusing you your dearest wish? Do you think I have enjoyed making cynical excuses for not giving you a child? I tell you I am a proud man. It is intolerable to me to be kept by you. If I have been difficult it's only because I have felt my position so dreadfully—not making enough at my writing to provide you with all you ought to have. Don't you see? Don't you understand what it all means to me? O, my God . . ."

Here came the climax of his performance. William put his arm against the door-frame and, leaning his head upon it, burst into tears.

Seeing him there, so beaten looking and done for, hearing him weep, thinking of his words that had rung so sincerely to her, and fearing that, after all, she had misjudged him, Veronica's resolution was swept away. She only knew that, somehow, he had to be restored.

Going to him she said breathlessly:

"William, don't, my dear. Hush, darling. It's all right. I'll get the money. I'll . . . O dear, don't, don't. I can't bear it if you . . . William!"

He took her in his arms, burying his triumphantly relaxed face on her shoulder.

"If you knew what it means to me . . ." he snuffled.

Wild with joy, he allowed her to pet him, and agreed to a cup of tea, the upset having exhausted him. Over their tea, he said, recovered and enthusiastic:

"Listen, Veronica, you must not worry, my precious. I know

that all will be well. You know it, too. We are both intelligent
people, and we know that since the woman did not give herself
up, she can hardly have waited for the police to come and pick
her up. No, no. She'll be well away by now. It's money for
nothing, and when you get it we'll go to Paris for the week-end.
Should you like that, Veronica?"

"Yes, I suppose so," she replied.

"Of course you would. Hang it, we must have a little gaiety.
We'll hop right off to-morrow afternoon. I'll meet you after
you've been to Scotland Yard, rush round to my friend with the
money, less twenty pounds which I'll 'borrow' for our Paris
expenses, and in the afternoon we'll catch the continental boat-
train. Right?"

"I only hope she's got away."

"Of course she has. What do *you* think? O, Veronica, I am
for celebrating. I think I'll go out and bring back half a bottle
of something so that we can drink to our glorious future."

Veronica wanted to be pleased about the future, too, but
when William had taken his blissful face out of the house, she
could only realize that her heart felt as if it had perished. She
thought of herself as one peering in at the fretted door of a vault,
determined to go in among the cold shadows in order to bring
out a new little life; for she could not make any mistake about
it—she was going to give Mrs. Christopher over to death so as
to get life for the child she had long been hankering after.

IV

The river was criss-crossed with the sludgy wash of four little
coasters that had gone flaunting and flittering one behind the
other down to the sea with coffins, kegs of liquid soap, waste-
paper and grain.

Veronica saw the troubled waters through the window when she was ushered into Hugh Christopher's office to tell her nice story about his mother. There was the river all pulled up as if by invisible kneading talons, running madly this way and that, hopelessly upset by an agent so inferior to itself that the disorder was an insult as well as being ridiculous.

Hugh sat at his desk and made full use of the insolence of officialdom as he allowed his eye to travel over Veronica's strained face and her well-made shabby clothes.

She's a cut above her poverty, he thought.

"Can I help you?" he asked.

"No," she replied, "I've come to help you."

"Interesting. What's it all about?"

"The . . . Highgate murder," said Veronica. She faltered, turned silent.

"Yes?" he said. "Get on with it."

Hugh heard her out in silence. When she had finished, he said, with an assumption of savage jocularity:

"Right. But, I say, the old girl did you rather a good turn, didn't she?"

"That could hardly have been her motive for murder," Veronica shrugged. "It just happened that I . . . that the man she killed . . ."

"Was blackmailing you, too," Hugh finished for her, "and now—why, you are no longer being blackmailed."

"You are endeavouring to make me feel rotten about this," Veronica rounded on him. "So I do, but I fancy it isn't your place to point that out."

She looked away from Hugh's icy gaze. He was protesting:

"I'm the last person in the world to point out to anyone where their gratitude should lie. Pray don't feel bad about coming here. Believe me, my dear woman, I don't know where we police would be without the public's sense of their duty. It is true, we usually have to help out their righteousness with certain little jobs of hard cash but, my word, the informer is worthy of his hire. Here's yours!"

He threw the bundle of notes across the desk at her. It bounced and fell on the floor.

If I hadn't come here to buy a baby, to buy a baby, to buy a baby, Veronica thought wildly, I'd pick up this money and I'd throw it straight in his face. As it was, she stooped, picked up the roll, and scrambled it into her old shabby handbag in a whirl of rage and shame.

"Don't offer rewards," said Veronica from the door, "if the occasion is to be used as a whipping-post as well."

"Poor old thing!" said Hugh with mock sympathy. "Does your reception here fill you with chagrin? But then, you don't really know the full circumstances."

"No, and neither do you," said Veronica, turning back. "What has just passed was a deal, after all, no different from political or stock exchange bartering. You wished to buy, I had it to sell. Keep your remarks to yourself in future—some people might think them actionable—and remember one thing—human beings can be driven far beyond the comprehension of an inflated idiot like you! Money has such a false and terrible value in this world and people will betray so much in order to get it when they need it, that those who offer rewards of it are more guilty than those who come to claim it."

"Outside," remarked Hugh, unimpressed. "We've paid you for your muck: we don't have to listen to your excuses as well!"

Shaken with anger and a sense of horror against herself, Veronica got down into the street. One of her ancestors, the general who had been a V.C., Indian Mutiny, now asserted himself and wished, through Veronica, to return and hit Hugh in the face. She began to make her way to the wine-house in the Strand where William was waiting for her.

Just as she came into Trafalgar Square she stopped dead on the

pavement with the crowd cursing round her for impeding them
and a fellow treading hard on her heels. For it had suddenly,
stabbingly come over her that she could not now have William's
child. Never, never could she allow a child to be born of such a
sordid bargain. A child bought with blood-money! Ugh! Bah!
And all your other exclamations as well! She would have to tell
William. She would tell him to-night in Paris that now they
were gorged with blood they must remain sterile! He would
think she was mad to be so changeable but . . . She continued
her way. Things were far more hopeless and unlovely than ever
they were before.

William got to his feet when she entered the wine-shop, and
gave a double order at the bar; he saw that Veronica needed a
drink.

Without speaking to him or taking the least notice of his
tender enquiries about the state of her nerves, Veronica waited
for her drink, and emptied the glass before she opened her
handbag and gave him the money.

"So you got cash, O, you clever little devil!" exclaimed
William jubilantly. He had been anticipating a cheque and had
made arrangements to cash it with a shady bookmaker he knew.
Now all that fuss and favour would be saved.

Five hundred pounds in cash! He had never held so much
money in his life. It awed him. He was so happy he was almost
in a trance. He hardly heard Veronica's story of how she had
fared at New Scotland Yard.

"Never mind," he soothed, "you've got it, you've got all this
beautiful money. You've done divinely! What does it matter to
you what *he* said!" Even in that moment he had to throw a few
spatterings of gall. "Remember," he went on, "how old your
family is, and he, no doubt, is one of the stinking proletariat
who has jumped into a good position by way of a scholarship
at Hendon!"

She looked at him sharply.

"Don't start anything," she said quietly. "I am quite the last person to goad at this minute!"

"All right," he said, smiling. He could afford to be amiable. "Now, I'm off to buy my prospects. You are to meet me at three sharp this afternoon, by the barrier at No. 1 platform, Victoria station. Got that in your head, you clever little darling?"

He squeezed her hand, smiled ardently down at her, and was gone.

Left alone, Veronica ordered another drink then went out and had lunch at the Strand Corner House.

Three o'clock found her standing at the arranged spot in Victoria station. She carried no luggage. For one thing she possessed very little apart from what she stood up in, and for another she was going to do some shopping in Paris. William had promised her that.

As she stood waiting for William, her mind took on an earnest engagement in which it strove to reverse her morning's humiliation, and simultaneously she tried to rid her heart of its oppressive burden of guilt. William was right—Mrs. Christopher must have got away by now. No one with a ha'porth of sense would have remained quietly waiting to be arrested.

But, O the mess, the mess. She had gone through all that for nothing because now she could not possibly have a baby. Two such conspirators as she and William could not buy a child with the proceeds of their bloody betrayal.

From the dusky width of the shrieking station she saw the platforms reaching out into the open sunlight—a marvellous beginning for a journey, that, to burst into light from shadow— something to remember whatever you started with, and whatever you found at the journey's end.

The great station clocks were all brazenly poking up their hands at one minute to three. Three o'clock he said. Three sharp. Where was William? Could anything have gone wrong? Could he have got so drunk that he had forgotten? Could he have . . .?

Three o'clock. The train began to bundle slowly out of the station; soon it had vanished in the sunlight. The empty platform had a vacant mournful look.

And what was this? A District Messenger boy come to deliver a note to the lady in the tweed coat standing at the barrier by platform one. Well, well! She took the note from the envelope, refraining from giving the boy a tip. William had all the money. She had three and twopence till her next wage packet which she ought to have received that very afternoon had she been in the office instead of loafing in Victoria station waiting to be taken to Paris.

But it looked as if, after all, she would not be going to Paris. In fact, it looked as if she would never be going anywhere again. Equipped with the five hundred pounds she had got so basely that morning, William had taken his leave for ever, accompanied, so he wrote, by a Russian princess. At South Kensington parties it is not difficult to pig-shove with many a fallen title and this delectable fate had overtaken William. Notwithstanding that the princess had had her day and was nearly twice his age, William wrote, with his bad-mannered insistence on frankness at all times, that he had fallen in love with her the minute he heard who she was. The princess had taken kindly to him in return.

But she had no money. This was a blow, especially as her blood was so blue. She was far superior to anything out of Burke's peerage, so it really was a tragedy that she was poor in cash. Veronica, however, had taken care of that for them. She had obtained five hundred pounds for them with which to set up housekeeping. He thanked her sincerely. It was the most worth-while action of all their time together. He was sorry he had to terminate that, but he had to think about his career, about getting his name known. He concluded his note:

I won't return, I never light a cigarette twice, so don't hope. This is rather a rotten way of bringing things to an end, but then, I am a rotter. I always told you that, but, like so many of your blasted sex, you saw yourself in the delicious rôle of one who would save a poor man from himself. I can't take any more of your medicine, it's too weak. You come from a windbag class that, at heart, has no real feelings, so you won't be hurt now except in your pride.

When Veronica had read this note and it fully appeared to her that the game was up, such a fierce sense of nothingness came to her that she wildly wept for perhaps a minute, standing there with her face uncovered, her hands in front of her clutching the note as if it were something precious and beloved. The tears slipped out of her eyes in big swift drops.

A station policeman watched her warily. A disastrously married man, he did not like women. He resolved not to go near her unless she attempted to do herself a mischief. No thought of prevention entered his head: he would only bestir himself after Veronica had acted. You never knew what women would do, it was best to wait and see!

But after that brief burst of uncontrol, as much an accumulated outbreak from her experience of the morning as reaction to William's note, Veronica continued to stand quietly where she was, her face stiffening under the drying mesh of her tears. Apart from tremors which attacked her now and then, Veronica seemed, to the policeman, to have completely calmed down. In a sense she was calm; compressed under the weight of the screams and warbles of the clutter of trains, a profound hush of depression was reigning in her mind. She had staked her all on one throw and lost. She became assured that life and all endeavour were so useless, so crushingly useless and boring, the mystery was how she had ever managed to reach this hour alive.

Life could, all at once, seem so relentlessly without purpose, it was no wonder some people could not continue on. It was easy enough to acquiesce that no one was given more trials than could be humanly borne. But what if one's whole vision of life became so foul and silly, so prancing mad, that not even the prospect of a perpetual happiness could tempt one to undertake five minutes more of it? Surely to those who wrecked themselves then, who had not given up for spite or defiance but because having come to the end of their endurance of so much strangeness they had changed beyond recognition to themselves—surely to those God, who understood all things, would show pity and mercy too.

All the time that Veronica had been indulging these high jinks of sanction to suicide, and for some time afterwards when her mind had returned to blankness, she had been staring, without seeing them, at a brace of station pigeons who were toddling round and round her feet looking for orts in a rapture of expectation. This fervent pair all at once became alive to her consciousness, and as Veronica gazed at their anxious little feet which kept breaking into brief comic runs, she was suddenly struck by the merriness of these birds, their beauty, and the wonder of these winged little lumps having life, anticipations, and nourishment amid the dirt and steam of the bellowing station. She had never thought of this before, she had hardly noticed station pigeons before. Yet now it seemed there were qualities in any one stalking pigeon that could speak of the qualities of the whole perspective of life. "Who can love anything that God made too much? What a world would this be, were everything beloved as it ought to be!" Words of love coming back from an early love, from afternoons in the classroom with the beloved teacher reading aloud from her desk the poems of Thomas Traherne.

O, thought Veronica then, all the delight and the grace ever given return, they come home. No, they don't return—they never depart, never depart, it is we who go away from them till some disaster reveals that the Kingdom of heaven is imperturbably within.

Wakefully she looked round the station. The fathers, mothers, children, luggage heaps, the dusty sunbeams entering through the glass roof, the trundling porters, the engines like enormous iron cows shuddering importantly between the platforms, and bright fruit on the stalls, all began to seem to Veronica as wonderful and unique as the industrious pigeons. This altogether unexpected and hitherto unglimpsed aspect of the brave and ardent essence of ordinary things whipped her heart now to respond to all kinds of other messages that had whispered and waited a long time to be let in. Before wonder resistance began to shuffle away. Impatience and bitterness gave way to acceptance and the beginnings of pleasure. She found herself thinking about the unknown travellers in the station with interest, comradely concern, even with feelings of affection. She thought: I suppose that's how God looks at the world and us though in an infinitely more understanding degree. But it's in this way, at any rate, that we can share His actual life, be in communication. Fancy! I've always made the mistake of supposing prayer to be only petition.

But what did this convey? Had shock and betrayal made the world and life so clear that she was seeing everything as though she had seen nothing before? For such a long time things had worn a crematory air, but now it was as if, for the first time in all her life, the light was right. All the mistakes, the blindness, the keen treacheries given and received seemed to be going up in the smoke from the locomotives as if from the barbecued remains of her past life. A splendour that hurt mingled with the sorrow in her mind.

Veronica looked away from the milling crowd to where, down every platform, the open air stood like a gracious presence, and the rails streamed steadily out into the sunshine towards the silver-fleshed sea. She thought of the journey she had been hoping to make and never would—now. But she had an alternative journey to go, and though her new way did not require a third-class railway carriage but rather a first-class resolution, there was something right and proper in her envisaging in a busy railway terminus the journey her spirit must take. The preparation, the setting-off, the withdrawal slowly but finally into the open—it was all symbolic of what she had to do.

She went through the forecourt of Victoria station into the afternoon streets. Going along Victoria Street she thought: I had to come to a stop with William some time, and it might as well be now. It's been like a short play—a curtain-raiser before the major piece—in which the heroine had no ease or safety, only excitement and pain which she mistook for happiness and plenty. It was bound to be destroyed—a union like ours—built on lies and dishonour.

But things were not altogether a tragedy. William had cracked up her life by the gates of No. 1 platform in Victoria station, and though she had known a desolation so horrible that living had seemed useless, touching rock bottom had knocked a very significant conclusion into her, nothing less than that life was a far bigger proposition than she was, even with the importance of her mangled heart and ruined schemes, and there was so much to wonder at, so much to love and be inspired by, it was a marvel how people ever got into unhappy and seedy relationships such as she had endured with William.

What a queer thing it was that right in the middle of total disaster a person should be given a wonderful interior vision from outward common things and find the way to begin again on better terms than any known before. Why, then, it was not really queer at all because life never changed from its own first benign aspect seen in the dawn of one's days, when the world and all that went on in it were surpassingly exciting and beautiful. Some people, and she was one of them, had to live a long time and suffer much before it could be realized that the original pattern never changed and never died. Only circumstances changed—never life. You had only to remember, do all in your power to remember what it had been like, and remembering, live in it, bring it forward so that the present took stature and glory from the ever-flowing past.

But she must have time in which to get used to all the terrible and wonderful things that had happened to her on this fateful day. But all would be well. She was sure of that as she had never been sure of anything before.

And why, O why, was she not missing William more than this? She had thought that she would never be able to free herself from the gyves that had bound her to him, yet here she was, bereft enough it was true, but not beaten, O, far from beaten. Besides, she knew that the affair with William had ceased that morning when she stood dead in Whitehall, and knew she could never have *his* baby. And now instead of an ending of all things she was facing the beginning—again. Good had come from what had been evil.

"You've killed my old useless self," said Veronica, addressing William then, "and for that I shall always be glad that I met you."

She was standing on Westminster Bridge staring up the sparkling river in the direction of Chelsea Reach. Buildings on either bank stood up albinoed in the intense white sunlight, and rows of sea-gulls brooding in the shining mud looked like mauve beads waiting to be threaded into a chaplet; a vibrant passage of colour held the eye in the geranium-red sail of a yacht. The scene was incredibly bright and heart-warming, and Veronica contrasted it with the river of that morning, grey and boiling up with disturbance, as an extension of her own feelings as she went to betray Mrs. Christopher.

Undoubtedly it was all hard and disgraceful but there was something else to think of besides. She had had the experience of seeing life without the inessentials, and she would be strengthened by such experiences again now that she had found the way to draw them to herself. Now she would live, not play at living. Repentance was action, not tears and the repeated word of self-accusation. Go and guard your gate!

There was, for everyone, someone to go back to when one had sunk to that familiar level when one was glad to eat the husks of the swine. And best of all, that someone would see the prodigal "from afar"—*from afar*—which meant, when you came to think of it, that the someone had obviously long been looking out for the prodigal.

Veronica went home. As she let herself into the cottage she looked at the almond tree and, for the first time, she saw it.

William, meantime, was being swiftly drawn through the northern shires in a train that was taking him and his Russian princess for a holiday to Scotland. He hoped and thought there would be no trouble with Veronica. His motive in breaking the news of his defection in a railway station had not only been a piece of decoration to his invented reason for wanting the money, it had been a safety device. In his cautious and touchy way he argued that Veronica left flat in a railway station, surrounded by lots of people and friendly book-stalls, would be less likely to do something violent than if news of his betrayal of her reached her when she was alone in the house. He fancied that if suicide entered her head in that bitter hour, she would be less likely, among holiday crowds, to throw herself under the wheels of a train like that silly bitch Anna Karenina, than put her head in the all too-handy gas-oven, alone, at home.

Alone—at home! Alone—at home! The train beat out the words through his head. He made so much of them, that he could have snivelled that night as he thought of the abandoned woman—alone, at home. Indeed, he felt for her so keenly that he quite overlooked the fact that of the little drama he was contemplating he himself was the undoubted villain.

V

A few evenings later, as Veronica was walking home from work through Kensington Gardens, she saw her old father sitting on one of the twopenny green chairs. About twenty minutes before, he had had one of his heart attacks as he was walking across the Gardens to keep an evening appointment in the Hyde Park Hotel. He had flopped like an old sick crane on to the green chair to recover, but it was not his habit to mention his infirmities, and he did not explain to Veronica why she found him so unusually disporting himself in the cool of the London evening. Instead he gave a tired but sweet smile to his wayward daughter, and politely said that it was nice, very nice, to see her in Kensington Gardens.

Veronica took one look at her father's face: it was an old elegantly cast face without clemency till a smile hinted that he had other things in his quiver besides a supercilious vigilance and pride. This face, with its tall forehead, violet-shadowed eyes, splayed haughty nose, and mouth that seemed to be getting ready to object to everything, suddenly evoked for Veronica the order, security, charm and integral loves that had made her old world—her happy childhood, with its sense of going on for ever and ever in jaunty innocence in a garden on endless summer afternoons, with a gay laughing mother sitting beside a table with silver and strawberries, under a trinity of lime trees; and wonderful beautiful grown-ups at tennis parties later on in August; and fruit off the walls; and picnics where the purple loosestrife flared beside the running stream, and when they left the picnic-place there would be marks with a look of suède on the ground where their fire had been: and nurse must not be forgotten—a nurse with old-fashioned streamers floating from her hair, who ran and scolded and slapped bottoms, doled out sugar biscuits, made cinnamon toast and lit lamps in the winter-time and told the story of the Wild Swans, the Ugly Duckling, and the Girl Who Trod on a Loaf. When Veronica remembered these things, which seemed to come at her now with golden speech, and her escapade of the last two years, the discrepancy was so jagged that public place though Kensington Gardens is, she dropped to her knees beside her father and held on to him as if she would never let him go.

"O, are you glad to see me, daddy?"

"Yes, of course, my dear, yes, vastly."

He held her away from him, seeing the trouble in her face, and he adjured her to tell her old daddy what ailed her. More than once old Lord L. sighed, passing his hand over his wan dry face, as Veronica brought out the full story of her decline and fall on the rocks of South Kensington with the type of person she never before had been familiar with.

It's not a bit of use, he was thinking disdainfully, the classes cannot be mixed; and he was assuring himself of the permanent inequality of man and congratulating himself on the virtue and superiority of his own strata when this courtly old man received a jolt that hit him to his foundations. He heard Veronica confessing to having gone and betrayed Mrs. Christopher for five hundred pounds. Veronica had saved this little bombshell till the last as being the most ignominious act she had committed in two years of getting pretty well through most of the weaknesses human kind is always ready for.

"Veronica! You couldn't have done such a thing!"

"Yes, I did. I did do it. He said she would have gone away, that the police would not find her. He said with five hundred we could have a baby. That's all I wanted, daddy, a baby, a . . ."

"But people like us don't do such things," protested poor Lord L., who always found himself bothered by the least impairment—and now, this! "It's . . . we . . ."

"We're no better than anyone else," said Veronica, "and I'm worse than most."

She burst into tears.

"Poor little puss!" Her father stroked her hair. When he was not wondering why a baby had to cost five hundred pounds when it was only too deucedly easy to get one for nothing, he was reflecting that, after all, he need not feel quite so superior. Here was behaviour that set breeding, gentle living, and honour all at nothing. Veronica, he reflected, always had had a knack for playing the fool but her going away to sell an old woman like that—he simply had no terms with which to assess such disorderliness. So he had better not be so proud, because he doubted if he had ever heard anything of his blood that was so humiliating, and so luridly shameful. He felt glad that his wife was dead and long dead so that she hadn't even only just escaped hearing this sidelight on the frailty of their proudly cherished daughter.

"My word! We must give that money back to the police at once," said Veronica's father, wondering at the same time just where such a sum was coming from.

"You can't refund blood-money," sobbed Veronica. "Think of what happened when Judas tried to give the silver back to the priests!"

"When *who*—O, Judas! No need to bring him into it. A pretty name to drag out just now, my dear!" he replied testily.

"Pretty appropriate," sniffed Veronica.

"Well, never mind *him*," said her father severely. "Judas!" He stifled fury. "O!" he cried in a burst of exasperation, "you were forced into it, you were forced into it. *That* bounder, that knavish fellow you ran off with—without him it would never have occurred to you to do such a shameful thing. I hope the poor old filly got away. Should hate to think of her going to the . . . well—being hanged, even if it's justice, through anyone belonging to me. I hope she got away."

"She must have," broke in Veronica eagerly. "I've been watching the papers. No arrest has been made."

"Thank heaven for that," replied her father. "But, of course, you know," his mouth looked as if it were full of something that had gone bad, "that doesn't excuse . . ."

"I know, I know," Veronica cried out. "Nothing can possibly excuse what I did. I tried to build a world by betraying another's life. What a horrible thing! I can hardly believe I ever stooped so low to do it."

Old Lord L. drew his grieving daughter towards him and murmured in her ear a consoling portion of loving and forgiving words; bad as things were, the comfort was that Veronica had come back. A cherished person had returned. It was something to be a father at a time like this.

Having less than an hour ago nearly died, Lord L. had been sitting thinking how pillaged his life was after one time high engagements on battlefield and estate. Almost ruined financially since the world depression of 1930, his sons earning mean and dreadful livings on the Stock Exchange and in Fleet Street, his horses, pictures, and once talked-of table gone, his only home a stuffy little house in a Bayswater Square, Lord L. had recently come to feel that life was reduced to a perpetual turning-over of *The Times* in order to see who had died or gone broke. But now he had his daughter to take care of—nurse her back to health and self-respect, nurse her right back to that decent cub of a husband of hers before he had finished! That's what he would do, by heaven! She could have all the babies she wanted *there!* He recalled for a minute Veronica's husband who had been so happy with her, who had said in his joy and simplicity:

"I go about with my head in the air because I am so proud of my wife."

Sitting on the green chair, with the tall trees glinting softly to each other in the rose-red evening light, old Lord L. thought he had never known till now how lovely and satisfying a thing it was to be the father of a girl. As he looked back, he wished he had taken more time off from his horses and dogs and devoted it to Veronica—there really was as much high purpose in begetting children as in breeding horses; he wondered why he had not thought of that before.

Indeed, when wincingly he thought over the years, he seemed to have wasted the devil of a lot of time, he seemed to have had some confoundedly queer sets of values, values which, when peered at after you'd been within an inch of losing your life, seemed to possess everything except value.

If one could only begin with what one had learnt at the end, sighed Lord L.

He now assisted Veronica to her feet.

"You will, of course, dine with me," he said. "I'm going over to the Hyde Park to meet Toddy, and we'll go and have a modest little celebration somewhere afterwards. Toddy'll do you good. He always could make you laugh."

Just here a youthful attendant came clumping round to extract the twopenny fee for Lord L.'s use of the green chair. A humorous search revealed the fact that neither Veronica nor her father had a penny of money on them.

"My boy," said Lord L. "I can hardly give you a cheque for twopence. You must take my card and I shall put two penny stamps in the post to-night as my payment. Shall I address them to you?"

"S'all right, sir, don't you worry, sir," replied the youth cheerfully. "No, I don't want to see no cards, sir. Knows a gent when I sees one, I should hope."

"Does he, by jove!" exclaimed old Lord L. to Veronica as they moved off arm-in-arm, "that's more than I can say, nowadays!"

"Speaking for myself," said Veronica, "I thought that boy himself was a gentleman!"

And then Veronica went on to say a little personal manifesto to her father, as they walked beneath the evening trees, which astonished and sobered him very much. She said that having knocked about a bit she'd had a few things knocked into her: that those who had nothing but wealth and worldly power were really the poverty-stricken; that Good Form often masked Bad Living; that the world was so wonderful a place you needed all your time for looking and listening and thinking about it, and there wasn't room for depression or self-pity; that the sin against the Holy Ghost wasn't a secret vice at all, it was simply— boredom; that plain simple goodness was better than the highest art or possession of the whole world, that she had only known it once and then in her own husband.

Lord L. made clicks with his dental fixtures partly to indicate sympathy and partly because words failed him. What with his heart attack and his daughter he decided he had pretty well had enough for one evening. So he blew his nose and said:

"Look, Veronica, how redly the sun is setting. It will be a fine day to-morrow."

The wind was getting up, too. It blew sharr-sharr, sharr-sharr, like a big broom thrusting at the gravel. Veronica listened, and looked at the sky which was prinked with many little sprigs of crimson cloud as if someone had just shaken out a great basket of fuchsias. She remembered the pigeons at Victoria station and how by the magic of imaginative will they had transformed her life for her, and she felt gladness returning. She said:

"How right you are! It will be a fine day to-morrow, and it's a wonderful night to-night!"

PART FOUR

FROM CAMDEN TOWN

I

THE last to leave Sine's house on the night of the murder was Giles Bilterland, the young doctor. Giles had done much in his short life for which he could have been blackmailed so he never had found it too oppressive that Sine had only been extorting for the obvious reason. Just the same, the tyranny had been hard to bear, and Giles, turning out the sputtering gaslights in the room of the dead, kissed his hand to the corpse, conscious of relief so prodigal it helped him not to panic when the dark swept in bringing the evil that had been waiting for the light to be doused. Whorls and spirals of uncanny presences seemed to gather in the room till the only free place was the hearth-rug on which Giles was standing with the fire dying in crimson clots behind him. So imperative was this sense of evil that Giles, seldom aware of the occult essences of things, knew he had not the courage to pass through the room to the black hall, grapple with the massive front door and so reach the safety of outside.

But what was he to do? He could not leave the gaslights burning. At some hour in the early morning a nosey-parker of a policeman might see chinks of light through the curtains and come to investigate. The longer discovery of the murder was held off the better for that strange woman, Mrs. Christopher, their benefactor, who deserved all the help she could get, poor ass.

Giles had not got a torch, but it occurred to him that a man such as Sine would practise certain household economies; there might be spills on the mantelpiece to save matches. Striking a light, Giles turned round; sure enough there was a pot of spills behind the marble clock. Lighting one, he held it aloft as a humble and precarious flambeau, and made a dash for the front door which he flung open just as his little flame wavered out and an odious humming swept down the staircase, flying male-volently about his head.

"Phew!" sighed Giles, remembering to close the door quietly as he went out into the night. Overcoat milling behind him, he hurried down Hampstead Lane, a small young man, no more than five foot four in his height, thick and dogged, his trilby pulled well down over his big puss-like face with its long upper lip and flat nose. He moved down the hill with determination and an ever-rising sense of freedom. Beyond the Spaniards Inn, he plunged off the road into the tangly down-dropping slopes of the East Heath, where he slackened his pace.

"No appointments, no pressure, no anything but me from now on!" declared Giles Bilterland with some mirth. His hand in his trouser-pocket lay on twenty-five pounds in notes that he had been taking to Sine. Bah! That frequent wicked toll of twenty-five pounds that had drained him so steadily, piled up debts, and promoted other irregularities to pay for silence on that one mischance of the past! The constant grinding anxiety of the thing! Why, he had been up all last night gambling to get together this money in his pocket, he, a doctor, and hell alone knew what old man or young woman might have come to knock him up for midnight cut-throats or confine-ments.

"Now we can do something—arrive somewhere!" crowed Giles, moving steadily across Hampstead Heath, his flat nose diving into the fresh night air.

"I've had to get used to a lot of things these last few years—the smell of dirt, the smell of death, the taste of bad food, the feel of rough clothes. The future need not be so sordid." He could not remember when he had been so exquisitely pleased —more than that, quite lifted up—as he dwelt on the neatness, the finality of the murder, and the escape it meant for himself.

He became aware of the moonshot night about him. The big pond in the Vale of Health lay in long silver folds, and the whey light shimmered and trembled through uptrailing gossamer sheets of moisture to the eerie splendour aloft where a vast bank of cloud was progressing with stateliness across the sky like a stretch of furrowed white grass.

Poo! What a beastly soapy light, thought Giles. This damned moonlight is corpse light! It's hideous, really, and only those fool poets have made it seem attractive to the mob who never think for themselves. Same with copulation—sheer brute pleasure—yet these poets, these tatty tricky poets have persuaded the men, and especially the women, that the activity of their paltry members is angels' joy! How I hate and despise poetry! Thank heaven an early and an exceedingly rank acquaintance with mortal limbs on the dissecting slab has given me the right perspective—the ability to see the world for what it is, a manure-heap round which everybody plays kiss-in-the-ring. That's reality, and no poetry has ever flecked my bloody eyes to it, and never will!

Before him London was smoking white in the moonlight. There's London lying before me! For the first time for a long time it really does lie before me and not on top of me. Everything is going to be different for me from now on, thanks to that fool of a Mrs. . . . what did she tell us her name was? Must remember that. Ah—Mrs. Christopher.

It thrilled him to remember the power which lay in his knowing a murderer. One up on the police, that!

It had been very obliging of this Mrs. Christopher to knock

Sine off. The only pity was—it had been too quick a death for him. I wonder why she did it, he thought. Wonder what he was drilling *her* for? She looked too respectable for words, and . . . yes, well, decent, somehow. Wonder what she's thinking now? Scared? Haunted by the hangman? What's it like to be a hangman? Does he enjoy his job? Are you happy in your work, mister . . . er . . . hangman? Are you a hanger-on? No, a hanger-up! They get twenty-five pounds a head, these undaunted chaps, these hanging fellows. Sounds a lot, but there aren't so many hanged per year, so they are barbers for the rest of the time. Wonder if my barber sneaks off every so often to officiate at Wandsworth? I don't know that I should like him messing about with my neck if *that's* what he's up to as a hobby. Who teaches 'em their anatomy? Where do they go to learn? If your son says to you: 'Dad, it is my dearest wish to be a hangman!' what do you do about it? To whom do you apprentice your up-and-coming brat? 'Meet my little boy, George, he's going to be a hangman. Yes, studying necks, rope textures and the mathematics of the drop. Takes after his grandfather who was the pioneer of the science of Morbid Psychology. Yes, I hope he'll be of service to you, one day!'

My God! What a business! I should not care to be Mrs. Christopher. I did not even relish the idea of remaining last in that house to partner the corpse. I always said that women were arrant fools, but this Mrs. Christopher seems to take the biscuit. She not only commits a murder but she tells three people all about herself. She substitutes one master for three! Any one of us now could . . . well . . . well . . . how my mind does run forward.

By now he had come to the Hampstead bus terminus and he went into a café and ordered a pot of strong tea.

With his hat removed it was plain that Giles looked older than his twenty-eight years. His features were regular, but the effect in totality was one of ugliness. His face was fish-white,

179

round and lumpy like a bag of nails, the skin being blanched as an almond. His eyes were curiously wide and full, and so brimming over that it seemed the rims must give way at any moment and his eyes dissolve down his cheeks. Thick tawny hair was brushed straightly across his head from a side-parting.

With one of his big, sinister-looking hands tapping the table, he sat supping cups of hot strong tea, building and breaking down a dozen schemes for his improved future.

"Like somethin' to eat?" the dark-faced waitress asked him.

"No. Go away," he begged insolently. He had a small tight voice as if he spoke against his clenched teeth.

Among the many abhorrences that complicated his life was a flaring dislike of women. No woman had ever harmed him—he had never given one of them such a chance—but he disliked all women on principle. His mother had used him with unfailing kindness and now to-night a woman had delivered him from an insupportable bondage, given him another chance. Even so, it did not occur to him to speak kindly to the waitress. He hated the individuality of women, their terrifying possessiveness, and the ruthless realities which lay behind even the tenderest and most charming façades. He saw women as beings occult, cretin, clever, all in one. He always suspected women of the worst intentions.

"Uppish, ain't you?" suggested the café-girl.

"I daresay," he retorted. "What about it?"

She could not meet his insolent stare and retired, muttering angrily.

He lit a cigarette and returned to his thoughts. On the café wall hung an exhortation to buy lavishly and consistently of a provincial make of chocolate. An ogling girl had been painted into the advertisement to lend some persuasion to the manufacturer's plea. Catching sight of this advertisement Giles frowned. The painted girl recalled someone to his mind, a face that came ducking in, highly rouged, impudent and seeking Mrs. Petromayne. Words jigged into his head.

"Mrs. Petromayne invites you to come and take her life this evening at nine o'clock precisely!"

That affair might very well have been so worded. Train wheels started up in his head. All that night train wheels had thudded through those insistent events, for Mrs. Petromayne's flat was built over the Underground permanent way, and the clamour of trains tearing through the long echoing vaults far below had belted its way into her rooms.

Knock! Knock! The wheels raced and the blood pelted out, jazzed out. Had there ever before been so much blood in all the world? Giles doubted it. Pails of it: blood everywhere, with its peculiar reek, and Giles had drawn it.

Poverty-stricken as now, Mrs. Petromayne had dangled a hundred pounds before him. A hundred pounds for a little operation, a little illegal operation. If successful and you were caught—six months in jail. If unsuccessful and you were caught . . . Mrs. Petromayne guaranteed that if things went wrong she would see that no questions were asked. Her lover guaranteed the same.

Things did go wrong, nightmarishly wrong, but they kept their word. She was buried without any scandal, and Giles did not stand his trial for manslaughter nor was he ignominiously struck off the Rolls. He would have remained quite safe had not the dead woman's lover been a friend of Montgomery Sine and, some months later, confided in him the whole affair.

Sine felt sorry for Giles. He felt so sorry that he found himself compelled to write to Giles and invite him to his house so that he could tell him his feelings in person. It did not do to lay one's heart bare in a letter. The jails were full of people who had been too fond of writing letters.

Giles went to see his sympathizer. Naturally, Sine told him, *he* was not going to go and lay information before the General

Medical Council to the effect that Dr. Giles Bilterland had procured an abortion, a highly successful operation, too, though the patient died! Such a course would ruin the young man, and he only just setting up in general practice for himself and desperately needing every guinea he could earn. Why, it was his poverty that had driven Giles to undertake that highly successful operation! Yes, yes, poor boy! Sine understood. He had made a study of human motives, he had every sympathy. At the same time he, too, had to live. His understanding, sympathy and, above all, his silence, were valuable. He was rather afraid that Giles would have to pay for them. No, it wasn't dirty of him at all, and certainly it was less criminal than Giles's own effort to earn cash by turning poor Mrs. Petromayne into a far too early corpse.

What? Giles would go to the police? Let him go, then! Sine would go with him. The police were as interested in illegal operations as they were in extortion. They would go arm-in-arm to the police and heartily ruin one another!

Ah, that was better! All along Sine had known how reasonable Giles would be. Giles had had a very expensive education. A lot of learning had been bought for him. Perhaps it had not done him very much good but, at least, he had been trained to use his reason.

How much did he want? Not very much. He was quite modest; there was nothing of the tyrant in his make-up. Twenty-five pounds whenever he needed it would be suitable. Probably he would not need it more often than once a month. Quite a trifle, really, to pay for immunity from total ruin. He would have asked for a lump sum and be done with it, but he knew very well that Giles had no lump sums, so he would be quite happy with an easy little twenty-five quid—once a month.

And so the extortion had begun and continued to this night. But now Mrs. Christopher, that rash and obliging woman, had cleared his path. Sine was dead. The woeful train-wheels need never revolve again. The incident for which he had been black-mailed seemed to fall away from him then to such an extent that he had the sensation of having lost a positive covering.

Giles motioned to the waitress.

"How much?"

"It'll be fourpence."

He gave her sixpence.

"You can keep the change," he said, his face eloquent of his contempt for waitresses and their kind.

"Thanks, I'm sure."

The girl threw a strange look after the little figure with its too-long, trailing overcoat. Inasmuch as her mind had never been directed towards set studies and she had not been grounded in the correct way to speak, the waitress was uneducated. In so far as she had acquired a knowledge of life and humanity from detailed observations of the daily horde she served with drink and victuals, she could have given points to many a university don. She was therefore uneducated as education is reckoned in terms of the right kind of academy and the veneer such institutions confer on those who can pay for it; but she was a cultured person in that she had learnt, in the humble means at her disposal, to widen her perceptions, and to respond to the signals which life and people threw her way.

And now as she stood gazing after Giles she was thinking:

That's a funny little carcase! He gives me a tip, a present, with *hate*. You could see it in those funny eyes of his! Call it kind-ness—to give a gift with no right feelings! There's more kindness in a criminal who gives you a stolen watch or somethin' with liking and respect, than in *him* and his sort who give tuppence or two thousand quid despising and loathing them they give it to, or worse, give it without any feelings whatever!

II

Outside the café Giles tramped on to a bus for home. He lived in the rooms above his surgery which lay in a waste of mean streets in Camden Town. These thoroughfares, when he came to them, had been transformed by the moonlight.

But to Giles, striding home, the moonlight only seemed to make more desolate the squalid district in which his poverty forced him to sustain an existence. He thought these streets were dismal enough by day, and now, to his perceptions, the moon had arrived to turn the district, in its eerie light, into some Dantesque realm which would not support life.

He came to his surgery which once had been a greengrocery and stood between a ham-and-beef shop and a working-men's club. Across the road there was a soap works, the machinery of which churned and crashed all day, and next to it a private house had turned its ground floor into a Turkish bath, though it was hard to see how its aged proprietor made money out of his idea which was much too advanced for that neighbourhood; no one ever went to taste of his wares, not even as a spree to a temple of mysteries. The wide shop window of Giles's establishment had been painted black up half its length and on this big brassy letters announced something of his activities.

DR. GILES BILTERLAND
Surgery Hours
Morning 9.30 till 10.30
Evening 5.30 ,, 6.30
Except Thursdays and Sundays

Every time Giles looked at this expression of a G.P. forced to practice in the nasty hurly-burly of poverty, all his nature reeled: It was an insult to him. The appalling street! The shameful surgery!

If ever I'm driven to the unspeakable, he thought, it will be because of this street! But I shall get away from it. That's the only vow I've ever made I'll ever keep. This rat-worn surgery was once a greengrocer's shop where they sold turnips and cabbages to a crew of unwashed females. It's still no better than a shop where I deal out penn'orths of pills and purges. I ought to be giving 'em poison! And he gave some covetous thoughts to a consulting-room in Harley Street—silver-plated fittings and glass, a morning rig and a monocle, a receptionist and a Rolls-Royce. There's power in all that, he thought. That's the absolute life, made possible by power. Of course, I became a doctor to rationalize my need for power. It's a profession conferring power on even the stupidest of its practitioners—power over life and threatening death. Naturally, most of us are strictly noble fellows, as noble as you please, and even the nobility can't help, from time to time, remembering the *power* and so getting the glory. Lot of glory in Camden Town!

If I'd had more time I might have gone in for psycho-analysis. That gives the practitioner a mangling sense of power, *mangling*. But I'm too snobbish for that stuff; it's the sort of thing that can put any little squirt with a good memory and a mechanical mind in the position of being able to dictate to his betters.

Meantime he was letting himself in at the side-door of his Camden Town premises and he went tumbling up the stairs. Here, bursting into a large and shabby sitting-room, his eyes fell on the only creature he had ever cherished, his young brother, Fred. The boy, nineteen years old, was sitting at the table, surrounded by books. The light from the two mottled gas-lamps above the chimney-board hardly touched his handsome harassed face, but there was enough light for Giles to be struck, as he so often was, with a pang of love for the lad. He used to say to himself, never to anyone else: "If it weren't for Fred I'd be damning myself even more than I do."

"What are you doing, darling?" Giles asked him friendlily.

"Reading poems about girls." The boy looked up, smiling. He had an air of being genially alert; there was nothing vague or mooning about him.

"My poor Fred!" exclaimed Giles with a show of mock concern. "That's unutterable saccharine. Here! Wait a minute."

Hat clasping the back of his head and coat still trailing open, Giles went across to his desk and rummaged about till he found some papers.

"Listen to this," he ordered, and began to read in a loud mincing voice specially assumed for his purpose:

" 'If men could see beneath the skin . . . the very sight of women would be disgusting to them. Consider what is hidden in women's nostrils, in their throats, in their stomachs: filth everywhere. . . . And we who would not touch with our finger-tips vomit or dung—how can we long to clasp in our arms a mere bag of excrements?' "

Giles leaned towards his brother with a triumphant leer.

"There, my dear Fred, isn't that much the prettier picture of the fair young maidens? Odo of Cluny—a discerning author!"

Fred, used to his brother, and gentle and forgiving, said:

"Does it say anywhere that our sex is free from similar disorders? I thought that we, too, had our snuffles and stinks. I've never read anywhere that men are formed as angels."

"Do you know what," said Giles, "you read far too much."

"No," replied Fred, "I don't read enough, truly I don't. Don't put me out of conceit with my books. Reading is all I can do. I'm not equipped to take up any profession, and you won't let me go to work in an office or somewhere where I could help you with a little money."

"I should think not," snorted Giles, beginning to throw off his outdoor clothes. He went and stood by the little fire.

"You don't know, Fred," he shot out suddenly, "how much it has been on my mind since you left Winton that I hadn't enough money to send you up to the 'Varsity or to one of those art schools you're always talking about. But our dear departed parents left only enough to see you through Winton after their debts had been paid, and I . . . well, you know it's been a struggle for me. I don't really know why parents bring children into the world, accustom them to easy living, and then suddenly die, within a few months of each other, without leaving the said children a ha'penny to carry on the sort of life they've been used to. Damned bad management somewhere!"

Fred looked at his brother kindly, thoughtfully.

"But Giles," he said, "father never anticipated that crash on the Stock Exchange, did he?"

"People should always anticipate crashes," retorted Giles ruthlessly, "because crashes are an essential order of life. Our father, my dear, was a fool. To invest all the coin he had collected in one undertaking was asking for the trouble he got."

"Well, don't make him out to be quite so useless. He was good to us. He loved us and was proud of us."

"Proud of himself, too," put in Giles. "Proud of being distantly related to a title or two—the rest is silence. If he'd thought a little more of his good money and less of his good name we should not now be existing in poverty. Unfortunately we shared in his disaster. But I'm not going into all that again. Let me tell you this—to-night, for the first time, I see an easier time ahead. It won't come all at once, but I've . . . had some good news; and if you'll be patient a little while longer I hope to be able to send you somewhere to study this precious painting of yours."

"Thank you, Giles," said Fred in his attractive husky voice. "But my painting can wait. I rejoice for you. I know how you have hated this place. O, I am so pleased for you, Giles, that things are looking better."

"Yes," pursued Giles with smugness, "I see a chance at last of getting what I want."

"You nearly always do get what you want, I find," said Fred, "so it's rather important to want the right kind of thing."

"What do you know about it?" exploded Giles derisively. "But that's enough. Just be patient, and don't read so much."

Giles had a furtive look at his brother's shabby flannel trousers and his shoes which were shapeless with much cobbling. He counted off twelve one-pound notes from the roll in his pocket.

"Here you are," he said, throwing the money on to the table. "Get yourself a suit, and what about some shoes? There's enough there, what?"

"Yes. I say! This is riches! But what about you, Giles?"

The elder brother scowled.

"I've said I shall be all right, haven't I? I'm going to bed now—unless you want me for anything. You don't? Well, I'm thankful for that. I had no sleep at all last night, I was . . . I didn't sleep. And to-night has been exhausting. Good news is always strange news and takes a person a-back as much as catastrophe. Good night, my dear."

When he heard Giles reach the floor above where their bedrooms were, Fred got up and went to his own little desk in the corner by the window. From it he took a battered tin cash-box which he unlocked and stuffed the twelve notes inside.

He'll be asking me for it back to-morrow or the next day, Fred thought, with a smile.

He found he could not return to his books. He closed them and with loving care put them back on his shelves. He stood looking down into the fire, thinking.

In the full light of the gas he looked as if he had been through a great deal; his young face was drawn-looking, with a pallor made more intense by his dark searching eyes. His habitual expression was gentle and reflective, and the light in his clear candid eyes, which seemed as if they looked into a distance beyond distance, mocked his frail flesh and its ruined tints. Fred's hair was darker than his brother's, being brown and curly, and he wore it with a centre parting. He was very thin and taller than Giles.

At school Fred had loved poetry, painting, and being quiet. No one there had taken much notice of him: he had not been an athlete or a scholar or one of those who contribute in an obvious way to the life of a school-house. He was still solitary, for he had no money to go out to places and make friends, and though Giles loved him he never made any attempt to be a companion to him. Fred scarcely ever saw him for when Giles's time was not taken up with his poverty-stricken patients, he was busy in the nefarious haunts he had made his own.

But Fred was not one to feel neglected. Poverty, which either embitters or redeems, had been his salvation. Through it he discovered the art of making something out of nothing, and learnt to live without expectations, and without fear. In the consequent clearing of his mind from the worries of multiplicity he began to comprehend in its highest implications the gift of life that had been given him. In this pursuit he was aided by three endowments—a simple patient heart, the serious intent to keep joy, and a loving response to life.

So it was not for his own future that he feared as he stood watching the flames roll themselves round the coals like pieces of apple-white silk. His tender anxiety was all for his brother. He was nowise moved to the sort of assurance that ought to have come to him by what Giles had told him of a change for the better. He was, in fact, more afraid for his elder brother than ever. I want him to be more comfortable, thought Fred, but success would be the ruin of him! He'll have to suffer to find his own true and wonderful self and I should like him to have been spared pain.

I'd have helped if I could, but he's never been interested in me, and why should he be? I'm not much, though I've been given a lot—allowed to find things out—like the little path, for instance. He looked pleased, thinking of the little path. Though muddied-o'er by the perplexities, trials, chunks of learning, and anxieties of the years of his adolescence, he had, somehow, contrived to leave open a shadowy little lane back to his childhood. In his humble, groping way he felt that the experiences he had known when a child were so much more significant and all-embracing than those he would ever know again, that he thought there was nothing more important in the art of living than to return as intimately as possible to those whole, unsoiled, and enlarging levels of comprehension, which had to be lived twice if God's face were to be seen—as his favourite poet, Henry Vaughan, had it. So Fred was always using the essences of the little things of daily existence, wresting the divine and the lasting from the common and taken-for-granted under their baffling façade, in order to try and establish contact once more with that open-eyed vision of the world, that first wisdom, the higher-than-reason wisdom, the wisdom of eternity which had once been his but had passed with his childhood.

He let his mind go out in companionship with all that was, from the moth sleeping the winter away in a hole in a paling to the glimmering stars in the long track of the Milky Way. He saw *himself* in all things about him, and consequently found everything interesting—nothing lost, senseless, or without affinity.

He saw that pure joy is something which flourishes quite separately from circumstances, as love does, something which can come to everybody. And his mind went back to countless occasions of joy, not in a romantically nostalgic mood, but recognizing that in them as nowhere else would he find the reality for which he was searching. When he thought of how a certain vista of downland going on and on into the infinite blue could yield up joy vivid enough almost to be a presence, he felt the reason must be that every tree and blade of grass, every

sparkling flint, bracken frond and foxglove hood possessed a
certain spirit which, when appreciated for its own sake, yielded
that gush of sheer pure happiness which seems to lay bare
fleetingly the whole significance of life, and intensify the longing
to draw ever more close to the joyful mystery investing even
the sands of the shore and the husk of a seed.

A glow-worm with its thin green light down in the grass,
an old tree mobbed by little birds, a blue-and-emerald dragon-
fly resting on the water forget-me-nots, or a hedgehog
apprehended with the sympathetic love their transcendent
perfection merited, could, in one dizzying flash, make it seem as
if a person had entered into harmony with all earth, all life, and
divinity.

When school was over for good and Fred found that home
was no longer to be the house built of golden Ham Hill stone in
the West Country valley amid the treed hills, but Camden Town,
he saw that he would have to transform the transformation and
he made an effort to clothe every dusty day with country
freshness.

Fred said to himself:

"You can always keep your heart alight!" And he tried
to.

When airs from the gasworks or brewery came stinking into
the room, Fred substituted the association. He made himself see
again the wild summer garden of the chalk down—the marvellous assault of colour at close range, yellow of the wild
parsley, meadow vetchling, bedstraw, wild mignonette, and
hawkbit; deep mauve of scabious; white of camomile, yarrow,
moon daisy, and wild carrot; flaring red of poppy; gold of
buttercups and bird's foot trefoil; purple of knapweed, clover,
wild geranium, Scotch thistle, and wild thyme.

Or he made himself see the woods in springtime rich with
dog-violets, primroses looking into small scummy ponds, wood
anemones, celandines, pink campions, speedwells, and the purple

orchis with sinister spotted leaves—all as a brilliant carpet under the white guelder rose and the pale pink blossoms of the crab-apple trees.

For every Camden Town event Fred substituted a country event. A dirty alley became a spinney blazing with bluebells, the tram trolleys whirring down the overhead wires changed to the singing of the chiff-chaff. When the glaring electric lights were lit in the evenings he would remember the railway halt at home—not even a proper station, simply two primitive wooden platforms, lit at night by oil lamps on posts; but these, far gleaming across the silent snow-packed meadows on a winter's night, could shine with an extraordinarily warm flaming clarity, as if these tongues of red-gold light were a manifestation of the Holy Ghost kindled there in that bitter dark to renew the heart.

And the thick yellow fog could fill his mind with a falling shower of golden flowers—ragwort, elecampane, St. John's wort, fleabane, cowslips, and marsh marigolds.

And, trailing the colours, scents and sounds of the country through the desert of Camden Town, Fred would see beside the mangy cat who sat nid-nod by the dustbins, the white road through the wood in July and a young stoat standing under the honey thistles looking like a miniature dragon.

But the memories were legion—dense and bright. The blackcap and the wood-wren singing; the comfrey by the running stream; the enchanter's nightshade in the cool woodland drives; the snow on the lawn pocked by the toes of birds; the flight of the silver-washed Fritillery and the Purple Hair Streak in the glade; the sad loving cry of the wood-pigeon; a road bordered with a fine cavalcade of stunted oaks; a currant-moth, beautifully speckled black and yellow, dreaming on a long green leaf of horseradish. And O, the heather, the harebells, and the wind from Weymouth! O, the meadow-sweet and the tufted vetch!

The thing was to live always with the "password primeval." Then you could not help going about with a perpetual sense of splendour in life and things.

But gradually it came home to Fred that since you don't *find* beauty, but take it with you, there was no need to invest the iron railings of a public convenience with the clinging con-volvulus to make it acceptable—the thing could appear pleasant in its own right. Sun, rain and drifting shadows, these could metamorphose anything. And in the fortitude of the London mangy cat, its affecting content as it felt the sun on its battered old head, there was a forth-showing of the undaunted spirit of life wonderful enough to refire the unhappiest. In Camden Town, no less than in the country, a person could look at the wispy new moon through the evening fog and see it red as the petal of a rose blowing on the sky. Camden Town roofs could take on the same tints of far immaculate light as those which transfigured the country village. The deep blue of twilight tipped itself behind the town chimney-pots as thrillingly as it had once closed in behind the spreading acacia tree in the garden at home, that friendly tree which, filling the whole of the great window of the drawing-room had made of it an ever-living tapestry. The light of dawn, sharp and colourless, could face with crystal the dirty stones of the town no less than the countless leaves trembling in the forest.

In the stuffy room in Camden Town, through the pain and through the fret, you could uncoil into the rustling wind or the flame on the hearth picking its way up the grey lines of smoke, as feathery as the wild white garlic in the dingle, and a marvellous tranquillity would come, obliterating the rush of the day from that eternal moment. You could find something to enkindle your inner life even in the trickle of coal-dust at the bottom of the scuttle. *That* was what having grace meant. *That* was having the right eyesight!

And as he stood on the evening of Giles's deliverance, thinking by the fire, Fred suddenly remembered that outside the moon would be full; turning out the gas he pulled back the window curtains and looked out.

From the height of this first-floor window he could see the lights of the railway signals twinkling above the roofs, climbing steadily up like hollyhock spires and turning gleaming yellow, crimson, and emerald rosettes at the mild night sky; these returned to Fred a throng of past nights when their carnival flowering in the dreaming dark had lifted the heart of a child.

Ah, the joy those lights bring back, thought Fred; it returns to me faintly now—such joy, and it seems to me that above my head the original bright essence is flying. Why, a person could not bear it if that lost joy returned Now exactly as it was Then!

His eager eyes searched the street below. Here flourished tones of lilac and iron and tinsel. In the wizardry of the narcissus light of the moon the mean houses seemed turned to blocks of soda, dimly shining; in these mysterious pallid-walled dens anything could be taking place. Pieces of broken bottle sparkled in the gutter. The asphalted road appeared to stream like a tranquil river into the lunar infinity of the charmed night. Above the crazy roofs the argent freckles of Orion's Belt were scattered to the south-west; and the burning moon had touched off a little cloud which lay to one side of it and now was breaking up, dropping swiftly down the sky in pieces like silvery ashes. In the far north more churned-up clouds, looking like glittering salt lagoons, were appearing in the vast trough of the dark blue sky. Water-clear reflections of the animated heavens beamed from the window panes in upper stories. It was Camden Town *en fête*.

"At such a time as this," said Fred, "I feel as whole as an angel."

He stood, with parted mouth and rapt eyes. "As whole as an angel," he repeated; and, touched to the heart by the sudden anguished dearness of things, his arm went up to his face and he gave way to grief.

It was then that he was wrenched round by an angry-faced Giles who had descended in order to speak to the lad about some forgotten household arrangement.

"Whatever are you doing?" demanded Giles.

He darted and lit the gas, then swept the curtains together. He was puzzled and disturbed to find his brother weeping, and he took refuge in the only way he knew of coping with the disturbances of the heart—he flew into a rage.

"What the hell's the matter?" he shouted. "This is something to see! What are you supposed to be at? Now dry that face quickly, Fred, quickly! Haven't I got enough without coming and finding you blubbering the minute my back is turned! Haven't I just given you twelve pounds? What more can you want? Lord God! I'm going to be driven completely loopy! I can see it coming. A person can go mad through constant vexations!" His big round face seemed to increase in size by his fury.

"I'm sorry, Giles," said his brother, drawing back from him. "I thought you'd gone to bed."

Giles stared with mingled disgust and pity into the gentle frightened face confronting him.

"You thought," he burst out. "By all that is miserable, what's the matter with you? What are you crying about?"

"It was nothing," pleaded Fred, down-glancing.

"Nothing! You aren't the sort who cries for nothing. Or are you? Are you, perhaps, turning into a lunarian? It's all that fool poetry. It's making you soft. I tell you, my fine fellow, you'll have to give it up. Life is too serious for poetry. Why, you're even beginning to *look* soft. You want to go and put your head down in a Rugger scrum, my boy. Get fit. Look as if you're all there! I'm still waiting to hear what you were crying for. Well, you?"

"O, Giles, I have told you. It was nothing. Just a mood. Can't people cry, sometimes?"

"Pshaw! Only weaklings cry," hectored the doctor. He seemed to shine with the hardness of his intolerance and self-regarding. "I won't have it, Fred, do you understand. Where would we be now if I had sat and blubbered? I can't do with you if you're going to be cowardly."

"Don't be so angry, Giles," the boy said. "I haven't done anything. You being so vexed and unfriendly when all I've done was to give way to a little private feeling—O, I do think it's such bad luck!"

"Aha! Private feelings! Now this is rather stunning," sneered Giles, then exploded: "I don't like those private feelings. I won't tolerate 'em! They . . . it upsets me. I don't understand it, I'm dashed if I do! I don't like what I don't understand. I'll not have you namby-pambying. I loath a coward. So don't let me see any more of your tears. And don't try it on when I'm not about, either."

He flounced off to bed.

Fred, left alone, gathered himself together. His tears were not usual. He could not remember when last he had cried.

In a corner he had pinned up a twopenny postcard reproduction of Rembrandt's "Christ Blessing Little Children." Fred went in for such things, and now he went to where this humble treasure was and, hands in his pockets, he stared at it like a mad man.

Outside a glib little wind was beginning to stir; Fred marked its wild humming.

"It's a tree-felling wind, that is!" he said. "The elms will be whanging down in the country before this night is much older!"

Comforted, he went into the kitchen and found a Bath Oliver biscuit. Munching its plastery bits, his mind began to rove up and out from the sudden grief that had assailed him.

But I have the assurance that all is well, Fred thought. What have I to cry for? Nothing is lost. What has come is best for me, certainly it is best. It is my life, *my life*. I shall do better to-morrow. Every day you have to keep on beginning again as though you've never done anything. But every day is wonderful—even the pain it brings is a marvel. From what I've learnt these last few months, it looks as if pain and beauty fuse, somehow, in a kind of sparkling acid, because since I've known suffering I've also had such experiences of beauty, it seems that pain has so revealing and repaying a side life would not be complete without it. Pain is not pleasure but it *is* possibility, infinite possibility. O, wherever there is anyone who suffers, I love you, not because I am sorry for you but because we share such a great illumination.

III

In the huddle of mean streets among which the Bilterlands had their home stood a small general shop on a dusty corner. It sold blue mottled soap, nutmegs, toffee, twopennyworths of jam and mustard pickles, starch, bundles of firewood, gills of vinegar, and watered milk which stood in a big white bowl that carried an indomitable lie in red lettering round its middle— "Pure and Unadulterated." Over the door a tin notice stated that the little place was licensed to sell tobacco. It was the small-time kind of a shop peculiar to such neighbourhoods where life and all is purchased in terms of twopences and tick.

The place was owned by a puce-coloured woman named Mrs. Clementina Portle. She moved heavily about her emporium, slapping down her squalid wares on the oilcloth-covered counter, and queening it over those who could not object because of the debits done in pencil against them in Mrs. Portle's greasy book of reckoning. She did not speak much; she was a listener who turned the droppings that came her way to the best account at the appointed time.

There was a Mr. Portle. He was a useful person to know. If you earned your living by supplying the Needful to Drug Addicts, Mr. Portle was willing to deliver the stuff for you to the various addresses of your eager clients. And did you suspect your wife of Nether Relations with a Cove, Mr. Portle would spy on her for you while you went out to earn the daily bread. You might be thinking of Asserting yourself with a little Vitriol Throwing; Mr. Portle would engage to get the juice for you. Perhaps you were engaged in the little sideline of Taking Jewels from people who had far too many: Mr. Portle knew the very fence to give you the highest price for your Haul. Mr. Portle performed all these services with rat-like daring for a Consideration. He had many other connections.

Certain Houses paid him a commission for introducing New Clients to the Disorderly Joys offered within. Similarly, proprietors of some Gambling Dens gave him a Percentage on all new victims brought to their Sacred Precincts. And Publishers of Very Choosy Literature gave him a Rake-Off on every book he managed to sell; he enjoyed similar Stipends from a few Producers of Very Natural Studies.

The Police would have liked to give Mr. Portle Something, too, had they been able to Prove Anything. But Mr. Portle was a Good Manager. He Played Safe. He betted only on Stone Jugs. He relied on his knowingness, happily unaware that he thought he knew a lot that he did not know at all. But he was always unwondering and cheerful, dreadfully self-assured, amazingly industrious, frighteningly competent, and inordinately vain. He had always held himself aloof from Law, Order, and the Salutary Virtues: they were Frivolities in a world of Serious Business. His life's motto could easily have been: Let there be darkness, then we can get at it!

Between them this remarkable pair had produced a daughter whom they called Agnes. She was a highly intelligent dwarf, a needle-sharp little object who was not ashamed of her stature, and resisted all her parents' attempts to clap her in a circus.

"I am as God Almighty made me," she used to say, "and there's no shame in taking anything from *that* quarter! Besides, people's got to be *chosen* to put up with special inconveniences. Not everybody could stand that sort of thing. Only some. They got to be selected. We're picked ones as rootle about near the ground. Anyway, there's as much to see on the floor as there is on the roof-top!"

Her face was large with smudged and flattened features as of a knocked-about old statue. And she had thick shining golden hair; there was something magical about it, and odd as she was, some people would have made a match with her for the sake of that wonderful hair.

Agnes, however, was not the marrying kind; neither was she one to remain dependent on her parents and their dubious earnings. When she left the local elementary school at the age of fourteen she went into domestic service of which she made a very good thing; she was immensely strong, willing, good-tempered, and kind. She was shrewd, too, and people liked her. When she was twenty-five she hired herself out as a housekeeper to Giles Bilterland and for two years she had slaved for him and Fred, especially Fred. She was in his confidence and she loved him beyond anyone.

On the morning following the murder, Giles called Agnes into his ground-floor consulting-room. She entered in her stumpy way, and he flourished a pound-note at her.

"Here you are. I want you to buy a few extra nourishing things for Mr. Fred," he instructed her. "I am not at all pleased with his general condition."

Agnes threw him a strange look.

Giles continued:

"He's not ill, of course. But he's been doing too much reading and is a little run-down, I fancy. I want you to get him plenty of eggs and cream and a chicken. Feed him up, you understand? I'll give you more money when this is spent."

"Yes, he does need extras," Agnes agreed. "People like him should be on extras all their life!"

"Really?" said Giles. "I wonder what you mean by that?"

"I mean that people like him are special—better than the rest of us, and they ought to be looked after more."

"Why are they better than the rest of us?" demanded Giles.

"Well," replied Agnes tartly, "if you can't see that there's no use telling. But Mr. Fred is better than most because, for a start, he's got the face of an angel such as you see in paintings in those little galleries that come ten a penny in Bond Street. And then everything in the whole world has meaning for him. Things *matter* to him."

"Dear me! How theatrical you are! Things matter to everyone, don't they, you ass!" said Giles curtly.

"Ay, usually the wrong things. But not with him. The right things matter to him in a . . . very special sort of way. He's always thinking. Thinks too much."

"Get out of my way," said Giles, suddenly enraged. "And mind your own business. It's a liberty for you to comment on my brother. What a liberty! Feed him properly, then he can't think."

"That's as much as you know," retorted Agnes who had never been anything but only baldly impressed by Giles either in his civilities or in his rage. She marched out leaving the door wide open.

Concerned for his brother, Giles hurried through his morning surgery. He then went out to pay a few calls on some sordid patients who were quietly rotting away in tenements unfit for human habitation; but the buildings were of the utmost importance to the remote and loving landlords who, on the

accumulative rents of these hovels and sties, were able to send
their children to the best schools in the country.

Following this disagreeable round, and having money in his
pocket, Giles walked to that part of Camden Town where taxis
plied, and drove to the Café Royal for his lunch. Over the meal
he came to the conclusion that he would have to do something
about Fred not in the distant future but now—at once, so that
the boy could *have* a future.

Ay, sneered Giles, I know *his* future—painting flowers and
bare bottoms! "*Voici des fruits et des fleurs!*" And then marriage
with some girl who colours her toe-nails, and likewise paints.
Or is, perhaps, literary. Ugh! She will certainly take everything
earnestly, as well as being arty, and will manage him like anything under the guise of helping him to realize himself, poor
devil!

Yet what the hell can I do, expostulated Giles with his roast
duck. I've got no money—only the freedom, at last, in which
I shall hope to make some money. What on earth was he crying
for last night? Bad—that. He's getting soft. But I put it about
him. We can't have tears.

He gobbled his food in a turmoil. Nothing—nothing ever
came about to his benefit. There must be some people, though,
who drew winning numbers. Giles looked round at the collection
of eating heads. There are far too many people in this blasted
world, he thought, too many looking for chances and too many
getting 'em to give me any satisfaction. He huddled over his
coffee, tossing off mean envying thoughts. Finally he took
himself off to the cinema, hoping that the crass realities of some
French film would take his mind from the painful facts of his
own life.

Emerging once more into the streets, he bought an early
evening paper, and went into a café for his tea. The newspaper
carried a lurid report of the discovery of the murdered man at
Highgate. "The police have not yet made an arrest."

No, and aren't likely to, thought Giles, cramming his mouth with hot toast, unless . . . unless . . .

Good God, I'm so harassed for money, so worried about Fred, so sick to death of the crimping, pimping way in which I'm forced to live, I could almost go now to that Mrs. Christopher, that murderess, and make her pay for *my* silence as much and more as she was giving Sine for his! And then—the *power* of such a position. I notice that Power pays a more immediate dividend when it is bent on destruction: the rake-off is deferred when it comes to a little construction.

O, it's nice, very nice to have thought of that, and it will never get beyond a thought. I'm too much of the nicely-brought-up middle-classes to attempt in fact most of the congenial goings-on that occur to me. I deeply regret that I was born a gentleman—if I am one, which I, and many another, could take leave to doubt!

He brought out his note-case and peered to see how much was left. Of Sine's twenty-five pounds, after the gift to Fred and to-day's expenses, Giles now had eleven pounds. He saw there was only one thing to do and he could not make up his mind whether necessity or arrant pleasure drove him, for since he had taken to gambling—in the first place to win enough to meet his blackmailer's demands—the habit had grown on him.

That's it, he sneered, you enter a thing as an expediency, and before you know where you are it has become something you can't do without—inescapable.

As it was a Thursday he had no evening surgery, and time was his own. He lingered over his tea and the newspaper, and frittered the night away with his mental strife till about half-past nine, when he might have been observed giving the pass-word at the door of the gambling club in Soho which he frequented.

His luck was good to begin with, but later the cards went against him, and he left the place at midnight owing nearly twenty pounds; fortunately he had lost to a lenient man who knew him; he was given a week in which to pay. As he had not enough for a taxi, and the last bus had gone, Giles began the long walk home. "So much for the pleasures of risk!" commented Giles.

Regent Street, as he turned into it, was getting lonely. A twittering pair or two in evening clothes clicked their way to a party or a night club, a furtive man hugged the plate-glass windows, and a few morose harlots were entreating with concentrated impudence. All was lit by the diffused rose-brown glow from the street lamps.

At Oxford Circus a street light had failed, but up the shadowy walls of the buildings some gigantic beams from a coffee-stall sent ladders of strong sunflower light. Giles dug into his pockets and discovered sixpence. He approached the mounds of saveloys and sandwiches and spent his money at the stall on a cup of coffee and a cheese-cake.

Thinking his intolerable thoughts he continued past Broadcasting House into the open elegant Regency-planned Portland Place. Here and there a reflection of street light glittered in a peerless fanlight or shone on a handsome massive door the wood of which seemed to have taken on some strange woodland potent now that the night was down. A roast-chestnut man went rattling home, in a fragrant cloud of nut fumes, the little charcoal fire on his barrow looking like the sinister red head of an opium poppy blinking knowingly in the dark.

Giles realized that on his walk he had been looking at people and objects as a writer or a painter sees them—finding them valid, enjoyable and important in their own right, in their own significance.

I'm not given to speculation of this kind, he thought: continual thwarting is enlarging my mind to lunacy.

It was the same when he came into the public roads of Regent's Park. Here where the spring was rising fresh and green among the galvanized trees, the soft roaring of the wind seemed to stir tender associations with old country places, and memories were ready to rise and flush Giles's heart. He successfully evaded all this.

"Be damned to you!" he growled. "This sort of thing is nothing but escape stuff from the worry of my gambling debts. I am deathlessly ready to defy any nonsense brought on by a few trees, the wind and lonely night-time! These gad-flies won't nip me! I'm up to the eyes in muck and worry: even so, why should I weaken towards the insinuations of a spring night through which I am traipsing only because I haven't got a bloody half-crown for a cab!"

Late as it was when he came to his dwelling, light shone out from the sitting-room windows, and when he reached it he found Fred with his books and a tray with tea-things at his elbow.

"Nose stuck in a book, as usual, my dear?" Giles greeted him.

"Hello," said Fred, holding out his hand; "the tea's still hot."

"Well, pour me a cup, and tell me how things have been."

"Fine," replied Fred. "Agnes gave me such jolly meals to-day —chicken and whipped cream and port wine and the lord knows what. She must think I need feeding up. You've paid for all those extras, of course."

"What about it?" said Giles. "You need stuffing. You're getting thin and bolt-eyed. I don't know how you young lads think you'll keep fit by moping at home. Why don't you get out to a gymnasium and exercise? O, well! Have you had a happy day?"

"Yes, thanks," Fred answered. "Most of the time I'm very happy, you know. There's no need to worry about me."

"All right, I won't," said Giles. "Ordered your suit yet?"

"Why, no. There's no hurry for that."

"I wonder—hmm—I've got a somewhat chilling request: could you let me have that money back?" Giles asked with a kind of insolent distress.

"Of course," Fred readily agreed. He went and got the money from his desk, and gave it to his brother with an affectionate gesture.

"A few debts rolled up," Giles explained brightly. "That's a regular thing, of course, and very stirring. But I really will give you something for keeps one of these days—don't let it knock a start out of you, dear boy!" He laughed painfully. "Well," he said, "I'm for bed." He turned at the door, and looked long at Fred. "I love you well. Good night."

IV

The announcement of the reward of five hundred pounds for information leading to the arrest of the Highgate murderer, which appeared in the newspapers during the next few days, was enough, in all its peculiar and forceful invitation, to throw Giles almost into convulsions.

Sitting in his dispensary, he kept reading the announcement, looking up from the printed sheet to the shelves of bottles which caught the clear cold light of the day in vitreous tints of emerald, sienna, and violet.

A perfect devil had grasped him by the face and was roaring in his ear:

"Whoop, what a lark! Five hundred pounds for Mrs. Christopher!"

Giles's face puckered with acid mirth.

"Shut your bloody mouth!" he told the tempter and to himself added:

"I'd do it to show I was above their petty silly notions of loyalty and right and all the rest of it. I've always been very amused at common decency and christian morality! I'd do it to show what real strength is, and if, afterwards, remorse set in, I'd then tell myself I did it for Fred!"

Five hundred pounds, eh? It was a nice lot of cash. A couple of hundred—perhaps one hundred—would fix Fred up in some art-school or another. He would pay off a hundred pounds of his own more insistent debts, and with the remaining three hundred he would gamble in an effort to turn the money into three thousand pounds—at least, that!

Before his eye he saw a thick wad of notes. "If thine eye offend thee . . ." Sportfully he smacked his eyes; let them offend and keep on offending! What was offence, anyway?

The way the mind ran! What levels it leapt down to! What was he thinking of? Why, he was only contemplating going and selling a woman to the police. They ought to have found her out for themselves. Offering rewards for lives! It was immoral of them, positively immoral. He would have nothing to do with it. Mrs. Christopher was his benefactor. It was idiotic and impossible for him to go to the police and sell them what he knew of this woman. He could not do it, not possibly.

He bent and committed to his memory the exact department in Scotland Yard where information was to be delivered.

What a fool Mrs. Christopher had been to give them her name and address—a stupid, wild, and daring fool who deserved all the trouble that might come her way.

What of those other two? What were they making up their minds to do as they read this announcement—that spry young woman who looked ready for anything, that amusing joker with the fringe of hair across his silly head. Giles suffered a spasm of fear—in case one of them would get to Scotland Yard first.

But no: they wouldn't do such a thing. He saw them as on the night of the murder, clamouring with gratitude round Mrs. Christopher as she wiped her little gun on her skirt. Those two would not tell. Only he was dangerous; only he had the courage to be vile.

All the day and through the night Giles worked on the problem. But there's no problem about it, he thought, tossing on his sleepless bed in the early hours of the morning. One does not do such things. One should not even think about them, because even the idlest thought produced *something*—the power of thought was awful, all the more so because what was called into being was unseen. Nevertheless, it was thrilling and bold to think about such things, to savour the power one had over another human being.

Why need we be grateful to Mrs. Christopher, demanded Giles, as the dawn gave shape to the little winged bulges that formed the pattern of the rough creamy ceiling-paper and reminded him of the swallow-tail moths that had flown in the dusk in the country long ago like ghosts of the insect world. And the brightening day picked out the one Hepplewhite chair saved from his old home, the pair of Gold Anchor Chelsea china vases on the mantelpiece, and the old carved chest, desperately held from sale-room and pawnbroker so as to have something for the last emergency.

Mrs. Christopher didn't murder for us. She did it to suit herself. Who knows what he was blackmailing her for? Perhaps another murder? Perhaps she's a dangerous criminal and it's my duty to go to the police.

On the other hand, ahem, she may just have been quixotic enough to have killed him so that we should all be free of Sine—a fresh start all round. If that was her idea, she only did it for vain-glory! She wanted to touch our hearts. Personally, I haven't got a heart. And I did not ask her to commit murder for me. If she *has* tasted the high delights of a supra self-sacrifice, I don't see why she should be deprived of the ultimate joy of standing her trial!

Of course by now the woman will have made a get-away. By now I daresay she's in America or the South of France. Even if I go and blab the police will never find her. Ah, but that's not the point. One simply does not . . . does not what? Here rises the gentleman again. He asks me to remember that remorse will follow any step taken towards Scotland Yard. But will it? Why the hell should remorse set in? Remorse can only rear its ugly head if a man is afflicted with a conscience. I can't be bound by such appendages. I shall rise superior to any niggling conscience. Sometimes decency would make us positively indecent. It's far more important that I should have freedom from debt and worry and so get forward with my humane profession, than this old woman should go scot-free for murder. My humane profession? That's a good one—coming from me!

Naturally, I don't like to do it. I feel sorry for Mrs. Christopher. She seemed decent, like my mother, somehow. It isn't pretty at all to think of them haling her away—through me. She'll probably hang. Full of hell the picture appears, and I am upset for the old woman. So would you be, too, he said, addressing no one.

But, he brooded, we must be strong—strong enough to rise above our own solicitude and suffering to create our own situations and fulfil ourselves. What's a betrayal or two? Loyalties are only weaknesses, and such small affairs as the conscience should not turn people from their way. Such little things put people off!

It's true, I vowed I'd never betray the woman, but I can't be tied to mere consistency. Moral misgivings are like the small-pox—we must get rid of them before they mark us.

There are great gifts in me—gifts which, so far, have been stifled for the want of proper exercise. I may not be better off than the majority, but I'm certainly better! And people with my positive sense of their own destiny must be ruthless—all great men have had to be ruthless—no sentimentality, no nonsense. It isn't as if I should be committing a crime, I'm only doing my duty. Moreover, she said we could tell about her—if suspicion fell on us, I'm bound to add. It hasn't, of course, but . . .

I wonder why the idea persists that I would be committing a crime if I went to tell the police about Mrs. Christopher, and not so much a crime against her as against myself.

Ah, to the devil with it! Men of my mark must not be hampered by scruples. Those are for women and boys—for my little brother, Fred; poor lad, I fear he will never get anywhere in this world. But it's different altogether for me. I know I am intended for importance. It's the one thing that keeps me going. And the first step towards this destiny is removal from Camden Town. Five hundred pounds would help that to happen. Free of debt I can begin to look round for a different practice. With a good name, I could borrow. Yes, I must go to Scotland Yard. What am I waiting for?

Having paid out these thoughts, Giles got up and made his own breakfast. He particularly did not wish to come into contact with Fred that morning. He went straight downstairs to his dispensary after his solitary meal, read the morning paper when it fell through the letter-box and, in due time, dealt with a row of sniffling patients. He prepared to go out. As he went down the passage to the front door he heard Fred calling to him from upstairs:

"Can you spare a minute, Giles?"

"No, I'm sorry, I can't."

"I wish you could just run up for a minute; it won't take long."

"You'll have to wait," Giles roared. "I'm late, I'm in a hurry."

He had got the street door open.

"Giles."

"Go to hell," said Giles, not caring whether the boy heard or not. He slammed the door and rushed for the 24 bus. All the way to Mornington Crescent the bus was compelled to mark time behind a great lorry carrying some doomed cattle to a slaughterhouse. But at last the road was clear, and Giles soon found himself at Scotland Yard.

Hugh Christopher received him at once.

"Information to sell," mumbled Giles without preamble.

"Let's have it," said Hugh, and when Giles had finished his story, Hugh remarked:

"It's very helpful—that. She certainly was good to you, silencing the fellow who was blackmailing you. You ought to have come to us about the extortion, you know, but, of course, we weren't offering rewards in that direction, were we?"

"I don't know," said Giles. "I'm not interested. I've done my part of the business. What about yours?"

"Yes, yes, I am coming to that, don't be afraid, you'll get your money," replied Hugh, unlocking a drawer of his desk and bringing out a bundle of notes. "You're a nice fellow," he continued, "I hope we meet again."

"I don't, thank you," said Giles. "I don't like your tone. When I come here to do my duty I don't appreciate insults."

"There!" exclaimed Hugh with ironic sympathy, "I've gone and offended you when, all the time, as you say, you were only doing your duty! We need people like you; in fact, to let you into a secret, we could not get on here without our Judas-trees. Don't look so vexed. Somehow, the Judas motif is part of the universal scheme. Without that bright lad even the Gospel would have had a different ending! So take your money, happy in the thought that you have played a very necessary, if a dirty rôle! Get out!"

"You don't give citizens any encouragement to do their duty," snorted Giles, taking up the money with a hand that was not steady.

"I said—Out, Get Out," said Hugh Christopher, "before I have you arrested."

"You can't do that," protested Giles from the door.

"Can't I?" said Hugh. "Jurisprudence may be such that one criminal goes free and is even paid for assisting another to face judge and jury, but remember one thing: there are very few people in this world who can truthfully say they've never done anything that wouldn't have landed them behind prison bars if all were known. The only people in jail are those who have been Found Out."

This was rather too near the bone for Giles to work out a retort. He turned on his heel and went downstairs into the open. It was a grey day with a silver sky pierced sometimes by brief flashes of sapphire. He brought up against a wall. He was stifling with rage. The outrageous way that fellow had spoken to him! Unbelievable! Of course, the police were always filthy to informers, filthy; and they wouldn't get far without that despised information, either, as well they knew, as that fellow had admitted. Here he was, helping them to track down a murderer and all he got for his pains—but, better not think of that. He must train himself not to think about Mrs. Christopher again. There had not been any fun in the power of holding her life on his tongue; it only might have been fun if he had chosen life for her instead of the hangman.

He began to feel cold and a sharp pain troubled his bowels. He moved off towards Whitehall where he went into a bar and drank two double whiskies. Warmed then, he began to concentrate on the money, feeling the big roll of notes and thinking that now he could buy Fred his entrance into an art school. O, the difference money could make! A person had a rebirth the minute it came into his possession. Money was the only thing that mattered in the world.

Fred would be delighted when he knew he could go to an art school. What an odd thing it was that he was not now rushing home to tell Fred of his good fortune. He hardly understood his reluctance to go home and tell Fred that a little money had come their way. Here he was lingering out his lunch and shunning the time of returning.

Once in the streets again, he moved up to Trafalgar Square. Beyond the fountains that pirouetted and toppled in the basins, stretched the unlovely façade of the National Gallery. In all his life he had never been inside the building. He now decided he would go in and look round.

But, to his perceptions, it was a dreadful place. He trudged from gallery to gallery, throwing looks of disgust at the great masterpieces, sniffing the combined aromas of varnish and polishing-wax and hot dusty sunshine.

"Such trash!" judged the young man. "It all ought to be burnt! Gives people silly ideas. There's nothing practical about art. It's totally unreal."

His irate gaze lingered on a gentle parson instructing his three children in Brueghel's "Adoration of the Kings."

"Old fool!" muttered Giles charitably. He began to make for the exit. It was then that his eye fell on a canvas by the painter Honthorst, "Christ Before Pilate." The faces of the subjects were dramatically lit up by a concentration of candlelight on the table at which the procurator was sitting. Christ, with big working hands bound at the wrists with rope, stood at the table gazing down at his accuser with mild thoughtfulness. All the light and force and searching poignancy of the picture were brought to focus in the candle's little ray and the two faces it illuminated.

Giles paused.

"Something missing," he said to himself. And then it came. "Where's Judas?" he said, and the answer was pat: "Standing not in the picture, but before it!"

He hurried away. "Mustn't get a Judas complex, must we?"

He went across the Square and into St. James's Park. He felt so chilled and agitated he thought he was going to be ill. "What's the matter with me?" he demanded irritably.

Under a tree he settled down on a green chair and spent a long time thinking, while round him a number of London's visiting sea-gulls flashed and screamed and flew down to the green felt of the lawns like showers of lilies. He wished he had someone he could go to—some friend—but he had no friends. Only a few

gambling companions. No friends. He was not the kind who
made friends.

But—he was forgetting. Fred was his friend. Fred loved him.
He had not been much of a friend to Fred but, in his own way,
he returned his brother's love. He would go home now and
break the good news to the lad. The *good* news? Well, the news.
Fred's delight would smash the persistent image of Mrs. Christopher—that silly woman who was, withal, so decent, so excellent,
who carried her good life in her face—a woman who had killed
but who was not the murdering type. No. She was a gentlewoman, a gentlewoman like his own mother, and, no doubt,
Mrs. Christopher *was* some man's mother. Some man's mother
whom he, Giles, had sent to the hangman.

Shut off! Shut off! Giles raved against himself. He got up and
went to look for a taxi. Fred would be staggered by the taxi.
The brothers seldom had the means to use taxis.

Evening was coming on. Soon he would have to deal with a
row of dreary patients. But first he would have this jolly talk
with Fred.

V

When Giles arrived home his brother was dead.

"Where's Mr. Fred?" he demanded of Agnes when he saw
that their sitting-room was deserted. She was standing in the
kitchen peeling potatoes. She did not answer him immediately.

"I said—where is my brother?"

She turned and began to wipe her hands.

"Mr. Fred died suddenly," she said, not looking at him.

"Dead? You mustn't say things like that, you know! Where is
my brother?" said Giles.

"I'm sorry. Mr. Fred died. He's in his room."

"He's dead! He's mad! He's in his room!" stuttered Giles; frightened smiles kept stretching his mouth. He turned and ran to Fred's room. Someone had lowered the white linen blind and in the diminished light Giles saw his brother lying on the bed—a credit to the ministrations of the district nurse. The hands were folded on the forbidding white sheet, and someone, probably Agnes, had enclosed within them a nosegay of little spring flowers.

"Fred! Fred!" Giles broke out, beginning to tremble. "Fred! Fred!"

He went on calling his brother in a loud violent way for quite a long time. At last Agnes went to him.

"You'd better come in the sitting-room, Mr. Giles," she said gently. "Come and sit down. It's the shock."

"What shock?" asked Giles, allowing her to lead him to the fire in the sitting-room. "You are wrong to be mentioning shocks. Who's had one? Have I got to treat somebody for shock?"

Agnes went to the cupboard where there was five shillings worth of brandy in a small bottle ready for an emergency. She poured some out and gave it to him. But the glass fell out of his nerveless fingers and smashed on the tiles of the hearth. Agnes looked at him worriedly. His face seemed to have caved in; it had become an old man's. In a little while he said dully:

"What happened?"

"He was taken bad soon after you left this morning," Agnes explained. "I didn't know where you had gone, so I couldn't get in touch with you. I telephoned his doctor."

"His doctor? What did he want a doctor for? Who was his doctor?"

"Dr. Inmyra of Hampstead."

"Inmyra? What was he treating him for?"

"Mr. Fred had cancer of the throat."

"What?" Giles was on his feet, the chair overturned.

Agnes repeated the intelligence.

"And I never knew! I was never told," said Giles in wonderment.

"Mr. Fred—he didn't want you to know. He didn't want to worry you. He said you had enough to think about. But he was going to tell you . . . this morning . . . only you wouldn't wait."

"No. I wouldn't wait," Giles agreed. He spoke with thick jerks as if he were throttling. He nodded his head sagely. "I even told him to go to hell. That's the usual form when your brother wants to confide in you that he is dying of cancer of the throat!"

Agnes looked at him with pity.

"His doctor told him yesterday the end would come at any time. That's why Mr. Fred thought he had better let you know this morning. Mr. Fred had known for a long time, of course, that he was dying. But he wouldn't have you worried."

"*You* knew," Giles shouted accusingly. "He told *you*." He began to blaze with indignation and grief.

"Yes. He had to tell someone. He was only young, you know, to go about realizing that he was done for. Besides, he needed someone—just lately, that is—to help him with the drug when the pain came on. This morning . . ."

"I want to know exactly what happened this morning."

"He was with me in the kitchen. I was giving him a drink of fruit juice—all he could get down this last two or three days. My mother sent a little girl round with some groceries and she brought that mongrel dog of ours. Mr. Fred said they were both to have something to eat and drink, and while I was getting 'em some cake and biscuits the dog jumped on his knee. Mr. Fred made a fuss of it, and began telling the little girl about some

215

supposed words of Jesus they found a few years ago about animals. I got it here in my pocket. I copied out what he said because such words seem precious."

Agnes drew a piece of paper from her pocket, and offered it to him. He began to read, not because he cared anything for the words of Jesus, but he would have read and listened to anything just then as if there were no telling what clues would be revealed that would clarify the terrible strangeness, and perhaps make things more understandable and easy for him.

"Ye ask who are those that draw us to the Kingdom if the Kingdom is in heaven? The fowls of the air, and all the beasts that are under the earth or upon the earth, and the fishes in the sea, these are they which draw you, and the Kingdom is within you." *

"Well?" said Giles to Agnes.

"Then the little girl said they would have to go, and Mr. Fred, he told the child to be good to the dog always because animals had been given us to love not to hunt and beat and kill. He was sitting at the table, and soon after a big hæmorrhage came on. He never got over it."

"What time? What time was that?" asked Giles, tremblingly.

"It was about an hour after you left, near as I can remember."

"I see," said Giles. "It was just about the time I was selling Mrs. Christopher. A life for a life, you see, Agnes."

Agnes did not see. She simply thought that her employer was going out of his mind, and begged God to come to his plight. Giles turned on her:

"*You* should have told me if he wouldn't. Inmyra should have told me! Why wasn't I told? To think that I have to listen to these intimacies about my brother from you—a servant and a stranger! It's impossible and revolting."

"It was Mr. Fred's wish that you should not know. Why shouldn't his wish be respected? It was his life—and his death,

* Oxyrhynchus Papyri, IV. 6.

too! He said he could bear things better if you did not have the worry of him. So I would not have told you for anything. Besides, he was right—you always did have a lot to think of, didn't you?"

"Certainly," replied Giles with dignity. "Certainly! I always had myself to think of! That's a whole time occupation, don't you know!"

"You needn't say all this now, Mr. Giles," said Agnes.

"No," admitted Giles, "it is rather late in the day to begin saying anything, God damn it! If only I had been told! But I should have known, I should have seen. I'm a doctor, you know. You're not forgetting that I'm a doctor, are you?"

"I'm not forgetting. Mr. Fred did not forget, either. He always kept in the shadow so's you would not notice his colour or . . . or anything. It was the only fear he had . . . that you would find out and be upset."

"He . . . Wasn't he afraid of . . . death?"

"No," replied Agnes, a smile making her battered face gentle and comely, "he wasn't afraid—not even during those last minutes. Those as lives the way he did has no cause to fear death. Ah, what pleasure he got from little things, from everything. He'd say: 'What thrills there are! Everywhere I look I see something that thrills me!' 'What?' I'd say, 'in Camden Town?' 'Yes,' he'd say, 'in Camden Town as ever was.' "

"Yes," commented Giles, "but he should have lived, not died to his famous thrills. O, I ought to have known what was wrong by the state of his skin. That disease leaves its evidence. Day after day he was getting to be a corpse before my very eyes and I never noticed it! Ha! Ha! The malevolent irony of it!"

"Don't take on so," said Agnes, trying to comfort him. "He wouldn't have wanted you to reproach yourself. You didn't know, and that was his wish. Think how blessed and happy his life was. 'Nothing is unfriendly,' he'd say, and, of course, if you believe that—it is so. He wasn't one of those chosen to have a wife and children to love, and he didn't get much chance of loving his parents, seeing that they were taken so early. But love can run other ways. Love is to love everything, it's to notice everything, the way he did, and be pleased with things just for what they are. That's how love can come into life every minute, it's how to be compassionate and kind, how to be happy. It's what Jesus meant about His Heavenly Father knowing what was happening to every sparrow, it's the life we were meant to live, and your brother lived it. He filled himself up with life, he lived with all he'd got."

"There's more in you than I thought," observed Giles. "You never told me these things before."

"You never let people near enough to tell such things."

"It's too late, now," said Giles. "If I'd let *him* 'near enough,' as you call it, he'd probably be alive now. I ought to have seen it from the first—we might have taken it in time. And now I realize that I perceived all the time how wrong things had gone, without taking it in. There was his pallor, his husky voice. He hadn't a husky voice when he was a little boy, when I used to say to him, 'Hope you have a good term, Fred.' His voice was clear and sweet then—they had him singing in fool choirs. *Of course*, I had noticed something; upon my word, I shall endeavour to give myself a little credit. I had noticed how pale he was, and I advised him to go out and play football! That does me great credit! That's the sort of thing I shall always remember! O, to think of him going through it all alone, marked down, with no one to tell, but you. If only I had *seen!*"

He thought of Emerson saying that for their living in the world invalids pay a high board. If anyone ever paid a high board, my brother did, he mourned.

"Well, don't reproach yourself," urged Agnes. "It could have happened to anyone. We all look at people and never *see* them till, often, it's too late."

"And yet," said Giles, "I'd made him my darling. O, yes.

I never loved anyone but him. Tell me, did he . . . suffer much?"

"Not till towards the end. That's why it got such a hold on him. He felt no pain, nothing, and then when he did notice something wrong, the disease was incurable."

"Was it very bad . . . the pain . . . towards the end?"

"Yes, it was. He used to say he felt as if he had been swallowing broken glass."

Giles winced, and hung his head. He knew, none better, how much has to be gone through before the body allows one to die in peace. Some got it easy—just lay back and dozed off for the last time. But with others it was a struggle, agonized and wild.

"But," cried Agnes, "he had the courage of a hundred, for all that he was young. No one knows how brave he was. But that isn't the best of it—he never grumbled, never complained—he was always gay and quoting poetry. By gay, I don't mean he was a clown. He knew and understood the sadness of things. But he had an idea that if you lived cheerfully yourself, that alone would do other people good. He always thought of other people. He was always delicate and considerate in his dealings with people. He was a child of Christ if ever there was one. Out of pain and loneliness he got a discipline which men twice or three times his age never know, and out of discipline he got what only a few find—he got the sight that finds beauty where it's never been before. Talk! I could talk about him and never be done. *His* religion wasn't long-faced church-going, without a heart. It was kindness, sympathy and tolerance, and it was delight in life—everything to be valued. He only ever railed against himself. Sometimes he had to vomit, poor lad, and then he'd say that he was a beast and a nuisance. He was no such thing. He was a saint, really. Too good for here. So good it sometimes used to seem to me as if he were mad—because, I suppose, real goodness is so seldom met with that when it does come our way it shows up *our* madness and, in defence, we have to think that what we see is dotty, not ourselves."

While she had been speaking Giles saw, in a stunning flash-back, his brother as a child of eight or nine. The little boy had gone to try his first fishing rod; from a footbridge he cast his bait of dough into the little river, felt a bite, and, with cries of pleasure, drew out of the water a glittering roach. The little boy stared at the beautiful fish with its silver scales and red fins. "Gosh, how ripping!" And then he hurriedly took the hook out of its mouth and dropped the fish back in the stream.

They say, Giles thought, that by the time you're twelve you've been everything that you'll be in later life.

He turned to Agnes:

"I'm going out," he said. "Go and tell those patients of mine that they'll get no attention from me this evening."

"But, Mr. Giles, what about your supper?"

"Burn it!"

"You ought not to go out now, you're not fit to go wandering about, you're not yourself."

"Thanks very much. Go and do as you are told."

"Mr. Giles—don't go out."

For answer he left the room and went down into the evening streets. A fog was coming on, silver-grey, tinged with rose from the unvanquished sun of the higher air; it lent a tremulous appearance to walls and buildings to the extent that it seemed as if they would waver off if a hand were put out to touch them. Giles wandered about in this dream landscape for a long time, empty of purpose but for one need, and that, to get rid of the money which bulged in his pocket and was his one point of focus.

Bloody stuff, he thought of it, bloody money, blood money, Mrs. Christopher's blood money, Fred's blood money, my blood money, it'll be a nice present for someone! Because I'm going to give it away—naturally—follow Judas, and I can't go wrong! Of course, I ought to go and give it back to the police, but those who offer blood money won't take it back. I know that from what happened to my prototype when he tried to palm back on the priests the thirty pieces of silver. So I'm going to give my informer's fee to some outside party—someone who'll appreciate it, someone *worthy* of it! But—who? All at once it occurred to him that Agnes's father, the busy Mr. Portle, would be ready to receive a gift of hard cash—damned hard cash!

The more Giles thought of it the more five hundred pounds of blood money seemed to be a very proper offering to Mr. Portle whose activities were well known to him, and who had, indeed, introduced him to the gambling club in Soho. Mr. Portle deserved some recognition, and towards his shop Giles hurried carrying the treat.

The cracked shop bell gave a metallic hiccup as Giles pushed open the door. While he waited for the gentleman of his choice, he gazed round at the shelves of seedy merchandise, the counter with its oilcloth cover and the glass case containing chocolate bars, pills, cards of hair clips, collar studs, and bottles of gum. A hanging lamp threw dingy brown rays about the shop and winked amorously at itself in a vast bottle of pickled onions.

Mr. Portle now ambled in. He was got up hotly in thick tweeds the colour of oatmeal, and instead of a collar and tie his neck was wound in a crimson wool scarf. He had a small pursed-up mouth which was altogether lost in two tremendous wobbling jaws, and a few locks of hair like grey cigars were piled forward with some artistry to mask tracts of bare speckled scalp.

"If it ain't Dr. Bilterland! How's tricks, Dr. B.?" said Mr. Portle in his sibilant voice. He made Giles a reverence that had nothing of respect about it. His sore pink-ringed eyes darted about like two minnows. "What can I do for you *now?* Or have you come to tell me that Agnes met with accident?"

Assured as to his daughter's well-being, Mr. Portle stood with his mouth open among the little mucks in the lamplit shop and heard of what he was about to receive. Very civilly he pawed this intelligence over, and at last delivered himself:

"You want to give me five 'undred pound!" said Mr. Portle with affecting docility. "For nothing? Is that really so? You know, you sound as if you're off your rocker!"

"You're not getting it for nothing," corrected Giles, with some semblance of his habitual bland insolence. "It's your *præmium extra ordinem.*"

"How much?" asked Mr. Portle.

"Your prize for the services you have for so long, if so surreptitiously rendered to the public! You know what I mean?"

"Ah, give over!" replied Mr. Portle with bold affability. "We get your meaning. What we don't get is why you're giving all this 'ere money away."

Giles had placed the big wad of notes on the counter. Mr. Portle patted it.

"I suppose," he suggested, "it is *your* money to give away?"

"Meaning—have I pinched it? The answer's No."

Mr. Portle stroked his gigantic jaw with a blackened forefinger.

"Perhaps you uttered it?" he leered.

"No," said Giles dreamily, "but I got it for uttering."

"Ah!" exclaimed Mr. Portle in a honeyed way. "So that's it, my pulse, my loving cup! Talkin' out of school! Blowing the gaff! *Informing!*"

"Hear the lout! But you're on the mark," said Giles.

Mr. Portle went off into a whirligig of thought. Big rewards like that weren't given every week. He went over the newspaper announcements that had caught his eye during the last few days—he had it.

"Scotland Yard, I suppose," said Mr. Portle.

"That was the bank."

"Lemme see, now. Something to do with the 'Ighgate murder case, was it?" asked Mr. Portle barbarously enjoying himself. All his person seemed to champ with raffish insolence.

"How do you get so spry?" asked Giles with mock admiration.

"I uses me loaf," said Mr. Portle with earnestness. "So you know the murderer, do you? And you went and give 'im away? You sing a full song, you do!"

"The point to concern you is that I find, after all, that I don't need the cash," said Giles.

"Black hell!" sniggered Mr. Portle. "Ain't you a one! Trying to cod me!" He pretended to be stricken with a very bad cough and surrounded himself with common noises.

"I don't often do my duty," said Giles.

"Evidently! It seems to have hurt you. But what is yer duty? Ask yerself that question! I keeps off duty, meself. Too risky, too expensive. And you want to give this blood money to me? You don't want it? You can't do with it?"

"Can you?" asked Giles.

Mr. Portle began to look as if something had gone sour. Mr. Portle's ethics had been dispensed in a cloudy infiltrated region where moth and rust did both corrupt, but he had his mouldering code. The staving-off had begun the minute he heard that he was to be given money for nothing; now he gave it the final twist—he said:

"You young gentlemen! My word! Full of skite, ain't you!" He wagged his dirty finger at Giles. "You makes your mistake in thinking that us as is without your advantages is ready to descend to your level. But, listen 'ere, Mr. doctor-clever-Dick, I may not chuck as fancy a front as you, but I've never sunk to what you are. I won't touch your bitching money. No fear!

And you can't get it and yourself outer my shop quick enough to please me."

"But what shall I do with the money if you won't take it?" Giles asked in a stilted far-away voice. His brimming eyes were opened to their widest extent and looked ready to leak straight out of his head.

"What will you do with the money?" repeated Mr. Portle in a high astonished voice, and then, changing his note to a lower, more confidential key, Mr. Portle told Giles what he could do with the money.

Giles gathered up the bundle of notes and wandered out. Presently he came to a hospital on the façade of which was a very large poster: "*WE WANT YOUR BLOOD AND YOUR MONEY.*"

"O," said Giles, "I can oblige these people. I can help these good folk out of their little hole." He poked round the building looking for the donation box and dropped into it the bundle of notes.

"There," said Giles, "you've got your Blood and your Money. Blood Money for short!"

Near the hospital crouched a church with a row of ugly stone saints moping on the façade, the wind blowing trash into their open mouths. Giles wandered in. Who knew but that in the church someone would be waiting to explain everything to him. A service had been going on and through the mist of incense, candle-flames at shrines sent out drowned gleams. But there was no one in the church except God, and Giles didn't recognize Him. He traipsed round, took a rose from a vase on a pedestal and put it in his coat; then he departed.

Much later he found himself in the bustle and glare of Euston Station, but he had no plans for a journey. The only journey he wanted to take was a long one—away from himself. He trundled up and down through the waiting-rooms and booking-halls, and somehow the place reminded him of the

National Gallery which he had visited that afternoon. He recalled the canvas—"Christ Before Pilate," and this gave way to two more pictures which he was busy titling as he walked along: "Fred Before the Judgment Seat"; "Mrs. Christopher Before the Jury."

Finally he bought a platform ticket and went and seated himself on the last bench before the platform dropped steeply down to the railway lines. Here he stared away from the bright station into the clamorous dark where clouds of steam hurtled up from incensed hoo-hooing locomotives, where the metals— shining like the leaves of the black bryony—swam away into the night, and a great forest of signal lights wavered and winked —the signal lights that Fred had once seen as luminous hollyhocks climbing to paradise. Here Giles sat, overwhelmed by the new areas of his consciousness which had been shocked into awareness by his withering remorse and loss.

More than once he had to control the impulse to go down the platform into the vast gleaming network of rails and hooded lights and walk about till one of the trains knocked the life out of him. He saw that he could not go on because he could go no further. From now on he could only submit or kill himself. But he knew he could never take that way out, though he would have been glad to be dead and safe, like Fred—Fred, a simple and unremarkable boy, who had met his end without fear, who had made even of death a graciousness.

> "To me the thought of death is terrible,
> Having such hold on life, to thee it is not
> So much even as the lifting of a latch.
> Only a step into the open air,
> Out of a tent already luminous
> With light that shines through its transparent walls,
> O pure in heart!"

Poetry now! How was it that such lines were stored in *his*

head. He frowned with painful wonderment. He hadn't looked at a book of poetry since under compulsion at school. That was it. School. Once he had had to memorize part of "The Golden Legend" and Longfellow's lines had come back to him as he thought of death for himself and his brother. Well, he couldn't die. He would have to Ancient Mariner it on and on, not having shot an albatross but having destroyed something as symbolic. Mrs. Christopher rose beyond her queer crime and her own dimensions and became to him a formless entity embodying higher loyalties, loftier aims, and wider visions than visited the generality of people.

But he had taken steps to destroy Mrs. Christopher—the symbol of better aims—and the world into which his betrayal of her had plunged him was a place of infinite disaster. He did not know how to deal with it. A man had no right to create a situation that was beyond him. He'd had no right to betray Mrs. Christopher. Such action had brought about a state beyond his control, a terribly dangerous state in which anything could happen to him and he had no protection—none—because he had cut himself off from protection. It was terrifying. It was sterile, abnormal. In buying Mrs. Christopher's death he had entered the tomb himself. He suddenly saw why virtue was desirable—it wasn't just a whim of the priests, it was sanity.

He wasn't so wonderful, after all; he was quite puny and futile, in fact. He was so gauche he had never asked what time it was till the clock stopped. Why had he gone and sold Mrs. Christopher? Because, of course, that was the easier thing to do. The really great personality would not have condescended to such meanness.

Life was a very queer game. Who'd have thought that to go free meant that you had to live under discipline! Who'd have thought that doing exactly as one liked was not freedom but captivity to a horror—the horror of realizing that without taboo everything was of equal value and, consequently, no value, and

the will so far from being an instrument of power became a mere
will-o'-the-wisp; that real freedom meant doing what somebody
else liked—what God liked—God whom he denied but in whom
he could not help believing.

He, Giles, had betrayed Mrs. Christopher to show what he
thought was power, and a higher Power had taken away his
beloved brother. His striving for power had led him only to
the conviction of a greater Power which, in its own time could
so throw down the mightiest, the subtlest, that there could be
no rising again without recourse to that same Power. It seemed,
after all, that true freedom consisted in stopping and enquiring
all day and every day what God's will was in this, that, and the
other. Paradise was here or anywhere at all if a man was living
in God's will and not in his own.

Well, he would have plenty of time in future for sizing up
God's will. He would never leave Camden Town now. He
would have to try and learn, somehow, to make of it the oasis
it had been to Fred, and he would have to begin without knowing anything of Fred's magic formula. He might make a start by
being kind to his patients—that occurred to him. It would be a
change not to receive them with a cold eye and the minimum
of bored attention. It would be something to see them as men
and women instead of "cases." In future when he swabbed a
little girl's sore eyes, or tapped some bony little chest, tenderness
might inform his competence.

He only wished that Fred were there to teach him how to be
kind. But Fred, the yearning dauntless boy, was dead and gone,
taking the passport. Fred, a young boy who had shown
that youth and immaturity are not the same! A heart-loose boy,
with nothing in his pockets, whom poverty had held back from
being a painter but who had been artist enough to see the world
ablaze in the colours of its first creation; who had learnt little at
school but knew how to find the eternal essences in the least
things; who had seen nothing of foreign countries and the

vaunted marvels abroad, but who had seen God in the rainy skies and streaming gutters of Camden Town.

Giles got up and shambled home. Agnes was waiting for him with hot milk. He noticed her relief at seeing him.

"Doubtless you thought I should finish up in the river or under a train!" he said. "I should like to be able to permit myself such a luxury. Get off home!"

Giles went to bed but not to sleep. He lay awake all night, while in the next room his brother's body, having been mortally vexed and debased by the suffering of the earlier day, lapsed further into its disintegration, its work and purpose finished. It had served Fred its last turn through dimming eyes that morning, for as he sat at the kitchen table with the oily dews of death upon him, there had been vouchsafed to him a peculiar triumph—the only sort of success he had ever wanted. As the shadows thronged round him, while anguish racked him, Fred had suddenly caught a gleam which, ever widening, obliterated the dark, the fear, the pain, and gradually became a mighty river of light upon which, before his entranced gaze, wheeled an articulation of the many things which had been offered to his childhood's interest and love, seen in the ideal Now as once perceived in the joyful innocent Then—memories of leaf and feather and star—memories that took him back to where a chaffinch was singing with the winds of spring-time, and the white admiral sailed over sprays of summer-hot bramble. He saw again an autumn hedge roaring red with maple leaves, and the blackthorn blossoming in sugary clots in the violent grey days of March; now a flock of wild swans flying low seemed like angels streaming into the sunset; in a mist the havana-brown moon lifted itself above the ebony line of the towering moor; bright cocks and hens in sparkling condition ran long-legged races after a girl strewing grain; in the January hedge the bare claret-coloured Dogwood shone among the pale green shoots, living up to its old country name of Bloody Twig; spindle berries hung their drops of fire in a leafless December; and in summer woods explosions of sunlight spirted between the silver firs and larches.

These things seemed to integrate with his sick labouring heart, and it was while Fred was caught away in all this beauty and light that he died, in a final all-embracing assertion of the sweetness of his days, his death the glory he himself had been making it in the midst of his simple lonely life.

PART FIVE

MRS. CHRISTOPHER

I

SOMETIMES on a night of early summer in London the stars take on a tinge which makes the sky seem as if it is decked with thousands of glittering buttercups. When dark falls those far blazing buttercup fields which, in the country, slope down to little rivers full of trout, seem as if they have been whisked to a reversed station overhead, and a few crazy Londoners lean back to stare upwards expecting a fall of flowers from the radiant night sky.

On such an evening Mrs. Christopher was sitting on a wooden chair in her dimly lit prison cell, the buttercups aloft (which she could see through the small panes of the window) playing upon her attention simultaneously with thoughts of Justice, Courage, Hanging, Jean Gabin in "Pépé le Moko," the Four Last Things, her Trial on the Morrow, and Oranges—she wished she had one. Percolating through her compendium of thoughts went a sea of Wagner which was pouring into the night from some Londoner's contiguous wireless.

Mrs. Christopher felt as one in convalescence; she had been through a gruelling experience and had recovered from the pains. She need not yet bother to assume the responsibility of living because she did not yet know the terms of her future existence. She did not even know where that existence was to be—here or elsewhere. That would be decided during the next few days. Meantime she need not determine anything except to show courage even if it should arise that courage was the one thing lacking to her.

Sitting opposite to Mrs. Christopher in the cell was her son Hugh. He was there by special permission of the prison governor, and the same authority had allowed him the privilege of an interview unmarred by the presence of a third party official of the jail. Hugh was leaning back, exhausted, having coached a very recalcitrant mother in the final details of what would be expected of her on the following morning.

"And I should not grin as much as you did at the first hearing, when you enter the Central Criminal Court to-morrow," he concluded darkly, "and come face to face with the paraphernalia of English justice! It's very old is English jurisprudence. It goes back to the Romans. Doesn't that mean something to you?"

"No grinning? Really? Blast it!" said Mrs. Christopher.

"There you are, you see. You're incorrigible. Remember something else, too: there must be no breaking off and interrupting yourself to ask the judge what his favourite author is, or if he has got a singing voice. Just remember that you'll be on trial for your life and . . ."

"Come off it!" said Mrs. Christopher. "You go on and on. Hasn't anything else happened recently in your life other than the murder your mother committed? It's a major happening, no doubt, but really, Hugh, you seem as if you can't get away from it."

"I can't," said Hugh glumly. "Is this a time for being facetious, Mamma?"

"I don't know," replied Mrs. Christopher, "but don't let us be too earnest. You'll have to go in a minute. Tell us something interesting. What did you have for your lunch? Food becomes an extraordinarily engrossing affair once a person has gone on to a prison diet. I sometimes spend a whole hour dreaming of food—endless varieties of food. I suppose strawberries are out now? I always did love strawberries and cream above every other dish in creation."

"Bah!" Hugh showed irritation in all his bulky person, relented, and said:

"If you don't go dictating to the judge and jury on how they should run your case, I daresay you'll be gobbling strawberries quite soon."

"I think you'll be mistaken."

"Maybe. You make whopping big mistakes yourself. What about those three who came and informed against you? You were sure they would never betray you—yet they did, every one."

"No," said Mrs. Christopher gently, "they did not betray me—they betrayed themselves!"

"That's it! Turn it off! Let's have the defence now for a parcel of beastly informers."

"O, Hugh, how awful it would be to hate them when we don't know what drove them to it."

"Mamma! Five hundred pounds drove them to it."

"You know what I meant, dear boy—the something that drove them to the five hundred."

"Ha-ha! Two of 'em pleaded that—shrieked that they'd been *driven* to selling you. Odd how much they suddenly needed five hundred pounds when they knew they only had to go and ask for it. There was a positive epidemic of this driving, I can tell you! But I let them have a few words! They didn't leave my premises feeling proud of themselves. I enjoyed rubbing their noses in it."

"Poor Hugh! It's bad when we're reduced to airing what bit of virtue we've kept intact. When people play what they imagine to be their trump card and you know it's their final throw, even if you hold a card of higher value, it's up to you to let them win."

"I ought not to have reproached them, you mean?"

"It wasn't necessary. I don't believe many people betray or do wrong because they like it. It's tiresome to cheat and steal and booze and lie, and no one in their right senses *enjoys* committing murder. I can vouch for that. But those things are done because we know no better, or because we do know better but are too weak, clever, or driven, to escape temptation. No one does bad because they *are bad*—see? Depend upon it, something silly rather than downright wickedness drove those people to claim the reward."

"But these particular three tale-bearers are so very unlovely!"

"Well, don't let us despise the unlovely. I remember that the only occasion in my life when I was aware of what Those In The Know call the Manifest Spirit, was entirely devoid of outer glamour."

"What happened?"

"I was gazing down into a dirty yard in which stood a derelict zinc bath full of stagnant green water, and there, for sure, I suddenly *knew* the presence of the Lord. Down in that yard! Nothing was changed to the outward eye, but I could not describe the wonder and happiness, the sense of a concentration of all the beauty in the world, which I knew for a few seconds. There it was. Since then I don't forget that the very place where God is to be found is in that place where no one thinks of looking."

"Of course, in a minute, dear, you'll be letting out that God is here, *here* in this stinking prison where half of the inmates are rotting to death on their feet. This cell of yours, you know, it smells musty, like the smell in a disused cellar—or a tomb. It's like being in a nightmare. It's god-forsaken!"

"If God isn't here," said Mrs. Christopher, "He isn't anywhere —there is no God. But the fact is, He's as much here as you and I are, and that's all in keeping with the notions of a God who allowed His son to be born in a stable out East, wrapped in rags for the want of warmer clothing!"

"I see. And what's God doing here? What's He doing about all these nice people in their pretty cages?"

"The nice people in their pretty cages have to do something before He can do anything. I must say there's not much encouragement. They keep us so short of toilet paper in this place that some of us have to tear out the pages of our Bibles to . . . well . . . and so we can't do very much in the way of reading about God. But all we have to do, if we want Him, is to ask, to speak up, to shout, to roar for the light of that gracious presence. God is doing here what God is doing everywhere—waiting about, in case of being wanted."

"Something is wanted here. O, the filthy place! The stifling hole! The little high-up locked window! The stink of lots of women together in very close quarters! These are realities which you don't seem to grasp—they don't appear to bother you."

"You have to grasp them, Hugh, and get over them—get beyond them. They even have their value by what happens to you in your efforts to get beyond 'em."

And while Hugh stared with disgust at the dirty cream-painted bricks of the cell walls and the narrow bed which he knew was not sprung, Mrs. Christopher was once again marvelling to herself that experiences of discomfort and horror could enable people to discover within themselves regions of personality hitherto unknown—vast territories of unexplored consciousness which, being tapped for the first time under the pressure of adversity, could reveal such riches, and give people an added aptitude for the transcendental and eternal; thus were they compelled to measure their own greatness which, of course, was the very reason why such experiences were allowed to happen to them.

Here a wardress peeped in through the spyhole in the door, and withdrew her face after a frigid look.

"God! What a face!" commented Hugh. "Absolutely insufferable! She ought to be locked up for wearing such an expression!"

"If you come to that, sometimes a person owns nothing else but a supercilious look. Be a tolerant boy."

"That may come in time—perhaps not in my time. Just the same, Mamma, I'm not altogether unredeemed. I've thought a good deal about things these last few weeks."

"A capital crime in a family usually provides food for thought," remarked Mrs. Christopher.

"I daresay you must have your little joke. But, do you know, your job of murder does not seem at all as serious to me as, say, a malicious lie, a piece of odious gossip, or some look of hatred from the very virtuous to the very unwise. A murder done in an excess of passion is not, perhaps, to be recommended as a means of settling disputes, but there are far worse things in this world than such a murder. Those three who betrayed you all committed a murder far worse than your little effort; theirs was calculated and they knew they were going to be paid."

Mrs. Christopher said nothing. She was seeing again the tale-bearers, Veronica, Edmund, and Giles, standing at Sine's desk with that beaten look on their faces. That they had been caused such a look at all, she judged, acquitted them of their sneaking journeys to Whitehall to sell her for five hundred pounds. She hoped that the money had done them some good. She broke the silence:

"Listen, Hugh," she said, "don't keep on ranting about those three. I have acquitted them but they are acquitted without my mangy forgiveness: they are acquitted by a truth as old as life, that though we all engage in any number of variations upon the seven deadly sins, we are all, in spite of ourselves, looking for goodness, being positive practical people, and goodness being the only positive practical force in the world. It's not what we've done that will matter—but what we'd like to have done. The real trouble with the world is not so much that people don't

235

believe in God as that they don't believe in the devil. He, unheeded, goes about bringing people down in all directions, and they wonder how they've gone wrong, and what they didn't allow for. Think of those three kindlily, and that of itself reduces whatever fault is in them. There's nothing for it but to accept people as they are, and if their mistakes get on your nerves take them as being *your own mistakes;* this at once alters your attitude."

"Why," protested Hugh, "I'd never betray anyone."

"Every time you refuse to forgive those three unfortunate people, you betray God."

"O, Him!" said Hugh. "But *He* never expects anything better of people!"

"No? Then who are you to go round setting up standards of behaviour?"

"I don't know," he confessed. "But who could help resenting their lack of loyalty? And then, they made such a fool of you. I resent that, too."

"Don't," said Mrs. Christopher. "Just be thankful that though I've lived a long time I've never grown so clever that I couldn't *be* fooled. Blessed are the foolish for they have room to learn."

"I wonder," said Hugh, "if you'd have forgiven them had you been running for your life from the police—if you had not already decided to give yourself up."

"If I'd been the sort who runs for its life, I should hardly have given those people my name and address in the first place, in case suspicion fell on any of them. And everything would have been quite different. People are always saying 'If only.' But life is 'This is it,' never 'If only.'"

"Well, the word now is 'Be Careful' and heaven send you luck to-morrow. Think of what is before you in the morning and less of this love mania of yours. What is the good of it? No one knows or cares."

He looked at his mother bunched up as she was in the prison

garb, the blue cotton dress with a tie which made her seem like a freak imitation of a nursery-governess, the thick woollen stockings, and big broken shoes; there she sat, completely undaunted, the embodiment of loving-kindness. All at once he felt like cheering.

He thought: I said I couldn't believe ever in the worth of the human race if all three of those people betrayed her. They all did, of course. Yet I find I can believe, after all, through her—Mamma—sitting here with her thin old prison frock and the silly tie and all! But his mother was answering him:

"My dear, my dear, you ask what good love is: it is the only good. Even to sit here," she said, "in this cell, among all the other cages with their bored tenants who have nothing more lovely to look at than a dirty floor and a chamber-pot, and send out to these prisoners thoughts which are not hateful and condemning—even that has good in it, and is equal to visiting them one by one, as you'd like to do, if they'd let you. When you see all the miseries and wrongs round you, you want to rush out and do something at once to change it all—something big and startling. Well, you can't. You can only try not to add to the woe at large, and keep a sympathetic mind. We don't know in what consoling way other people are shown the loving impulses sent in their direction by those thinking of them kindly—thinking of them kindly not out of condescension and smugness, but because we, too, are the same as they. I *am* those three who betrayed me, just as, if I hang, they will hang with me. In this world *we're all in it*, that's why notions of one race, one nation, and one class being better than another, are stupid and vulgar. We're all in it!

"Go home, Hugh, and sleep well, as I shall. No one has hurt me but myself. Whatever happens to-morrow, I'm not far off the end of my life, anyway, but you and the younger generation have to go on with the battle against men's inhumanity to each other, and you've only one weapon—I mean love. Yes, I know the word has lost its meaning: the twentieth century will be remembered for its attempt to destroy love and kill the heart. Yet the better outward way of living for which we all long will never come but from within, from ready hearts. For this world's plight there is only one remedy, and it lies in the reality of love. Don't let it put you off that you hear such things from a murderer. Sinners are the ones who best understand love because sin asks for love, calls it out and creates it more poignantly than anything else on earth.

"Don't forget your gloves, and don't forget to forgive our three tale-bearers, as I hope they will forgive us for tempting them. Still, that experiment has taught me something: now I have some faint idea of what it is like to be God, to be betrayed over and over again, even by those you thought were loyal, yet able to forgive and, better still, able to love."

*   *   *   *   *

Because of statements like these, repeated during the course of her trial, a jury of three frail women and nine strong men found Mrs. Christopher—GUILTY BUT INSANE.

THE END